*Praise for*
# THE HAZARDS OF SLEEPING ALONE

"In this poignant and often funny novel, Elise Juska does the work of an archaeologist; she digs deep to uncover subterranean truths about loneliness, the mysteries of human connection and the delicate push-pull of mother-daughter relationships. She excavates, she reveals, and she gets it exactly right."

—Carolyn Parkhurst, bestselling author of
*The Dogs of Babel*

"Elise Juska writes of real people and her voice rings true. Charlotte is an utterly original character: at once fearful and hopeful, honest and funny, naive and wise. This is a wonderful novel."

—Lisa Tucker, author of *The Song Reader* and
*Once Upon a Day*

"Juska's portrait of [Charlotte] is an exacting one and hews, however uncomfortably, close to the truth. . . . A powerful success."

—*Kirkus Reviews*

"[A] revealing and realistic portrait of a woman who's always been so afraid of what she can't see that she's never realized what she can become."

—*Romantic Times*

"Read *The Hazards of Sleeping Alone* yourself and then pass it on to your mother or daughter."

—*BookLoons*

"Anyone who has awakened in the night alone and afraid will rejoice at Charlotte's transformation."

—*Booklist*

also by elise juska

*Getting Over Jack Wagner*

*The Hazards of Sleeping Alone*

a novel

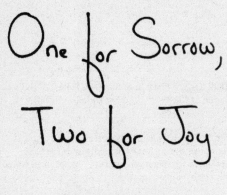

# One for Sorrow, Two for Joy

## ELISE JUSKA

POCKET BOOKS

NEW YORK   LONDON   TORONTO   SYDNEY

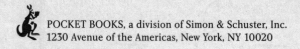 POCKET BOOKS, a division of Simon & Schuster, Inc.
1230 Avenue of the Americas, New York, NY 10020

ISBN-13: 978-1-4165-1692-7
ISBN-10:     1-4165-1692-1

Library of Congress Cataloging-in-Publication Data is available

This Pocket Books trade paperback edition June 2007

10  9  8  7  6  5  4  3  2  1

*Designed by Mary Austin Speaker*

Manufactured in the United States of America

For information regarding special discounts for bulk purchases, please contact Simon & Schuster Special Sales at 1-800-456-6798 or business@simonandschuster.com.

for my sister sally

# ACKNOWLEDGMENTS

I wish to thank editors Christine Weiser and Carla Spataro at *Philadelphia Stories* and Henry Israeli at *Dragonfire* for publishing early excerpts from this book in their great magazines. For helping coax the final manuscript to light, I am very grateful for the quick reflexes of Shana Kelly at William Morris and the efforts of many creative people at Simon & Schuster, especially Lauren McKenna, Louise Burke, and Megan McKeever.

Louise McLeod, Laoise Hogan, Sharon Clancy, and Maura Mulligan provided generous and patient fact-checking on many Irish details, from Limerick street maps to grilled cheese sandwiches. Thank you to Shelley Barber at Boston College Library for her helpfulness in researching Yeats and to real-life crossword puzzle constructor Jonathan Schmalzbach for his enthusiastic insights into the cruciverbal world.

I am grateful to many friends and readers for their comments on this manuscript in various stages: Allison Amend, Tanya Barrientos, Tenaya Darlington, Derek Dressler, Melissa Dribben, Greg Downs, Diana Kash, Clark Knowles, Emily Miller, Laura Miller, Michele Reale, Kerry Reilly, Eric Rivera, Shauna Seliy, Curtis Sittenfeld, Elizabeth Thorpe, and especially my mom, who read portions of this book an outrageous number of times and never wavered in her patience or her insights.

Many thanks to Whitney Lee for her hard work and enthusiasm, Ann Kimmage for her healthy perspectives on writing and life, and Shawn McBride for emails that kept me laughing. Maureen Gillespie, Kieran Juska, Amanda Strachan, and Emily Woods provided last-minute advice and old friendship. Christian Barter gave me perfect words in many forms.

My family, especially Mom, Dad, and Sally, has always been my most consistent and important source of support. Thanks to my grandmother, Muriel Juska, for getting me hooked on quick-n-easy crosswords at an early age, and to my cousins for their expertise on many subjects, from bugs to school uniforms to the rides at Wonderland Pier.

Finally, I could not have written this book were it not for the memorable months I spent, and for the friends I made, in Galway, Ireland. *Go raibh maith agat.*

# CONTENTS

One for Sorrow,
Two for Joy

# CHAPTER ONE: Bugs

The fascinating thing about bugs—all living creatures, really—is that they are designed to save themselves. Nothing is extraneous, nothing decorative; every feature is part of an intricate mechanism of survival. Some disguise themselves as thorns or sand, others as dead leaves or tropical flowers. The damselfly poses as a blade of grass; the golden wheel spider rolls into a ball and tumbles away. The walking stick can assume different forms. Sometimes it looks like a twig: thin, mottled brown, a cinnamon stick with feet. Other times it's gold or green, splayed open like a ragged leaf. When the bug is sitting on a tree branch, it's impossible to know it's there.

As Claire looks at her hand resting on the kitchen counter, a walking stick appears in her mind's eye. Her pale skin is the same shade as her Formica. The freckles sprinkled across the back of her hand merge with a smattering of dots the color of sand. Claire raises a finger, slightly, then lowers it. She has become indistinguishable from her kitchen.

She crosses the kitchen and pushes open the back door. It's been raining all morning, a steady rain, the temperature hovering just above freezing. She steps into the backyard— half-mown, half-ragged—and shuffles across the long side, wet fronds darkening her slippers like paintbrush tips. She is wearing her bug slippers, a gift she received from Bob shortly after they moved to New Hampshire. They are difficult to walk in, like shuffling inside two couch pillows. A year ago, the beetles' heads were bright yellow; now they are faded, their antennae limp, chins angled toward the ground in defeat.

She grips the handle of Bob's garage-turned-office and heaves the door open to the screech of rusty metal. Bob looks surprised to see her there; rarely does she interrupt his work. Claire is equally surprised by this vision of her husband. Whenever she pictures Bob in his office, it's with head bent studiously over research. Instead, he is just sitting there, slack-jawed, eyes trained not on a slide or book or specimen but gazing into the dull vortex of his office, a nest of computer wires clustered at his feet.

"Claire?" Bob says, sitting up straight. "What's—"

"Nothing's wrong," Claire says. She pauses a beat. "I need to go."

"Okay," he says.

"No. I mean, I need to—leave."

Bob's lips, at rest, are always slightly parted. Claire drops her eyes from his face. She focuses on the long, low cabinet behind him: a card catalog of insects, a hundred tiny coffins, glass-flattened, toe-tagged, angel-winged. The wall above it is covered with important papers in brown frames—diplomas, citations, their wedding photo, a merit certificate from YES, the Young Entomologists' Society.

"Maybe just for a while," Claire says. "I just have to. I need to get away."

Bob has taken off his glasses and is rubbing them with a satiny red square, plucked from his pocket like a magician's scarf. It's one of his signature habits, reverted to in moments of disorientation: as if by cleaning the lenses the problem on the other side will become clear.

"But," he says, pushing his glasses back on. "But, ah, where would you go?"

Bob is a rational man; it is a large part of why Claire married him. He is steady with his emotions, realistic in his expectations, quick to unclog a sink. He is the kind of man who would never do a crossword puzzle in anything but pencil, who will always cut bagels in half before he freezes them. But when it comes to life's more complicated moments, situations that demand emotion—in which another husband might ask why or how or what had he done or, my *God*, what could he do to change her mind—Bob's first priority, always, would be logistics.

Claire tightens her arms across her chest. She feels disengaged from herself, her mind from her mouth, hearing her own words as if spoken by someone else. She must hold herself in place carefully—too much talk, too much motion, and she might splinter apart. Then Bob stands up and takes a step toward her.

"I'm sorry," Claire says. Her voice is trembling. She unclasps her arms, slides her wedding ring off, and drops it in an empty kill jar on the end of Bob's desk.

CHAPTER TWO: } Bob

**W**hen they met, Bob was studying entomology and Claire was studying etymology. This seemed, if not predestined, at least cute. It was only fitting that Claire would meet her future husband this way: standing in the middle of a university campus on a crisp fall afternoon. It had always been through school that Claire experienced the world.

She loved school, loved learning, though even by first grade she knew better than to admit it out loud. She got straight A's, but this never felt like an effort. Secretly, she even liked homework: the sense of a task needing completion, the satisfaction when it was zippered into her book bag and waiting by the door. To Claire, the inside of a classroom on a rainy afternoon was the most comforting place in the world: a roomful of girls and boys sharing a common space, chins lowered over pulpy yellow paper, sniffling, breathing, pencils scratching, the rain pattering the windows, and the teacher rubbing the eraser in slow, thoughtful circles across the board. She preferred school days to weekends, and felt a heaviness whenever another summer stretched before her, hot and empty and endless. Nothing important would happen to her over the summer.

Even her bedroom as a child was less an extension of home than of school. The shelves were clogged with books, the nubbly red bulletin board papered with certificates— PERFECT ATTENDANCE. BOOKWORM. LITERACY CHAMP! Her desk drawers were filled with lists of words she'd learned and loved. *Galaxy. Bubblicious. Cashmere. Cacti. Acquiesce.* She dismantled her spelling and vocab lists sound by sound, syllable by syllable. She cared less about the meanings than the feelings, and sometimes whispered the words just to feel them in her mouth.

Whatever slight interactions Claire had with boys were, like most of life's pivotal experiences, a function of school. The first time she danced with a boy was in gym, during the exquisitely humiliating square dance unit. In health ed, while practicing taking one another's blood pressure, she touched the soft inside of a boy's wrist. It was in earth science, sixth grade, that Claire first held a boy's hand. While Mr. Frick pressed his finger to the buzzer on Lab Table One, the class clasped hands in a sloppy, sweaty chain of electrical conductivity, brave smiles frozen to their faces, compelled in the name of science and their precarious spot in the pecking order to not let go.

It wasn't that Claire was unpopular exactly, just unremarkable. She was sturdy, more big-boned than chubby, with red hair she wore in a single braid and freckles that bloomed like constellations of stars on her round cheeks. Each of her elementary school pictures was essentially this: a thick fringe of bangs, a tentative smile, a missing tooth. Jennifer Kelly, who was popular, once told Claire that she looked like a Campbell's Soup Kid; this was a compliment at the time. Claire wasn't made fun of by the popular kids, nor was she invited to their parties. She had a few equally shy, unremarkable friends with whom she discussed the popular crowd so thoroughly she felt a part of their world, even if they wouldn't have known her name.

What small but increasing notice Claire attracted at school was because of schoolwork. She had the highest GPA in the class. She set the annual record for the MS Readathon, collecting several Pizza Hut gift certificates. By middle school she had discovered a quietly fierce competitive streak, evident in her grades and awards and propensity for games like Merlin, Simon, and Boggle. In eighth grade she made it to the finals of the schoolwide spelling bee, broadcast to all the classrooms by closed-circuit TV. On the day of the finals she wore her hair unbraided. A sticker on the front of her uniform said Homeroom 19. The bee came down to two spellers; Claire's final word was *sciatica*, the winner's was *balloon*. The sense of humiliation and mild injustice that trailed her from the broadcast booth was unalleviated by her return to language arts, where the class offered a dribbling of applause and her teacher whispered fiercely, "You were *robbed*."

At St. James Catholic High School, Claire thrived on AP English classes, the literary magazine, the yearbook copyediting team. In her junior year, she agreed to go to her first dance with a boy not because she liked him, or even really knew him, but because his name was Percival Percivont. When she was accepted to college (Ivy League, early decision) she ordered a stack of trendy sweaters based on color names alone—*sassafras, sterling, lawn, lime*.

In college, she harbored an unoriginal crush on Professor Collins, who taught her freshman romanticism seminar, wore lambswool sweaters, and spoke in iambic pentameter. At a keg party, she met a rugby player, Leo, who confided that he was "secretly shy" and working on a novel no one knew about. Claire instantly imagined herself in the role of Leo's girlfriend: quietly supportive, a book lover with few good friends to tell. She lost her virginity to Leo that night after several rum and Diet Cokes. He left her room before dawn, and when they passed each other on the quad, they didn't say hello.

When Claire graduated (Phi Beta Kappa, summa cum laude) her parents and little sister attended the ceremony. Her father kissed her dryly in the middle of her forehead. Her mother kept loudly referring to her as "Beta Kappa Claire," which had the effect of making Claire feel dumb. Noelle, just finishing her junior year of high school, told Claire she was crazy to keep going to school when she didn't have to—Claire would be starting a PhD program in linguistics in the fall. Claire had smiled down at her sister. The truth was, she wouldn't have minded staying in school forever. *Academia*—how she loved this word, the forward march of it, the two genteel vowels bookending the sophisticated nut in the center. Higher education agreed with her; it confirmed her. Within the firm structure of brick buildings and twelve-credit semesters, she was at home.

In grad school, Claire drowned happily in her schoolwork. She began smoking occasionally, lost ten pounds (not to be confused with the fifteen she dutifully put on her freshman year in college) and got straight A's (even if no one said "straight A's" in grad school). It wasn't until the beginning of her third year that, as Claire was leaving the library, she noticed a blond man with a backpack crouched awkwardly outside the Social Sciences building. He seemed as choreographed a part of the academic setting as the hallowed gong of the clock on the steeple or the trees with their leaves gently turning or the group of high school students drifting in a small, nervous cloud across the quad.

As Claire drew closer, she saw the man was peering at his hand. A thick, bright stripe of a worm lay across his index finger, mint green, like toothpaste on a brush.

"Beautiful," he murmured.

The man had on a green barn coat, thin-rimmed glasses, and wrinkled khakis. A shock of thin blond hair spilled across his forehead—he was handsome, in a scholastic sort of way.

"Black swallowtail," he said.

Claire paused. She had never looked at a worm up close,

except for the one she found curled up next to the crispy prawns in the $3.99 college student all-you-can-eat Chinese buffet. But she had to agree: In the world of worms, this one did seem unusually attractive, leaf green with dramatic black stripes and yellow splashes.

"*Papilio polyxenes*," the man said.

Claire stepped closer. Though she never initiated conversations with strange men—or any men—she heard herself ask, "Is it a worm or a caterpillar?"

The man looked up in surprise. She wondered if he had been speaking to the worm all along.

"Oh, ah, a caterpillar," he said, pushing himself up from the ground. He was tall, his knees plastered with a few dewy strands of grass. "Also called a parsley worm."

"Parsley worm," Claire repeated.

"Soon it will go into its, ah, chrysalis."

"Chrysalis." The word slid between her teeth like liquid gold. "And then what?" she asked. Maybe it was his fitful speech that was making her feel braver.

"Well, then, it becomes—" He tugged on one ear. "It becomes a butterfly."

The metaphorical undertones were absurd. But in that moment, the very idea—that this chubby, sluggish creature nestled on this man's finger would go into hiding and emerge with wings—struck Claire as the most poetic thing she'd ever heard. The man leaned down and placed the caterpillar gently on the pavement. Like proud parents, they watched as it inched away, dragging itself behind itself stripe by stripe.

Then, just like parents, left alone after the kids leave home, they stopped communicating. She pinched the air with her thumb and forefinger, wishing she had a cigarette. He pulled his glasses off, one wiry arm snagging on his ear. They were the kind of glasses that were spindly, unbreakable, the kind Claire associated with professors and violinists, the end of each arm curved like a teacup handle. She watched as he began to clean them, massaging the lenses with a satiny red cloth. As he coaxed each arm snugly around each ear, Claire realized she craved this kind of care. Then his hand was waiting before her.

"Bob Wells," he said.

As his hand folded around her hand, Claire felt a profound calmness start in her chest and travel outward, the kind of contentment she felt in a classroom in the rain. This man felt steady, safe. She found herself smiling at his every detail: his damp, grass-stained knees, his unintentional metaphors, the sunlight glinting off his glasses, and his serious, pale-blue eyes.

"Claire Gallagher," she said, and even though she'd spent four semesters studying linguistics, she managed to overlook his most pressing, most ominous detail: His first name was spelled the same way forward and back.

Bob, it turned out, was the pride of the Entomology Department. His research on environmental toxicology had won him the Handelman Award for Excellence two years running. True, he wasn't a writer; he wouldn't dazzle her with his words. But, Claire reasoned, he didn't have to. From Bob's brain to his lips, every sentence seemed to undergo a patient process of internal editing, an effort to express himself rightly—as close to truthfully—as he could.

"I love . . ."

Claire was sitting on his lap, in the brown leather chair that swallowed half of Bob's tiny office. It was late October, one of those perfect fall evenings when a college campus was at its finest and walking across a quad felt a little bit like falling in love. Everything was right with the world, every detail in agreement—the golden light warming the dorm windows, the purplish afterglow of an early sunset, the sounds of feet shushing through red-gold leaf piles and snatches of laughter from some unseen conversation. The feeling was equal parts joy and sadness, hope and nostalgia; impossible to look forward without looking back.

". . . your nose . . ."

Bob was wearing only his glasses and boxers, his legs stretched beneath her like a lanky seesaw covered with light blond hair. Claire hooked her legs under the insides of his knees. There was something thrilling about it, the proximity of flesh and academia, the body and mind sharing the same four-by-ten square of rough mulberry carpet, Bob's baggy tweeds and Claire's sassafras sweater mingling with the dusty brown hardcovers that littered the office floor.

"I love your nose . . ."

He was older, thirty-two to her twenty-four, and this implied maturity, yet it was always Bob who seemed more nervous. He often dissected her this way, breaking her body down into its carefully adored parts. Claire had always hated her freckles—as a child, she'd scratched at one until her skin turned black—but Bob traced them slowly, like the coordinates of some delicate constellation, so genuinely enamored of her that Claire couldn't help but feel pretty in his arms.

"I love your nose"—he concluded, cheeks flushing spectacularly—"because it's, ah, attached to your face."

The following winter, Bob was offered a job at the Institute for Biological Sciences, a research training facility in Roan, New Hampshire. Claire was still a year away from finishing her dissertation. The plan was for her to put it on hold until after the move. To delay finishing a crucial paper—much less an entire degree—went against every grain in Claire's body, but she reminded herself that she had a move to organize and a wedding to plan. Plus, saving her dissertation would give her something to do in New Hampshire. What more perfect place to write a dissertation?

That spring, she and Bob huddled over the fax machine in his office, watching as rental ads came inching through. Bob scrutinized them like chemical formulas, circling the "AC" and "utils incl." Claire found herself charmed by descriptors like "sun-filled," "cozy," and "unique space." Though Claire was immersed in words on a technical level—phonetics and semantics, morphologies and roots—she was still prone to falling into ill-advised love with them. She told the linguistics department that she was excited about New Hampshire because this position was "a great opportunity for Bob," but the real reason, which she told no one, was that he had described it as "sylvan." She had focused on that droplet of a word—*sylvan, sylvan, sylvan*—not just its meaning, but the fact that Bob chose it. So he could be a little dry, a little clinical, but deep down where it mattered—*sylvan!*

Eventually, it was a "2BR/1B+" that caught both their

eyes. Claire was charmed by the "homey" and "secluded" and unabashed "little slice of heaven." Bob approved of "near highway" and "W/D." Both were enticed by the "+" dangling off the end like a dripping cherry on a fork. As a symbol, it satisfied both of their most basic instincts: It had a mathematical quality that appealed to Bob, and a suggestiveness that played to Claire's powers of imagination. When the realtor explained that the "+" was a partially renovated garage set twenty feet from the main house, they decided Bob could adopt it as his office. The realtor sent Polaroids and they took it, sight unseen.

A month after the wedding, Claire and Bob pulled into their new driveway with a U-Haul groaning behind them. As she walked through the empty rooms, Claire felt giddy, hopeful. She didn't see the house; she saw the life they would have inside it. She lingered on the fireplace and pictured snowy winter nights, foreign films, good wines. In the kitchen, she conjured scenes of hyperliterate dinner parties, complicated appetizers, and witty, erudite conversations. She imagined herself adopting a look of sloppy buns and embroidered ponchos, becoming well versed in olives and cheeses. She imagined herself *worldly*—though this, she would learn, is the trick of academia. It lets you believe you're engaged with the world even if that world exists only theoretically, even if the very word *academia* begins to sound like some sort of disease. Even if what you really are is not worldly, but *wordly*—concocting realities that exist only in your head.

That first night, lying among the stacks of unopened wedding gifts and cardboard boxes, Claire listened for what she'd counted on being a clean, perfect, rural silence. Instead it was a cacophony of buzzing and chirping, grasshoppers and field crickets and katydids.

"It's loud," she said.

She was staring at the ceiling, at a long thin crack running through the plaster. Bob's arm felt warm beneath her neck.

"That's because most predators sleep at night," he whispered, as if to not disturb them. "So the insects can afford to be noisy."

Claire pulled the comforter to her chin. Her face was itchy.

"Listen," he said. "Hear that?"

"What?"

"That."

Claire listened. The chirps sounded in threes, a thick, drowsy waltz; gradually she distinguished one set as louder and faster than the others.

"It's a love song," Bob said excitedly, as the chirps rose in pitch. "Someone caught his eye. Or his wing."

Claire smiled. As the sound peaked and softened, she asked, "What's happening now?"

"She came over," Bob said. "She likes him too."

Claire rolled toward him, pressing her face into his warm chest. This man, her husband, was a romantic. It may have been accidental, but he was a romantic all the same. Closing her eyes, she listened as the world outside sang and serenaded. What was she complaining about? This place was their very own sleep machine—people paid good money for these things! She was drifting off as she heard another chirp grow louder. This one sounded arrhythmic, agitated.

"What's wrong with that one?" she asked.

"He attracted an enemy," Bob said. "They'll fight to the death."

For a while, the arrangement seemed as ideal as it appeared. Claire stored her books and laptop in the spare BR, Bob worked outside in the +. This separation seemed healthy, even necessary. No matter that the backyard was crawling with ticks and blackflies—"Think of it as *Wild Kingdom*," the realtor had said—a discouragement to anyone else, but to Bob, a windfall. Claire outfitted her study with new file cabinets, made colored labels, and arranged her dissertation notes in three-ring binders. She filled the shelves, built into New Englandy nooks and crannies, sometimes sliding books on top sideways for a haphazard, distracted effect. Out in the garage, Bob laid carpet and installed space heaters. He bought a "bug hat," a netted helmet that made him look like an insect superhero (*The Exterminator*, Claire thought). In the interest of experimentation, Bob kept one side of the backyard cut short while the other grew wild. The split extended from the back door to the woods at the edge of their property, like a stripe of duct tape bisecting the bedroom floor of siblings who don't get along.

In mid-September, Claire and Bob attended their first interdepartmental potluck, a monthly gathering hosted by a different institute researcher and spouse. The researchers Claire found smart and serious and, surprisingly, not unsocial. She would have preferred—understood—unsocial, but Bob's new colleagues were gregarious in a way that felt specialized and strenuous. They played a game in which everyone was required to guess the name of the famous scientist written on an index card and taped to his or her back. Claire spent three hours trying to come up with ALESSANDRO VOLTA while researchers poked her in the arm, flailing as if electrocuted.

"Ben Franklin?" she guessed.

One scientist shook his head. Another bent toward a floor lamp pretending to jab his finger in the socket.

"Watt?"

She felt a hard poke on the shoulder and turned to see another one on the floor convulsing. "Bacon?" she guessed. "Francis Bacon?" The room regarded her, pasty and concerned. It was the only word game Claire had ever despised.

"Claire?" She felt a hand on her arm. It was Terry, one of the faculty wives. She was holding Claire's elbow in one hand and a paper plate in the other. "Did you make this quiche?"

Claire had in fact made the quiche, and had spent an embarrassingly long time doing it, despite the fact that the slice on Terry's plate looked disturbingly wet.

"It's delish!" Terry approved, and Claire smiled, because Terry was trying to be kind, but inside she felt her first flicker of despair. She had hoped the wives might be her friends, women with whom she could roll her eyes and sigh, maybe share an ironic laugh now and then. But this, she could tell already, was not to be. These women had no irony. They wore only earth-toned sweaters and squelchy, sensible boots. Most of them, like Terry, were older than Claire by at least a decade. Claire was twenty-six, and even though so far in life her age had recommended her—marked her as "impressive for someone so young"—here it rendered her inexperienced, adorable, her quiche a puddle of spinachy water, and her open-toed sandals a rookie mistake.

As Terry gamely dug into the crust, it struck Claire forcibly that she did not want to become this woman: grazing the outskirts of academia hooked to her husband's arm. It was her first surge of edginess, near-meanness, though this was a feeling she would come to rely on soon. Anger was easy.

"Yes," entered another woman, a plant biologist named Julia. She wore narrow, rectangular glasses and, maybe by virtue of her faculty status, had arrived with a store-bought ham. "Very nice quiche."

"Did you make the crust yourself?" Terry said, but the way she asked, she might have been referring to an imaginary pie cooked by a child in a sandbox.

"I don't even know how to turn my oven on," Julia said.

Claire felt the smile tense on her face. She wanted to set the record straight, to let these women know she had four-fifths of a PhD and had scored a perfect on the logic section of the GRE. She sought Bob's gaze across the room, silently imploring him to jump in and preserve her dignity. But Bob just smiled. Her husband did not detect the subtleties of human behavior, especially female human behavior, or the behavior of anything, really, unless it molted and ate its own skin.

"I'm writing my dissertation," Claire blurted, turning back to the quiche eaters.

Terry looked at her in kind, crumpled confusion. "I thought you were Bob's wife?"

"I am. But I'm still writing my dissertation."

"What field?" Julia asked, gripping her glasses by one corner and straightening them on her face.

"Linguistics," Claire said. "Language acquisition. Dialectology and phonology. The way a language is acquired, evolves, and varies depending on social and cultural contexts."

Terry smiled. Julia said, "And you still have time to cook!" before dissolving politely into the party, an index card marked LOUIS LEAKEY stuck to her back.

That night, driving home after the party, Claire waited for Bob to tell her how much he'd hated it. She was dying to commiserate, to talk about the people—as she saw it, one of the best parts of being a couple was leaving parties and talking about the people—but Bob said, "I had fun. Didn't you?"

In the darkness, Claire couldn't see his face. "Sure," she replied, and stared out the window, half a quiche heavy in her lap. She was afraid her real opinion would sound too critical. Or worse, that Bob just wouldn't understand. To find something funny no one else did, be saddened by something other people shrugged off—under normal circumstances this felt lonely, but trying and failing to explain it to your husband would feel even worse.

Then Bob asked, "Want to know something?"

Claire turned, feeling a spike of hope. "Yes?"

"It's fifty-one degrees."

She surveyed the world out the window: an empty road, a slivered moon, a row of bagged leaves lined up on the curb. "How can you tell?"

"Male snowy field cricket," Bob said, then went on to explain that this insect functioned like a natural thermometer—count the number of chirps in fifteen seconds, add thirty-nine, and you had the degrees Fahrenheit.

It wasn't what she was looking for, but Claire had to admit she liked this nugget; it seemed like it could come in handy,

maybe be useful at parties. That night, and every night there-
after, she would lie in bed listening for the male snowy—in
her version, there was only one—watching the second hand
and counting chirps until she fell asleep. But as the nights got
colder, the chirps got slower. The cricket was winding down as
winter approached. It was poetic. Unbearable.

Bob, meanwhile, was experimenting with increased vigor,
sometimes getting up to check his traps in the middle of the
night. The inside of their house had become a minefield of
organic pest control: bay leaves, mint leaves, garlic cloves,
cucumber slices, jagged green chunks of Irish Spring soap.
Claire once found Bob kneeling with his nose to the baseboard
in the kitchen—the ants' "point of entry," he explained—
sprinkling a mixture of cayenne pepper, cinnamon, and coffee
grounds in a spicy, militant line he swore no ant would cross.
Claire tried to work on her dissertation, but couldn't seem to get
traction. She told herself this was temporary—new house, new
husband, garden-variety growing pains—and occupied herself
making address labels, compiling wedding albums, composing
group e-mails that sounded thrilled and witty. She would make
this life work; it was inconceivable that it wouldn't.

Until the afternoon Claire opened the refrigerator and
found dead ladybugs inside—hundreds of them, boxed in
pale green Tupperware, bookended by lunch meat and cream
cheese. Bob had heard her scream from across the yard.

"It's okay," he said, stroking her hair and panting slightly.
"I put them there, Claire. This, ah, morning. It's fine."

"It's not fine! How is it fine?"

"They're ladybugs. Insect control. They eat more than five
thousand aphids a year."

She stared at him. "But why are they in my refrigerator?"

"Storage," Bob replied.

This, she realized, was a man she did not understand. This was a man who had reduced her to a woman who said "my refrigerator."

"It's okay," Bob repeated. "No reason to get, ah, alarmed."

*But ladybugs!* Claire knew it was too illogical, too unscientific an argument to admit out loud. She was embarrassed to even be thinking it, but there it was lurking inside her, a flaw in her biology, like a lazy eye or a dead tooth. *Ladybugs are good luck! You don't mess with good luck!*

"It's just that it's better to let them out after nightfall," Bob added. He was trying to reassure her. She recalled him once explaining that the reason ladybugs were so brightly colored was to warn other bugs they didn't taste good. "They're perfectly safe. Just as long as the temperature doesn't go below freezing."

"What?" Claire paused. She yanked open the door again and peered inside. Sure enough, the ladybugs were still alive, twitching, as if crippled. She wrested away from Bob's hands. "Are they dying?" she whispered. She felt suddenly on the verge of tears. "They look like they're dying."

"They're not dying. I glued their wings so they can't fly. Ginger ale and soda water."

When she looked at him, his proud smile faded.

"Claire," he said. "It's just science."

"But ladybugs," she said, unable to control herself. "Ladybugs are *good luck*."

The look he gave her then was the kind you give a crazy person, equal parts bewilderment and concern. As Bob put his arms around her, promising to free the bugs by dinner, Claire felt her panic evaporate, replaced by something hard, absolute. Her husband didn't get her. It was so clear; it was devastating.

After the first frost, the male snowy field cricket vanished, like everything else, under a heavy coat of white. As the snow mounted, so did Claire's restlessness. Antsiness—though she banished this word from her repertoire. This house, this entire sylvan state, was making her sharp-cornered, nervy, the kind of person who chewed her nails and spat them on the ground. She discovered twin pockets of flesh at the backs of her thighs. She hadn't noticed them before—easy to miss under all that wool!—but suddenly they felt like sandbags. She blamed her dissertation. She blamed New Hampshire. There was nothing to do in this place but eat!

Then one evening in November, at an environmental fund-raiser, Claire was introduced to the mayor of Sylvan County. She froze, her hand clasped in his. The mayor was short, fat, and balding. As Claire fought to keep smiling, she realized "sylvan" was not Bob's description of the area—"sylvan" *was* the area. From then on, Claire knew that when her husband said "sylvan," what he really meant was Sylvan, and this dis-crepancy summed up their new life in New Hampshire: the difference between how a thing seemed and how it truly was.

As winter took hold, Bob published an article on inte-grated pest control. He attended the annual convention of the Entomology Society of America and returned with a pair of souvenir bug slippers and a hangover. Claire went to all his campus lectures, smiling and absorbing compliments on his behalf. She had given up trying to make real friends; once the possibility was gone, it was easier. She became surprisingly adept at mingling, her absorption in the role so convincing that sometimes she could step outside herself, look at her and Bob standing together, nodding and laughing, and see them as likable as everybody else did.

"Still working on my dissertation," she piped up, if anybody asked. The reality was, the dissertation was stagnant. For the first time since kindergarten, Claire was not in school; without the structure, she was useless. Really, what was the point? She began to resent the very idea of writing a dissertation, that she should be expected to sit here, trapped in the middle of nowhere slaving over this paper like it might change anything. No one in Roan knew if she was working on it, no one cared. And once it was written: What then? As long as Claire was still working on her dissertation, she was in a state of working on her dissertation, and this was something she vitally needed to be.

If she was sinking into disuse, Bob didn't seem to mind. This struck Claire as a sign of, if not weakness, at least obliviousness beyond repair. Maybe she was wrong about Bob. Maybe he'd never taken her work seriously. Maybe he didn't mind if she was pathetic—*wanted* her to be pathetic! Claire tried to quash these thoughts, but sometimes a triple wave of doubt and guilt and resentment blindsided her out of nowhere. Other times it rose gradually, from prickles of annoyance over Bob's mint leaves or netted hat to amazement that anyone could get a sweater quite so wrinkled to moments of despair that her degree was unfinished, that she felt so purposeless, that she had followed her husband to fucking Roan, New Hampshire, and her husband would never say "fucking."

"I love you," Bob said.

Every night and every morning, the endearments seeming to increase in proportion to her duress. Was he just trying to make her feel better? Was that pity in his voice? Secretly, Claire had begun to suspect Bob *didn't* love her. Not that he was lying on purpose, but that what he said and felt didn't mesh and, whether from lack of intuition or experience, he didn't know the difference. There wasn't enough intensity behind his words—the "love's" drifted down like snow in a plastic globe, light, barely there, the way he inexplicably kissed her over her padded bras. He would claim to love her unfailingly, and maybe this was his failing. He would love her, in spite of anything and in spite of everything. But what kind of love was that? How was she supposed to trust it? She could do nothing, and Bob's feelings for her wouldn't change, and sometimes this felt more like an insult than a relief.

Claire was overjoyed to see the end of that first bleak winter, only to find herself in the middle of an itchy, wet, endless spring. Mentally, at least, she still kept herself limber. She worked her way through the shelves of the Roan Public Library. She played *Jeopardy!* every night and did the syndicated crossword in the *Roan Gazette* every morning. For dessert, she polished off the cryptogram, and if desperate, the seek-and-find. Sometimes, hungry for more, she went out and bought an easy puzzle book—or more accurately, EZ puzzle book—the pulpy paperbacks sold in the Naber Market for ninety-nine cents. The covers boasted words like *Presto, Quickie, Jiffy,* and *Jumbo,* sometimes cartoon pictures of magicians or bunnies. She felt covert buying them, a junkie in need of a cheap fix. She got a rush speeding through the downs and acrosses, filling up the empty boxes to arrive at an unambiguous whole. The EZs were instant gratification, the street crack of linguistics, and in the messy world of life beyond school, by God she needed this.

On campus, she kept the puzzles tucked out of sight, though it wouldn't have mattered had anyone seen. Her life was merely a function of her husband's. When she went to campus, people smiled, but she knew how they saw her: the bug guy's wife. When she ran into women in the supermarket, she would nod at their comments about sale prices or winterizing or the scandal spattering the cover of the *National Enquirer* while inside she shouted: *I was valedictorian in high school!* When the cashier asked if she'd found everything she needed, on the inside she railed: *Lady, not even close!* Only after she was strapped in her car would she yield to the rage inside her. She sped home, flying through the potholes. *Take that!* She liked the satisfyingly hard bounce in her seat. *And that!* These rural potholes were awesome, otherworldly, huge and untouched as craters on the moon. *Andthatandthatandthat!* Back at home she swallowed her anger, tossing the groceries in the refrigerator and tearing through an EZ until she heard the bang of the garage door that meant Bob was on his way inside.

The March morning a pothole ripped open her front tire, Claire found herself stranded at George's Auto Shop—not so much a shop as it was George's front yard—and walked a mile to the Naber, bought a pack of Merit Lights and a Jumbo Puzzle Fun, and binged. Sitting on the curb, she filled up grid upon grid, smoking one cigarette after the next until her stomach was queasy and her head pounding so hard she could barely see. When she finished the last puzzle, she found herself staring at the inside back cover like the bottom of a ravaged cake pan: WRITE PUZZLES FROM HOME!

Despite her nausea, she felt a faint stir of something. Claire didn't believe in signs, but if she had, this would have come close. To not just finish puzzles, but to make them—*create* them. A crossword puzzle writer.

Better yet: A *cruciverbalist.*

It wasn't steady pay, wasn't even a steady job, but this wasn't about the money. You submitted a puzzle and, if published, were paid a small fee. Creating them, she found, came easy. Most of the puzzle consisted of tiny, EZ words, with two or three long ones bracing the middle to unify title and theme.

Claire's first puzzle was titled BUGGED!

The long words were:

Honeybees (Sweet stingers)

Butterfly (Ex-caterpillar)

La Cucaracha (Roach, south of the border)

Grasshopper (Drink with crème de menthe?)

It appeared in Deluxe EZ Crosswords, Volume 53, Number 8. Claire bought a bulletin board and tacked it above her desk.

Gradually, she began to fill her life with words again. Short words mostly, three and four letters. She became well versed in suffixes, prefixes, state abbreviations, compass points. She grew obsessed with short, vowel-bloated words like *nee, roe, oleo, olio, ewer, era.* Old English: *ne'er, e'er, o'er.* Celebrities: *Erma, Pia, Ella, Mia, Etta, Lou.* She dismantled words to consider all their possible permutations, examining the hairline differences between *relieve* and *relive, martial* and *marital, fall* and *fail.* She grew increasingly aware of the fickle nature of language, how easily it could mislead. *Bug,* for example, could be a flaw or a flea. Pest or pester, eavesdrop or annoy. In her head, she was constantly dissecting new words, boiling them down to their elements, scrutinizing every angle, every atom, all the many ways a thing could be defined.

BOB:

Mr. Newhart

Female haircut

Wobble

Pageboy

Aim for apples

It was in May, the end of the academic year, that it was Claire and Bob's turn to host the potluck. When Bob mentioned it one night after dinner, Claire's stomach sank. "But," he added quickly, "they said we don't have to."

"They?"

"Only, ah, if we want to."

"Why wouldn't we want to?" Claire snapped, and stood up to clear the table. More alarming than the prospect of hosting the faculty potluck was the possibility that her uselessness had become so visible, so known. Maybe this was her chance to start over and impress these people: to throw the perfect party she'd imagined when they first moved here. As this plan took root, Claire felt a faint but determined excitement. The next day she went out and bought new dishes, heavy blue earthenware. She got online and found recipes for organic cheesecakes, provocative salads with chickpeas and pears. The night of the party, she wore chandelier earrings and a long skirt that nearly grazed the floor. But by ten after seven, her attempt at a more sophisticated potluck had already devolved into just one more big fat bug joke when Terry arrived with a "dirt cake" (chocolate pudding mud, crushed Oreo dirt, gummy worms) that prompted so much strenuous laughter Claire felt like crying, like saying, "I married an entomologist—you think I've never seen a *dirt cake* before?"

By nine, the guests were gone. Claire stepped back into her bug slippers and laid her earrings on the windowsill. She faced the sink, piled high with earthenware, and stared out the window. The night sky was deep black and filled with bright stars, but they were just that: no shooting, twinkling, wishing. Her unhappiness had never looked clearer.

"Claire?"

It was the concern in Bob's voice that made Claire's eyes fill, the sound of her own sadness confirmed by someone else. When she turned, Bob was standing close but not touching, four earthenware goblets caught in his hands. Claire stepped forward and pressed her face to his neck. It was the closest she came to telling him—what? This thing, whatever was making her unhappy, wasn't small and fixable. To say it out loud might set in motion something she couldn't undo. Once she admitted she wasn't happy, their marriage became an unhappy marriage, and one of two things happened next: It fell apart or became the source of constant fear and stress and scrutiny, and she wasn't ready for either of those things.

"I'm just tired," she said, knowing he wouldn't push harder than this. Though in his work Bob was constantly posing questions, in life he always seemed to defer to what was happening around him, as if accepting that people behaved in ways he didn't understand. He didn't examine the life he was in, didn't analyze what he had or long for what he didn't. Even their relationship seemed like something he had tumbled into contentedly, and with little struggle, by virtue of looking up on the quad that October afternoon and seeing Claire standing there.

———

Claire lingers in the quiet. The only sound in the kitchen is the sprinkling of rain, a patter so delicate it's almost insulting. She stares out the window, caught in the pause between what just happened and what will happen next. The world outside is touched with a soft gray light, the light of dinners being almost ready and backyard games ending, the beginning of the day's end. When you love your life, this light may be the day's most comforting; when you don't, the most depressing.

Claire's gaze veers toward the garage, her heart pounding. One of them will have to be the first to emerge. She wonders what Bob is doing, if he's still standing in the spot she left him—the thought is too much to bear. She turns from the window and surveys the kitchen, hunting for some small acknowledgment of what just happened, but everything looks impossibly the same. The breakfast dishes in the sink, the last murky inch of coffee in the pot. The chicken she was making for dinner simmers in the slow cooker, languishing in a soy-sesame marinade.

On the floor beside the oven, four cucumber slices perch on a dish, glaring up at Claire with their rubbery green eyes. She looks away, toward the cookbook still splayed open on the counter. It was a wedding gift she and Bob received right before they moved here, along with a fondue set, cappuccino maker, snow shovel, flannel sheets, movie rental certificates—gifts for living together and, in retrospect, living together somewhere far away and cold. Those first few valiant months,

Claire had started working her way through the recipes, even penciling comments in the margins. TOO FRUITY. NEEDS DIJON! Seeing it now, she cannot imagine ever having been the kind of woman with the energy or the optimism to write something like NEEDS DIJON!

The room swells toward her. Claire leans back against the counter as a hail of small white spots bursts before her eyes. She closes them, tries to breathe, but the breath gets stuck in her chest. She remembers her college roommate, Erica, who once told her it was always smart to break up outside—that way the memory doesn't stick to anything, it breaks into particles, floats. Now Claire senses the minefield of memories lying in wait around her, jostling each other like children in the fading light. She opens her eyes only to see insects swarming the refrigerator door—magnets. Brown and green, generic-looking, interspersed with snippets of the Magnetic Poetry Book Lovers series. She scrapes the *Love* from the refrigerator door and stares down at it. What is a woman supposed to do in the moments after she decides to leave her husband? Take an aspirin? Heat some chicken soup? Pull down a suitcase and start to pack?

*Where would you go?* Bob had asked. There was more than curiosity in his tone—there was incredulity too. He didn't say "will," but "would," and in the world of verb tenses Claire knew what this implied. It was the second conditional: the hypothetical conditional, the "imaginary" conditional. It meant that Bob didn't believe she would actually go through with it. The assumption makes her angry, but the tiniest bit tempted. The prospect of figuring out what comes next feels terrifying—all the dismantling, the explaining, and worst of all, the shame she would—*will*—feel when admitting to the world that her life wasn't what it seemed.

Claire feels her throat tighten. She crosses the room, picks up the cucumber dish, and dumps it in the sink. The slices land with four disgusted splats. As she turns the water on, dish still in hand, she spots something moving. A spider, trundling its way across the sink floor. She jerks the faucet off and leans down, peering at it. Bob once told her that the spiders found roaming sinks are males who have fallen off their webs looking for mates, and this story struck her as so tragic, so undignified, that from then on whenever she saw one, absurd as she felt, she guided him onto her fingertip and set him free. This one is navigating an obstacle course of unwashed coffee mugs and milk-stained cereal spoons with admirable tenacity, skirting the four mossy craters that just came plummeting from the sky and nearly ended his life. How valiant, his efforts to survive. Entomology, Claire thinks, is not just science. Like everything else, it boils down to love and death.

"Claire."

She turns so quickly the dish slips from her hand and shatters on the floor. She stares at Bob, and Bob stares back, their eyes locked in surprised silence. Neither makes a move to clean up the mess.

"When did you come in?" she asks.

"Just now," he says.

Bob looks defeated: shoulders sagging, hands limp at his sides. Claire is struck suddenly by how much he has aged. It's easy to miss, living with a person, but now she notices the thickness in his face, the hair receding at the temples, blond yielding to gray. Next month, he will be thirty-six. For a moment, she is overcome with regret that she didn't wait a few weeks so he wouldn't celebrate his birthday alone.

"I thought maybe you'd already be packed," Bob says.

"Oh, no," Claire says quickly. "I wouldn't do that." It is weak reassurance, given the circumstances.

Bob sits down at the table. Claire crosses the room, side-stepping the broken dish, and sits in the opposite chair. She wishes now she'd turned off the crockpot. The sound of chicken bubbling and smell of dinner cooking seem sad.

"So are you really, ah, are you—" Bob fumbles, then stops, letting her finish the thought, but all she can come up with is, "Yes."

"Just for a while?"

"I think so. I don't really know."

Claire folds her hands in her lap. She wishes she hadn't taken her ring off with such a flourish; to put it back on now, though, might seem unfairly optimistic.

"So you're just leaving," Bob says, with a sudden bitterness. "Just like that."

"No," Claire says. "Not just like that. I—I've been feeling this way for a while."

He pulls his glasses off and sets them on the table, rubbing his eyes with the heels of his hands.

"I know. I should have said something. I guess I just thought that it would go away. That it was me."

"So it's me," he snaps, and Claire has the incongruous thought that finally, Bob is angry, and she likes him better this way.

"I don't know if it's us," she says. "Or this place. Or both."

He drops his hands back to the table. His eyes, without the glasses, look vulnerable and small.

"I guess I need to find out if it feels different," she says. "Somewhere else."

"Don't forget, wherever you go, there you are," Bob says, and it is completely uncharacteristic, but then so is the spiteful tone of his voice, and the trembling hand raking through his hair, and the fact that they are sitting here at all having this conversation.

"I know," Claire says. "I know that." She hears her voice catch. She will not cry; it would be unfair to cry. Then Bob is reaching for her hand across the table, and as sweet and selfless a gesture as this is, it makes her feel unbearably lonely.

He is quiet for a minute. "If you want," he says, "we can have a baby."

Claire has to bite her lip to keep from sobbing. "That's not it," she says. "I'm not sure I want to be married anymore."

Outside the window, a tree branch snaps, unleashing a flurry of snow. Minutes pass. Claire doesn't know if he's still holding her hand on purpose or has forgotten it's there.

Finally he says, "How long will it take? Before you know?" and it is such a classic Bob response that it might be funny, even endearing, if it weren't so exactly indicative of what the problem is.

She shakes her head. He lets go of her hand.

"I love you," he tells her, but it sounds flat and formal, a last attempt at a remedy that's failed many times before. When she doesn't respond, he scrapes his chair back roughly. "Why don't you call me when you get where you're going," he says, and starts toward the door. Halfway across the room, he turns. Claire looks up—was there more? *Please, let there be more.* Without meeting her eyes he walks back to the table, grabs his glasses, then crunches back across the kitchen, and slams the door.

Claire keeps her eyes on the table. She listens to the engine rev and the anxious spin of tires on snow. She stands, watching out the window, as the car pulls off down the street, faster and jerkier than usual, white exhaust pluming behind it like a cape. Sound dissolves. The ticking of the oven clock emerges from the quiet. She turns again to face the kitchen, heart pounding. When Bob gets back, she needs to be gone.

First, she retrieves the broom and dustpan from the closet and kneels on the floor, sweeping up the broken dish, and tries, calmly, to review her options. She could stay in a hotel tonight, just for a night, but it seems too sad, too desperate. She can't bear the details: the plastic key card, the drinking glasses topped with pleated paper crowns. She could call one of the wives, but isn't close enough with any of them; it would trigger too much gossip, require too much explanation. She wishes she had an old close friend, one with a big house and a warm heart. With a bearish husband who would welcome Claire inside, taking her suitcase and giving her elbow a reassuring squeeze. He'd say something corny like, "I know, time to make like a tree and leave," then carry the kids upstairs while the friend steered Claire to the kitchen, poured her tea or bourbon, and told her she was absolutely doing the right thing.

Her last close friend was Erica, but that was back in college. The truth is, Claire has no friend close enough to call at a moment like this.

Claire stands. A few splinters of broken china stick to the knees of her jeans. She could drive to her parents' house, sitting empty in Philadelphia, but even in a crisis this is the last place she wants to be. She considers her father, in his new Jersey shore condo, and imagines pulling up there in the middle of the night: the soft crunch of tires over pink pebbles, the tinge of salt in the air. For a moment the prospect is comforting, the two of them sitting at the kitchen table tomorrow morning, quietly drinking coffee and trading sections of the paper. But it isn't the condo's kitchen she's imagining; it's a different kitchen, and a different father. These days her contact with Gene is infrequent enough that the prospect of staying with him is awkward, not to mention depressing: some attenuated version of their former family in some attenuated version of their former home in some attenuated version of their former summer vacation. Claire spent Christmas there, convincing herself the Jersey shore off-season might feel blustery and dramatic. Instead it was near-deserted and freezing, a fossil of its summer self. The amusement rides were frozen, the boardwalk stores sleeping under dead signs and chain metal. But the worst was the condo itself, sparse, scary-clean, furnished with the few things Gene had decided to bring with him. Two rocking chairs, three plates, a cuckoo clock—there wasn't enough there to constitute new rooms; they felt more like tributes to old rooms. When Claire asked why he didn't take something more comfortable he said, "I didn't bring anything I couldn't carry," which sounded like the rationale of a man with too much pride, or an emergency evacuee.

The room is darkening at the edges, the rain lashing the

window in sharp, icy flecks. Claire empties the dustpan into the trash, then pulls off her bug slippers and shoves them on top. As she scans the floor for any missed shards, something on the far side of the room catches her eye—a tiny black squiggle. Could it be the spider? Escaped from the sink and running for his life? She practically runs across the room. It isn't the spider, of course. It's the magnet she must have dropped on the floor.

LOVE:

Valentine catchphrase

Makes the world go 'round

TV's *Boat*

Term of endearment

"Crazy," acc. to Van Morrison

Placing it on the tip of her finger, Claire closes her eyes, makes a wish, and blows. When she opens them, the *Love* hasn't budged. She returns the magnet to the refrigerator door, next to the gaping maw of a magnetic spider. Outside, the sleet is turning to snow. The ruts from Bob's tires have disappeared.

Claire moves quickly toward the phone and flips through her address book. Cradling the receiver under her chin, she dials. The ringing on the other end sounds as far away as it is.

"Hello?"

It is her voice, no question about it.

"Hi," Claire says. "It's me."

A pause: "Claire?" Then: "Oh my God. What's wrong?"

It is then that the tears spill over, the first Claire has cried all day, because she realizes her sister would instantly, and correctly, assume a call from her means that something must be wrong.

"What happened?" Noelle is saying. Her voice is crackling. "Are you okay?"

"No." Claire waits for the explanation to assemble itself, but when it does, the words are simple. "I'm leaving Bob."

Claire waits, pressing the receiver hard against her ear, and despite the bad reception she can hear the moment a smile cracks her sister's face. "I never thought you'd have the guts."

# CHAPTER THREE: Guts

No _____, no glory
Abdominal workings
Beer-drinking casualty (pl.)
Easy college courses
Courage
Nerve

So you're bugging out," Noelle says.

The joke catches Claire off guard, and she's laughing and crying at the same time. "It isn't funny," she says, even though it kind of is.

"Well, I give you props," Noelle tells her. "I mean, I know I barely knew the guy, but I mean, the bug thing? It always sounded kind of gross. And was he bad in bed? It kind of seemed like he'd be bad in bed—I can stay this stuff now, right? Is this helping?"

Claire feels a pinch of defensiveness, though it's not like Noelle's candor should surprise her.

"I'd rather you didn't," she says. "I mean, it's more like a break. I don't even know what I'm going to do yet."

"Oh. Sorry." Noelle pauses. "Well, how did he take it? When you said you were leaving? Was there a big blow-out?"

Claire shakes her head into the phone.

"Did he cry?"

Has she ever really seen Bob cry? His eyes had watered sometimes, near onions and in strong winds.

"Did he try to, like, win you back? What did he say?" The line crackles. "Are you still there?"

"Where would you go."

"What?"

"That was the first thing he said—where would you go."

"Oh."

Claire can hear her disappointment, and she is right to be disappointed. Had it been Noelle's story, it would have been better. For all her love of words, Claire could never tell a story like her sister. Even if the reality of a situation was under-whelming, Noelle could cobble together some drama from its ruins, exaggerating this detail, inventing that one.

"Then he said we could have a baby," Claire said.

"Because you wanted one and he didn't?"

"No. Not really."

"Oh," Noelle says, clearly confused. "Well, so, back up. Where *will* you go?"

"What?"

"Where . . . will . . ."

"Right." Claire had heard her the first time. Though she is grateful for the implied confidence of *will* instead of *would*, she doesn't want to admit she has no answer. "I guess I'm still figuring it out."

"Well you don't have to. You're coming here."

"Where?" Claire pauses. "Ireland?"

"Why not?"

Claire turns toward the wall, as if not wanting to be overheard. "Because it's a different country, Noe. Because I have nowhere to live there. I have nothing to *do* there—"

"What are you doing where you are? Like, cooking and cleaning?"

"I'm working on my dissertation."

"Can't you put that on hold until you get back?"

"And also, I write crossword puzzles." The word *cruciverbalist* wriggles in her jaw. "I construct them."

"But you're just a freelancer, right?"

Claire closes her eyes. She reminds herself that not everyone chooses words as carefully as she does, as Bob does.

"Seriously, and I know this goes against every responsible bone in your body, but you shouldn't think, just act. Do you have a passport?"

"Of course." Claire thinks fleetingly of her honeymoon in the Caribbean. Even that vacation had seemed a function of Bob's research: a bioluminescent bay, a swath of mosquito netting.

"So grab it. Fly standby—to Shannon, not Dublin—and call me when you get here. The timing is perfect. We'll drink some pints and figure this all out."

"Wait—" Claire presses the phone tight to her ear, as if doing so will tether her sister to the line. "I would have nowhere to stay."

"What's that supposed to mean? You'd stay with us."

By us, Noelle means herself and Paul, the boyfriend, the reason she moved to Ireland in the first place.

"I'd feel like I was imposing," Claire says.

"Oh my God, please. Haven't you heard of the Irish hospitality? Making tea and having guests—they live for this shite."

Claire stalls, submerged in the static. She imagines the distance between herself and her sister—a snowstorm, an ocean, five time zones, God knows what else.

"Listen, I'm not going to beg," Noelle says. Her voice is getting flat, impatient, maybe bored. "If you don't want to come, don't come. But I think it would be good for you."

Claire throws a panicked glance around the kitchen. The reality, she reminds herself, is that she has no other choice.

"Fine," she says.

"Seriously?"

"But only for a few days—"

"Brilliant!" Noelle says, already not listening. She affects a thick brogue and sings out: "May the road rise to meet you!"

The last two times Claire saw her sister were for sacraments—marriage and death. The marriage was Claire's, two summers before. Against her better judgment, she had succumbed to superstition about the groom not seeing the bride the night before the wedding and agreed to stay at the house. Noelle was home for the weekend, prepared to wrestle her way into a pale blue bridesmaid dress she openly despised. It wasn't unusual for Noelle to be home on weekends; she went to college less than an hour from there, at a state school she despised too. On this visit, she had announced her arrival with a new metal-rimmed hole in each earlobe: round as a hubcap, wide enough to drop loose change through. Noelle had a reputation for empty threats—she'd sworn many times to get a tattoo, become a vegan, a Scientologist—but that day, her recklessness felt earnest. There was the proof, yawning in her earlobes. Even their mother winced, telling Noelle to wear her hair long for the wedding so she could pick up boys.

"I don't *want* to pick up boys," Noelle said. She was sprawled on one end of the sofa, Deirdre on the other. Claire and her father were sitting in the rocking chairs. The TV was tuned to the Home Shopping Network, which they weren't watching so much as letting fill up space. Only Deirdre was paying attention, sipping a can of Miller High Life with eyes fixed on the screen.

"I already met one," Noelle reminded them.

This was the romance proving to dominate the wedding weekend, not Claire and Bob but Noelle and Paul, the Irish bartender she'd spent the summer with on the Jersey shore. Now that the summer was over, Paul had returned to Ireland, for which Claire was secretly thankful. She didn't want a stranger in her wedding pictures, and it was just the kind of thing Noelle would have insisted on.

"I won't ever want to meet another boy again," Noelle said. "Swear to God."

"Watch it," said Deirdre.

Though she wouldn't hesitate to swear in fifty different languages, their mother got nervous whenever God was involved. It terrified her that Claire wasn't getting married in a Catholic church, so much so that she'd called her in the graduate dorm.

"What did you say he is?" Deirdre asked, when Claire picked up. "An atheist?"

"Mom?"

It was rare that Claire and her mother spoke on the phone, something Claire's college roommates had always found sad and fascinating. Claire made the obligatory calls home to check in now and then, but spoke mostly to her father; Deirdre often didn't feel well enough to get on.

"What are you talking about?"

"Your bug man." Her mother's voice sounded smaller than it did in person, her puff-chestedness almost cartoonish. "Who won't get married in a church. He's an atheist?"

"It wasn't just his decision. It was both—"

"Atheist?"

"No," Claire said. "He's an agnostic."

"A snot?"

"An *agnostic.*"

"Never heard of it."

"It means someone who believes—that we can't know what to believe," Claire said. "That it's impossible to prove either way. That God exists, or doesn't exist."

Claire was glad she didn't have to see the expression on her mother's face. If pressed—say, in multiple-choice format—she would have labeled herself an agnostic too. In her mind, it was the only logical way to go. But she had so far avoided having to admit this out loud, and was grateful, plagued as she was by the faint but nagging fear that if she did she might be damned to hell.

Sitting in the living room the night before her godless or possibly Godless wedding, Claire shot Noelle a look of warning. The last thing she needed was to reawaken the church debate. When it came to religion, like most things, Noelle had aligned herself with Deirdre. She had sung in the children's church choir, helped make floats for CYO parades, claimed to sacrifice something for Lent every spring. She had worn a cross on a chain around her neck since her First Communion, though over the years it had morphed from a delicate silver necklace to a variety of cheap, chunky pendants bought at the mall, attached to plastic backings labeled FASHION JEWELRY. Unlike taking the Lord's name in vain, this never seemed to worry Deirdre; if it wasn't explicitly a commandment, she let it slide.

"Sorry, Mom," Noelle said. "But I'm telling you, this guy is the one. The man I'm going to marry."

Deirdre's eyes didn't stray from the TV.

"Noelle Conneely," Noelle mused. "Noelle Conneely . . . Mr. and Mrs. Paul Conneely . . ."

"Noelle," their father said.

"What?" Noelle pounced. "You didn't think I'd take his last name?"

"Let's just take this one wedding at a time."

"I bet I'm way more traditional than you think, Dad. Did I tell you Paul goes to church? Every week? Like, voluntary? Last year he gave up beer for Lent."

This news had seemingly no effect on Gene, though of course it wasn't him it was intended for.

"I know he's the one. I just do. I feel it in my *bones*." Noelle glanced again at Deirdre; this was one of their mother's signature lines, though in Deirdre's case the feeling was literal too.

Deirdre was still fixed on the TV, where a coiffed saleswoman was peddling aquamarine anklets.

"Maybe I'll drop out of school," Noelle said, fingering the metal in her ears.

"Noelle, please," from their father.

"Why not? It didn't hurt Mom any." She reached behind the couch for Deirdre's cane. "I bet you a million dollars I'm not learning anything I'll need to know in ten years. I mean, bio? Algebra? Proofs? *Proofs*? Dad, seriously, in your entire life, have you ever sat down to do a proof?"

"You just don't like your school," Claire said, unable to help herself.

"Yeah," Noelle said, throwing her a glance. "Thanks for reminding me."

"I'm just saying, there are alternatives—" Claire began, then stopped. She had given Noelle college advice before and sworn never to do it again.

Noelle had laid the cane across her knees and was holding her hands under her chin, chipping polish from one thumbnail with the other thumbnail. "I think I'm more like one of those students of the world types," she said, flecks of pink polish drifting into her lap. "Dad, think of it this way—if I drop out, I save you money. You and Mom can take that cruise you always wanted to."

It was hard to tell if Noelle actually believed this or had performed some mental manipulation to convince herself it was true. Gene and Deirdre had absolutely never mentioned wanting to take a cruise.

"I'll go live in Ireland," Noelle said. "Paul already invited me. I can stay with him for a while, travel around and soak up the culture—"

"No you don't," Deirdre cut her off.

Noelle paused. It wasn't like their mother not to support her unconditionally. That was their deal.

"But Ireland, Mom," she said. "My whole life you've been saying I should get in touch with my roots—"

"I don't mean not ever," Deirdre said. "Just not now."

Noelle had her mouth open to protest, but the look on Deirdre's face was enough to make her reconsider. Their mother's eyes were hard, bright with fever, or fervor, Claire was never sure.

"I couldn't be prouder to see you become an Irish barmaid, honey," Deirdre said, eyes still on the TV. "But I could drop dead any day. Do your traveling on your time, not mine."

In the silence that followed, tears began slipping down Noelle's cheeks.

"For God's sake, Dee," Gene said, standing up and knocking his rocking chair backward. He stalked from the room and left it there, like a beached animal, curved claws pointed toward the ceiling and rolled helplessly onto its back.

From the corner of her eye, Claire watched Noelle. Still crying, she had turned her attention to the cane, on which she had started writing, in blue nail polish, MOTHER OF THE BRIDE.

Later that night, after Gene and Deirdre had gone to bed, Claire went looking for her sister. Maybe it was the scene in the living room, the quietness of Noelle's crying, the undeniability of those holes gaping in her ears, or the finality of this, Claire's last night as a single woman, but she had the urge to offer her little sister some advice. She found Noelle facedown on her bed, paging through a magazine and attacking a Charleston Chew. The marshmallow fudge stretched from her mouth like a lavish white tongue.

"Can I come in?" Claire asked.

"You are in." Noelle didn't look up.

Claire looked for a place to sit, bypassing the foot of the bed in favor of the floor, where she lowered herself to an orange beanbag that crunched when she sat on it. "So," she said, struggling to sit up straight. "How are you doing? Are you doing okay?"

"I'm doing fucking awesome," Noelle said. She tossed her magazine in Claire's lap. "According to this."

Claire let the magazine unfurl. It was a quiz. *Are You Settling Down—or Just Settling?* The photo was of a couple sitting on a couch, the guy pointing the remote at the TV, holding a bowl of cheese curls in his lap and draping a loose arm across the woman's shoulders. She was looking away and biting her lip, her face a mask of doubt and oil-free foundation.

"I got an eighty-eight." Noelle balled her candy wrapper and aimed for the wastebasket, hitting it in a perfect arc. "You try."

"I'm not really in the mood, Noelle. I just came to make sure you were—"

"Oh, come on, tonight's *perfect*. Brink of being a grown-up and all that. Are you afraid of what it's going to say?"

"No." Claire picked up the magazine. "Fine. Give me the pen."

Noelle tossed her pen on the carpet, leaving a blue smear on the fuzzy orange thread. As Claire picked it up, the mere weight of a pen in her hand poised over a list of questions was enough to give her confidence. She was good at tests. Tests were her thing. She'd scored a perfect 800 on the logic portion of the GRE. But as she began wading through the questions, she found all of her check marks falling in the "no" column. No to skydiving, no to karaoke, no to sex on a beach. For the first time ever, she was thankful for that one-night stand in college. As she moved down the list, the experiences grew progressively more adventurous.

*Bungee jumping: no.*

*Sex in an elevator: no.*

*No.*

*No.*

*No.*

*No.*

Claire began to panic. It wasn't a real test, she reminded herself, it was in a fashion magazine. It was designed to make you feel you needed self-improvement, which translated to buying more magazines. Who cared that she hadn't had sex on her parents' bed—who would *want* to? She was marrying a smart man, a smart and well-respected man. It was actually horrifying to know Noelle had scored so high.

Claire's score: nine.

Her prescription: *Girl, loosen up!*

Her sound inside: a faint alarm.

"So?" Noelle said. She was slicking her nails a garish blue, to match the cane and clash with the bridesmaid dress. "What'd you get?"

Claire pushed herself up off the floor. "Sixty," she said, and as the word came out, she felt justified stretching the truth. The test was unfair in the first place.

Noelle looked up. "Really?"

Claire looked pointedly at her blue nails. "Could you not wear that tomorrow, please?" she said, and walked out, taking the magazine with her. She tossed it in the bathroom trash can, but minutes later fished it out and stuffed it in the back of her dresser drawer.

———

*Bob,*
*Went to Ireland to visit my sister.*
*I'll call when I get there.*
*I'm sorry.*

Claire reads her note once more before turning off the light. She picks up her suitcase and walks across the kitchen floor, treading lightly, carefully, the way you treat a thing as you're leaving it. Outside, the snow is falling steadily, the stripe of garage windows silvery in the moonlight. Claire pictures her wedding ring, sitting on Bob's desk in the bottom of the jar and, as she shuts the back door, feels the judging eyes of a hundred dead bugs.

For the first time in a long while, Claire is grateful Bob is a scientist. Even though when he took his vows he meant them literally, she knows Bob knows marriage is an inexact science; he understands its likelihood of success. Her husband is woefully realistic, and if it's part of what made their marriage difficult, she hopes it will be part of what makes her leaving, if not easy, at least easier for him to understand.

The cab is waiting by the curb. As Claire starts across the moonlit snow, relief and fear collide in her chest. It is the dead of winter. The woods are silent, except for her footsteps and breath.

## CHAPTER FOUR:  Eire

**T**o make a crossword puzzle, you begin with the theme. Fill in the long crossbars up and down the middle—these words should be cleverly, conceptually related and, if parallel, contain the same number of letters. Most EZ freelancers download the grids from crossword software. At first, this seemed to Claire like cheating, yet there was something about starting with an empty grid she found irresistible: preset, prelettered, ghost words waiting to be filled. Some software programs also offer suggestions for the words themselves but these, she promised herself, she would never use.

After the theme is in place, the long words spawn small words, and small ones spawn smaller ones—*ibids, eons, okos*—like a branch growing twigs. Claire is careful to avoid anything too negative. Curse words, obviously. References to illness, politics, war. She tries to be original and come up with fresh three- and four-letter combinations, but sometimes, out of necessity, she must revert to one of the standbys. *O'er, ore, e'er, ewe, stet, eke, eire.* It's good to know words like these are out there—bite-size, full of vowels, useful in a pinch. They are words rarely used in actual conversation, their primary function crossword filler, to bridge the gaps between awkward consonants or plug an empty corner of an unfinished puzzle like spackle on a hole.

EIRE:

Ireland

Erin

Emerald Isle

Bono's homeland

Where eyes are smilin'!

Sitting on a plane headed to Eire, Claire stares at her crossword notebook sitting open on her plastic tray table. When she is anxious, her mind usually lapses instinctively into puzzle mode, but tonight she can't concentrate. She is imagining Bob's surprise when he finds her note on the kitchen table. Once, before they were married, Claire had overheard him explaining her family to his. "Claire's mother has, ah, a chronic sickness," Bob said.

Claire was in the next room doing the dinner dishes, but when she realized what they were talking about, stepped closer to the door.

"But it isn't, ah, fatal," he said, followed by a long pause. Claire tried to imagine what Bob might be doing—miming a bottle raised to the lips? A pill tossed down the hatch? Twirling a long finger beside his ear? "Her father's a carpet salesman."

"Are they still married?" asked Bob's sister, Susan, and Claire was grateful that he could answer that one with a firm yes. But in describing Claire's relationship with Noelle, Bob hesitated again. "They're, ah, estranged."

On autopilot, Claire walked briskly into the living room, asking, "Anyone for coffee?" Later she told Bob *estranged* was the wrong word: It implied some kind of horrible betrayal, some hidden family secret. It wasn't accurate, she said, and this was true. No dramatic rift had come between Claire and Noelle. They were seven years apart. When Claire left for college, Noelle was still wearing braces and selling Girl Scout cookies. As siblings go, they just weren't close. The month after Deirdre died, when Gene retired abruptly and bought the condo, Noelle made good on her promise: quit college, took off for Ireland, and hadn't been back since.

Claire stares at the empty grid. The squares are beginning to blur. On the screen in the seat back in front of her, a little digital airplane is painstakingly tracking her journey from one country to the next. She closes her eyes, wishing for sleep, but her mind is alert, racing. Her anxiety isn't just about seeing Noelle. But to see her here, of all places—the country her mother had made impossible to love. The country responsible for all her broguing and dancing and, what the hell, drinking. "May the road rise to meet you!"—do real Irish people even *say* that? Deirdre had been born in Ireland, but lived there only thirteen months; nonetheless, they were the months that most defined her. She claimed to remember a few choice details: a fog that blanketed the streets like soft yarn, a pink house with a red door, uncles who played violins in the evenings, and an aunt who ate a pound of chocolate and a scrambled egg for breakfast every morning. An only child of dead parents, Deirdre had no one to confirm or deny her stories, and though the precision of the details belied her age no one dared suggest they weren't true. The only real proof was the birth certificate—Deirdre O'Hanlan, County Limerick, 1952—hanging in the living room, like a diploma, in a cheap gold frame. More than evidence of her mother's birth, it was proof of her very self: her claim to an entire country, a heritage, a history. It was permission to be who she was.

In Claire's opinion, most of that heritage had amounted to accessorizing—the CDs, the green sweaters, the sinks and showers stocked unironically with pungent bars of Irish Spring soap. Deirdre even professed to love Yeats—her sole concession to "literature," though she still managed to undermine it by holding her nose to affect a pinched, snooty tone. Several volumes of his *Collected Works* lurked under the glass-topped coffee table in the living room, his face staring up from the top of the stack: thin, craggy, bespectacled, carved from rock and shadow. Under the warped glass, his features looked muted, as if underwater, their dignity chipped away by the remote controls and wadded tissues and soda cans. Only on Saint Pat's did he experience a brief, voracious freedom. Hours of eating and drinking and dancing culminated, with a kind of sloppy inevitability, in reading. Deirdre would hoist up a heavy volume and brogue her way through one or two or four or eighteen poems, depending on how many cans of High Life she had had. "Let us rise and go now!" she would recite, voice cresting and faltering, blue eyes pooling in her rough, red face, and Claire had to fight the urge to look away.

She had always felt dubious, and somewhat embarrassed, about her mother's Irish nostalgia. Even Deirdre's rigorous Catholicism seemed to rely heavily on the accents: rosaries wound around bedposts, dramatic arcs of palm stuck in mirror frames, snippets of manger hay tucked in wallets, and plastic spritzers of ocean water collected every summer in Ocean City. Every August, their family vacation was timed to coincide with the fifteenth—the Feast of the Assumption, a Catholic holy day of obligation and old Irish tradition. It was, for Deirdre, a fantastic convergence of her own holy trinity: Ireland, Catholicism, and the Jersey shore.

The morning of the fifteenth, Deirdre would head to 8:00 a.m. Mass, alone with an empty plastic soda bottle clamped under her arm. When Mass ended, the priest led all the parishioners to the beach, where he blessed the ocean and the crowd waded in up to their knees, dunking their containers under and letting the "miraculous water" fill them. Claire and Noelle sat on the porch of their rented house, nibbling doughnuts, waiting. Gene read the paper, keeping one eye on the shore. Much as having Deirdre at home felt turbulent, stressful, not having her there was a different kind of unsettling—even Noelle sensed it, staying uncharacteristically quiet—like the uneasy tension that befalls a town after a storm. Eventually, the group appeared in the distance, making their way along the boardwalk from the beach. They made an unusual pilgrimage, a small mob of what were clearly vacationers, sporting various degrees of suntans and sunburns, T-shirts and sweatshirts that said OCBP, carrying their heavy, sloshing jars and bottles in front of their bellies. Noelle would be the one to yell, "I see them!" and scramble to the porch railing. When Deirdre arrived, she didn't say a word, but went upstairs to bed, setting the bottle of miraculous water on the kitchen counter.

Claire could not keep her eyes off that bottle. In the light from the window, salt and silt swirled like a glittery, holy fish tank behind the most mundane of labels: Birch Beer, Black Cherry Wishniak, orange stickers that said NICE PRICE or 99c! It seemed not unlike her mother, common on the outside—lowbrow even—but possessed of some mysterious, elevated inner workings. It intimidated Claire like the smudge of ash that appeared each year in the middle of her mother's forehead. It was her mother and not her mother. It was a soda bottle and something more. *I know more than you do*, said the bottle, majestic in the sunlight and somehow morally superior to the wrinkled, fleshy jelly doughnut they'd saved for her on the plate beside it.

Back in Philadelphia, Deirdre would transfer the water into plastic plant spritzers she labeled MW—not to be confused with regular, nonmiraculous water—to spray on their foreheads when they were sick. Sometimes she even spritzed her own joints, like an oilcan. Whenever Claire went back to college, Deirdre followed her to the car and doused the windshield, broguing, "May the road rise to meet you!" She claimed that she used it to boil the potatoes on Saint Patrick's Day, but of this there was no proof.

Claire presses the Off button on the screen, the little airplane evaporating blissfully into dark. She turns to the little window, scraping back the shade to look out at the empty sky. She can practically hear her mother's triumphant chuckle. *I know more than you do.* Deirdre had never gone to college, worked the same Sears jewelry counter for twenty years, but spoken or unspoken, those six words were the addendum to every sentence she delivered: her stamp of wisdom, earned through age or chronic sickness or simply maternal rank. She'd always sworn Claire would one day come to Ireland, a prospect Claire thought about as likely as her moving back home. Now it feels as if her mother has won something—a double victory. Not only is Claire running to the country her mother loved, she's running from the husband her mother never liked.

"*What* does he do?" Deirdre had asked, cornering Claire in the kitchen the first time she brought Bob home. It was Saint Patrick's Day, and though Deirdre wasn't feeling well, nothing would keep her out of commission. Every year, she cooked the traditional corned beef and cabbage. She smothered the house in gaudy green decorations, paper leprechauns—LUCK O' THE IRISH!—and withered green streamers that looked like the stems of dying plants. In the background, musical Irish brothers— the Makems, the Clancys—played jigs and reels and mournful ballads. Like Deirdre, the music of Ireland could swing from cheerful to melancholy in a blink. When Claire was small, before Noelle was born, Deirdre used to play her the Clare Reels, a series of step dances from County Clare, clasping her hand to her chest and swinging her in giggling, dizzy circles. Years later, Claire could remember the beer on her breath, the firmness of her grasp, the warmth that emanated like an oven from beneath her skin, like cooking and sweat and the deodorant that wore off under her sleeves in pasty white half-moons.

In the car with Bob, on the way there, Claire had heard herself quoting her father: "The only thing predictable about lupus is its unpredictability." This was Gene's party line whenever they had to cancel plans at the last minute because Deirdre felt a flare coming on. Even as a child, Claire had never needed to be told. She was seven when Deirdre was diagnosed, and from then on, their house was dictated by the ebb and flow of the disease: fever and fatigue lurking and leaving, a constant game of attack and retreat. She grew attuned to the shift in the air as the "impending flare"—that's what her father called it, like a foreboding weather system—approached their house, a cloud crawling over the sun, the shadows in the house growing darker and longer. "Impending flare?" Claire would ask, and her father would nod, and she would nod back, solemn as an army nurse. For years, Claire clung tightly to that word: *flare*. It was one of only a few words she had to explain her mother, even if she didn't fully understand it. She knew *flares* were the names of the flaming sticks set up around car accidents, and *flair* was something her mother praised Blanche on *The Golden Girls* for having. These colliding definitions confused her, yet also made a certain sense, for the same quality that existed in funny, fearless Blanche and the bright drama of those flaming sticks were qualities she sensed existed somewhere in her mother too.

On this particular Saint Pat's, Deirdre had a temporary shamrock tattoo on her left cheek, a green plastic top hat perched on her head, a green streamer wound around her cane like a barber shop pole. But beneath the jauntiness of the costume, Claire saw that the joints in her hands and feet were swollen. Her skin was flushed, her red hair sweat-flattened. A butterfly rash spread like a stripe of sunburn under her eyes and across the bridge of her nose. Her attempts to conceal it had only made it more conspicuous, liquid base several degrees darker than her skin tone spackled on so starkly it looked like war paint. And yet, behind her cane and hat and thick, botched makeup job, she had never looked more formidable.

"What's his job again?" Deirdre asked. She was holding a Miller High Life in one hand, leaning on her cane with the other. As she spoke, she screwed up her face as if she smelled something rotten, something besides the warm, cabbagey fog that filled the kitchen and, Claire knew too well, would linger there for days. "Something with bugs?"

"Yes." Claire lowered her voice. "He studies insects."

"He's an exterminator?"

"He's an entomologist." They had covered these details before, but Claire knew to expect this from her mother. Despite her air of superiority, Deirdre was ornery in any situation that highlighted things she didn't know—books she hadn't read, references she'd never heard. She dismissed any movie with subtitles as "artsy fartsy" and had long ago forbidden Gene to join the neighborhood book club. When confronted with an unfamiliar word, Deirdre made a great show of bungling it, reducing it to something unglamorous—"What's that you said? Hypocrite? Oh excuse me, I heard hippo shit."

"Bob is very well respected," Claire said. "He's very smart."

Deirdre rolled her eyes and took a swig of beer. "Smart, shmart," she said.

Claire looked at the floor. She reminded herself that Deir-dre's condescension was about her own discomfort. And on that particular night, as Claire took in her mother's knuckles gripping the head of her cane, the rash sprinkling her face, pain flashing in her eyes, Claire saw, too, that she couldn't begin to appreciate how real, how literal, that discomfort was.

Suddenly, Deirdre set her beer down on the kitchen table. She crossed the room slowly, leaning on her cane, and reached for a bottle of painkillers from the windowsill. It was a new bottle, the cap screwed tight; because of her weak grip, the caps were usually left on loosely, sitting on top of the bottles at odd angles like jaunty sailors' hats. Claire watched her mother's pinky finger crumple as she struggled with the lid.

"Here, let me—" Claire said, just as she heard the top pop off, followed by the sound of rain, the fleshy silence.

"Hand me my beer."

Claire reached for the High Life on the table and passed it to her mother. Deirdre dropped a pill on her tongue. Claire kept her eyes on the row of bottles, interspersed with jars of spices—Naprosyn, Red Pepper Flakes, Plaquenil, Daypro, Ital-ian Seasoning. With her back still turned, Deirdre tilted her chin back and poured the rest of the beer down her throat.

Claire dropped her eyes to the floor, said nothing. Her mother was sick, had always been sick; she had learned to say nothing.

"Does he make you laugh?" Deirdre said.

Claire looked up. Her mother was heading slowly back across the room.

"Does he write you love letters?" Deirdre wiped a stripe of

foam from her top lip. Her eyes were wet. "Does he give you butterflies? Does he make your heart go pitty-pat?"

Then Deirdre was standing in front of her, reaching out to cup Claire's cheek. Claire stiffened, then the hand was gone, so quickly Deirdre might have been picking off an eyelash. Deirdre looked at her evenly. "I want you to fall in love," she said.

Claire held her gaze and replied, "I am."

Looking out the window at the dark, endless sky, Claire imagines her mother lounging on some paunchy celestial cloud, dressed in her favorite fake-silk bathrobe and chugging a can of High Life. In the background, an Irish jig blasts from some hidden sound system, until Claire realizes that it's coming from a real sound system, and that she is about to begin her descent.

———

Shannon Airport feels oddly leisurely, more like a shopping mall than a center of international transportation. People are dressed in the colors of dirt and oatmeal. On a television mounted to the wall, newscasters laugh and sip tea. Across the lobby, travelers are lined up at counters raising glasses, dipping spoons in soup bowls, spearing sausages the size of rolling pins with forks gripped in left fists, all of it so casual they could be sitting in their own kitchens. All this tea and ease seems designed to undermine Claire's own sense of urgency. Noelle, whom Claire called twice with her flight information, is nowhere to be found.

Claire stares at her lap, feeling conspicuous in her J. Crew cypress coat. She is annoyed at Noelle already, for letting her *be* this person—a woman who's just left her husband, sitting in an airport alone. Though as she scans the airport, Claire concedes that there is no place she could blend in more. Noelle was the one who had inherited the Germanic half of their Irish-Germanic father—her skin tanned and her hair was mud brown, despite several botched attempts to Irishize it with powdered cherry Kool-Aid mix. And yet, it was Noelle who embraced her 75 percent Irishness. When she was six, she asked to take Irish dancing lessons, sensing even then the most direct route to their mother's heart. Even as a teenager she never quit her dancing, performing in competitions and VFW halls and, the high point of Deirdre's year, the local Saint Patrick's Day parade. The girls in Noelle's troupe all looked identical: row after row of full-skirted green dresses, sweetly freckled faces, arms straight at sides, knees hiked to chins, expressions blank as plates. But Noelle looked different; it was more than physical. Her body moved in step with the others, but her face was always working, revealing something the others' didn't, some sweat or struggle that was about more than the exertion of the dance. Deirdre attended every performance. If she wasn't feeling well, she brought her cane, all the better for banging on the ground.

Claire thinks she sees Noelle and feels a splash of nerves, but no—a different young, thin, dark-haired girl. She checks her watch: 7:35 a.m. The streets in New Hampshire must be plowed by now, the morning still and quiet, the frosted apostrophes of snow arching over the curbs. She pictures Bob asleep, mouth parted and blond hair spilling onto the pillow. She knows these thoughts are not nostalgia necessarily, but displacement; still, as she looks at the pale stripe on her ring finger, she wonders if she was too rash.

RASH:

Reckless

Skin affliction

In her tired mind the definitions merge, separate but connected, as memories of the butterfly rashes that spread across her mother's face are linked, vaguely but definitely, to the itchy, hasty, impulsive feeling that brought her here.

"Claire!"

Blurriness sharpens to a point: a quick, thin figure with dark hair and blue jeans, flushed and waving, running toward her.

Claire stands, bracing herself for Noelle to grab her, but once there, Noelle hesitates. They hug from the shoulders up, leaning across the moat of luggage. Noelle clutches one arm tight around Claire's neck; Claire presses both palms flat against Noelle's back.

"I am so sorry I'm late," Noelle says, when Claire steps back.

She looks different, Claire thinks. Older. Softer. Her face is rosy and damp with rain and her hair has returned to its natural brown, a dark, tousled curtain with a crooked part down the middle. She is wearing dark blue jeans and a nondescript brown wool sweater. If Noelle doesn't look like an Irish person, she's at least dressed like one.

"So what happened is, Paul loaned the car to his friend Rodger," Noelle says, slightly out of breath. "And Rodg was late returning it, so I got a wee bit of a late start. Then on the way here I got mixed up—you wouldn't believe the roads, there are no signs *any*where—so I stopped and asked this woman who was in her front yard, like, tending sheep. Before you know it she's inviting me in for tea, and I didn't want to say no since she was being really sweet—plus it's considered, like, morally rude if someone offers you tea here and you don't take it—" Noelle's hands are flying around, conducting her fantastic excuse. "So I go inside—and before you freak out, trusting strangers is like a thing here—and I told this lady, her name was Mary, I told her I was going to the airport and she said I had loads of time, but she might have been slagging me because, get this, it turns out she had an ulterior *motive*. Her *son*. Who she thought I was supposed to *marry*. She thought me showing up at their house was some kind of sign I was the daughter she never had. I swear! There are Irish people who believe in this kind of thing, Claire. And not just old people either, young people, like they don't even know each other, they just have this *feeling* and they get married on the spot—isn't that brilliant?"

It sounds insane. Noelle tucks her hair behind her ear, and Claire notes the metal hubcaps are gone now, the holes collapsed like small, fleshy mouths.

"So her son, my future husband, was out working on the farm—I mean, the farm? a farmhand? how hot is that?—and then he came in and looked exactly like Colin Farrell. He was *nice*—that means hot in Irish—so we're all sitting there drinking tea, and I break it to Mary that I have a boyfriend and I swear, she starts to *cry*. The woman is *crying*. Do you believe it?"

Noelle grabs a suitcase without waiting for an answer. As her hair falls forward Claire notices the essential detail she hadn't before: a long streak of artificial red racing brightly down one side. Correction, she thinks, Noelle is exactly the same.

"So that's why I'm late," she concludes. "Let's go get a drink."

"Drink?" But Claire is already speaking to the back of Noelle's sweater as it heads toward the exit. She still walks slightly duck-toed, bouncing on the balls of her feet the way she did as a little girl.

"Why not?" Noelle says.

"Isn't it kind of early?"

"You're on vacation! In Ireland! Land of drinking in the afternoon!"

EIRE:

Land of drinking in the afternoon

The double exit doors part to reveal a wet stage, gauzy with fog and spotted with flat gray puddles. Noelle points her chin at a little red car double-parked on the other side of the road, then turns to Claire. She pauses, and her face grows thoughtful. Smiling, she pushes a shock of hair out of her eye.

"What?"

"You look different."

"No, I don't," Claire says. "How?"

"You look unmarried. Or, at least, less married." As Noelle starts toward the car, she says over her shoulder, "That's a good thing."

———◡———

Claire had expected this to be a gleaming, charming island. Gemlike, quiltlike, the *Land of Leprechauns,* the *Birthplace of Blarney.* Instead there is a near-grimness about it, all this untamed brown and green, muck and stone. As the car hurtles down the Galway–Limerick Road, the landscape unravels indistinguishably on all sides: raw, haphazard, a loose grid of soggy sheep, ragged fields, low stone walls, and random boulders like the ruins of some ancient playground. Bristled brown hills jut from the earth like the chins of gods.

Noelle is sustaining a near-breathless monologue. Claire tries to decide if her semblance of a brogue is completely or only partially fake. Either way, it needles Claire's linguistic nerve. To adopt any tongue that isn't yours—Noelle's Irish slang or the leprechaunish brogue Deirdre trotted out for holidays and wedding toasts—seems, in some small but decided way, like deceit.

"So I work at the pub—I mean, *the* pub, the only one in town. It's called Conneely's, because it's owned by Paul's family. They pay me under the table but don't worry, they're totally sound. And the pub is great craic—but in Ireland craic doesn't mean drugs, it means good times . . ."

Claire gnaws on the inside of her cheek. She is annoyed by Noelle already, a feeling so familiar it's almost reassuring. How many times has Claire been strapped in a car beside her sister? She remembers the 1978 Datsun with the strawberry-shaped air freshener, the miraculous medal Deirdre kept mixed with the change compartment's sticky coins. On long rides, Claire and Noelle used to play car games. Claire won the wordy ones, like Twenty Questions and Going to California. Noelle won the ones that relied on reflexes and observations: license plates, cows, cemeteries, Volkswagens. "Punch buggy blue!" she would yell, hurling her hard little fist at Claire's soft shoulder.

"I didn't even know we were playing!" Claire would protest.

"You don't have to know," Noelle would reply. "We're playing all the time."

Now Claire stares out the window, at the mounds of thick, shadowy peat racing through the hills like veins. As a child, she could never return those punches, or admit how much they hurt. She was seven years older. Instead, shoulder smarting, she would press her palms to the window and search for the car in question, unconvinced it had ever been there.

Noelle cuts a corner hard, almost colliding with a low stone wall. "Watch it!" Claire says.

"I am watching it."

"You know where you're going, right?"

"Of course." Noelle delivers this with a confidence not exactly earned after getting lost on her way to the airport. She steps lightly on the brake. "You can never really get lost in Ireland because you can stop and ask anyone and they point you in the right direction. It's, like, a thing here to trust people."

"You mentioned that."

"Plus, the country's so small, it's hard to get lost." She leans over and starts rummaging in the glove compartment, keeping one eye on the road.

"What's the name of your town?" Claire asks.

"Killylickey."

"Seriously?" she says. "Killylickey?" It sounds like a name in a fable, a tongue twister, some tortured game of S and M. "Killylickey?"

"Yeah." Noelle pulls a cigarette from a crumpled pack. "Fag?"

"No, thanks," Claire says, though she does want one, surprisingly badly, but feels some old, sisterly sense of responsibility to set a good example. She hasn't smoked in almost a year, not since the crossword-and-cigarette binge last summer. It was accidental aversion therapy; from then on cigarettes had repulsed her, but apparently the feeling doesn't cross international lines.

"I took the week off, by the way," Noelle says, steering with one hand as she flicks a stubborn lighter. "But that doesn't mean you can't stay longer."

Claire glances at Noelle, tousled hair falling forward over the cigarette. "I don't know if I'll be here that long, Noe. It might just be a few days."

"Oh," Noelle says flatly. She churns her window down.

"We said that on the phone, remember?"

"I guess I didn't think you were serious. Who comes all the way to Ireland and only stays a few days?" Noelle looks like she's about to say more, then thinks better of it. She inhales and angles the cigarette out the crack at the top of her window, seemingly oblivious to the rain falling in.

Claire turns back to the road. "How far do we have to go?"

"Just over the hedge," Noelle says. "But that's Irish for, like, anywhere."

                       ~

Conneely's Pub looks like something plucked out of an Irish storybook, an Ireland-of-Hollywood soundstage. Thick sod roof, smooth white walls, adorable huffing chimney.

"Do Smurfs live here?" Claire shouts, over the rain pelting the roof of the car. Noelle gives the floor a cursory search for an umbrella but comes up empty-handed. "Get ready to run," she says.

It's less than a block from the car to the pub, but by the time they get there Claire's khakis are slicked to her thighs, her macintosh coat darkened to a moss green. Her shoes are waterlogged, recalling the slippers that bowed their heavy heads from her feet yesterday morning. Yesterday morning? Is that possible?

"Best way to step into a pub is soaking wet!" Noelle sings, shoving open the wooden door.

Inside, Claire is assaulted by a different kind of weather: dim and warm and cavelike. The interior of the pub is like an extension of the natural landscape—dull dark woods and dull darker woods, glass lamps and framed pictures—a cross between a bog and a family den. Softly glowing glass lamps hang in even intervals above the bar like a row of inverted green bowls. The only real light comes from the fire leaping in a giant stone hearth. The place seems packed for midafternoon on a Thursday, filled with people of all ages, books and newspapers and sweaters, dark pints and soup bowls, a two-year-old girl, a ninety-nine-year-old man. So far, Ireland doesn't seem so different from New Hampshire: lots of lousy weather and wool and soup.

"Claire!"

She turns to see Paul leaping from behind the bar. He is spindly and tall, with a thick pelt of dark blond hair pulled into a ponytail. "Sláinte!"

"That means cheers," Noelle translates, as Paul clasps Claire in a tight hug. He is wearing a rugby shirt that says CONVERSE GENERATION and smells like sweat and cigarettes. She remembers the first time she met Paul, at the funeral home. She had just spent twenty minutes assuring people that she was "fine" and New Hampshire was "beautiful" and agreeing that, yes, her mother would have been "so proud," when a skinny young man in a leather jacket gripped her by the shoulders and kissed her hard on both cheeks.

"Fucking tragic," Paul said. "My sympathies, Claire. This is bloody fucking miserable."

Claire had been living in Roan for almost a year, and though she often wished her husband said "fucking" at least sometimes, she was glad to know he'd never say it at someone's mother's funeral.

"Thank you," Claire said, and turned to Bob. "This is my—"

"It *is* bloody fucking miserable!" Noelle interrupted, appearing by Paul's side, her huge, full eyes turned on Claire as if in reproach for her pale, dry ones. "Why is everybody being so *polite*? Why not tell it like it *is*?"

Now Noelle is smiling as Paul says, "Welcome to our humble country."

"Thanks," Claire says.

"This one managed to find you, did she?" He palms Noelle's head like a basketball. "Surprised you aren't lost somewhere in Donegal."

Noelle rears her head back, flinging her damp hair like a whip. "I did *not* get lost, FYI. I even managed to score a marriage proposal."

"Did you now?" Paul says, resuming his post behind the bar as Noelle climbs onto a stool. "Who's the lucky bastard?"

"His name is Morten, and he's a farmer, and he's cut like a rock. Mary—that's my new mother-in-law—she thinks we're meant to be."

"Is that right?"

"Famous last words!" shouts one of the men at the bar.

"Lads," Paul says, "meet Claire. Just in from the States."

Three heads turn in Claire's direction. The lads range in age from twenty to eighty, but they all have the same face. At the top, it is most defined and dramatic—a thick crown of hair, a broad sweep of brow—then tapers to watery blue eyes, narrow slices of cheekbone, and vague, whiskerless chins. As they age, their complexions deepen, the flushing pink of youth giving way to a steady wind-red ruddiness. The old man's face betrays a lifetime of drinking, the rubbery bulb of his nose threaded with a delicate explosion of burst blood vessels. Each of the older men wears a flat plaid tweed cap; the youngest has a tiny gold hoop in one ear. They could be Youth, Middle Age, and Old Age: three versions of the same man.

"How long are you here?" Middle Age asks.

"I just got here. About two hours ago."

"He means," Noelle interjects, "how long are you staying."

"Oh." Claire perches on the edge of the stool next to Noelle's. "I'm not sure yet. Maybe just a few days."

"Probably longer," says Noelle.

"Old schoolmates?" asks Middle.

"No!" Noelle laughs, probably at the thought of them being friends by choice. "Sisters."

Middle narrows his eyes, hunting for the resemblance. It's the same look guests used to wear peering at photos in their house in Philadelphia. The pictures were all double frames—hinged, gilt-edged, like prayer books—half Claire, half Noelle. They were usually paired thematically: two squalling baptism photos, two serene Communion photos, two softly retouched high school senior portraits. In the other half of Claire's college portrait was a shot of Noelle holding an Irish dancing trophy. The double frames always invited comparison, exaggerating their differences, and Claire suspects that sitting beside each other at the bar has the same effect. Claire's skin looks paler than usual, her thighs and fingers extra-thick. Noelle's dark hair seems darker, the splashes of rose on her cheeks even redder. Her body is skinny as a piece of string, clavicle so pronounced you could set a teacup on it.

Middle shakes his head and smiles. "Like chalk and cheese."

"That means black and white," says Noelle.

"Got it," Claire says, and can't help but think that in that scenario, she is the cheese.

Middle isn't finished. "This one's a plastic paddy," he says, jutting a thumb toward Claire and grinning. "Where'd you get that hair? Mother leave you out to rust in the rain?"

Claire forces a polite smile, hoping to steer clear of any conversation about her mother, as Noelle bangs a loud fist on the bar. "Bartender!"

"Not serving today?" Youth asks her.

"Nope." Noelle smiles. "I'm off for the week."

"You're on holiday, then?" Middle says, to Claire.

"Sort of," she says.

Noelle leans toward the lads confidentially. "She just left her husband."

Claire feels her face flush with heat. Middle is smiling, Youth blushing. Old Age just gives her an even look.

"She's here to find herself," Noelle adds.

Is she kidding? Claire glances at her, annoyed, but can't tell.

"But don't go getting any ideas," Paul warns, setting two pints on the bar. "She's here to get away from arseholes like yourselves."

"She's out of your league anyway," Noelle says. "My sister's, like, a genius."

"That so?" says Middle.

"She's a writer."

"I'm not a writer," Claire says.

"Hey, Ferg's a writer!" Paul shouts, as Youth turns a quick shade of plum red. "Isn't that right, Fergie? Get another two pints in him and he'll bring tears to your eyes. Fucking poet."

"Well, I'm not." Claire is beginning to feel like a detail in one of Noelle's stories, expanding as she struggles to retain her true proportions. "I'm not that kind of writer," she says.

"What kind of writer are you, then?" prods Middle.

"A cruciverbalist," Claire says, regretting the word even as it leaves her lips. She reaches for her pint but Paul puts a hand out, saying, "Let it settle," as Middle asks, "What the fuck's a cruciverbalist?"

Claire pulls her hand into her lap.

"What did I tell you?" Noelle says, and Claire is surprised to hear the ring of pride in her voice. "She's, like, the smartest person in the world."

"But what's it mean?" says Middle.

"Claire," Noelle says, "tell him what it means."

"It means, I make crossword puzzles."

"Puzzles!" Paul crows, slapping the bar with his palm.

"Talk to yer man Ferg! Fergie's a puzzle. Puzzle of human nature!"

"Different kind of puzzles," she says, but is trampled by Middle shouting, "Austin fucking Powers! International man of mystery!"

They laugh, all except Claire and Youth/Ferg, who looks pained and purple, muttering, "Shut your hole."

Middle shakes his head. "Cruciverbalist," he repeats, drawing the word out as if it's some newfangled American invention.

Claire fixes her eyes on the pint. Its black insides are rolling, roiling, a storm cloud in a glass.

Then Youth/Ferg looks up. "So what's it really mean, then?"

He is looking right at Claire. His tone is quietly serious, his blush narrowed to two spots of color, one blazing on each cheek. It's not criticism in his voice, but curiosity; Claire knows the difference.

"The first bit," he says. "The *cruci*. That's crucifying, like? Christ on the cross?"

"There's a good Catholic," says Middle.

"You crucify words, then?" Youth/Ferg goes on, ignoring him. "Kill words? Murder the English language?"

"Sort of." Claire has never thought of it in quite those terms; for all her dissection of words, she's never dissected the act of the dissection. "I guess."

Old Age speaks then for the first time, gazing into the bottom of his empty glass. "If you're looking for a dead language," he says, "you've come to the right country."

Two pints sit between them, solid columns of black with foam crowns. "The secret is," Noelle instructs, "think coffee milkshake."

Moments ago she announced to the lads that they needed girl time, kissing Paul on the forehead and weaving her way toward the back of the pub in a flurry of hellos. Now Noelle leans across the table on the points of her elbows, fists buried in her cheeks. In the firelight, her face looks even rosier.

"I totally couldn't get into the taste when I first came here," she says excitedly. "I would order Bud and get *slagged*—even though the Bud here is, like, a thousand times stronger than in the States—so I finally decided to suck it up and learn to like it. And now I love it. I seriously do." As if to prove it, she dunks her face in.

Claire takes a sip. It tastes thick, dark, loamy. Nothing at all like a coffee milkshake. It tastes, she thinks, like this country looks.

"Do you like it?"

Claire swallows. "It's heavy."

HEAVY:

Filling

Overweight

Burdensome, Difficult, Intense, Significant

"Yeah." Noelle leans back, sounding only slightly disappointed. She surveys the pub and pushes one hand through her hair. "It's healthy too. Vitamins, nutrients. 'Guinness is good for you' and all that shite. Irish mothers even feed it to wimpy babies to make them tougher." Noelle picks up her coaster, a slice of cardboard with a cartoon of a thick-bodied little man wearing overalls and carrying an enormous steel beam. GUINNESS FOR STRENGTH! it says.

"Maybe Bob could have used some," she grins.

"Noelle."

"What? Doesn't it help to be—"

"No," Claire cuts her off, picking up her glass. It doesn't matter if there's some truth to what Noelle is saying. Noelle barely knows him; she hasn't earned the right.

Noelle crunches her coaster in half. Claire looks down at hers: the same cartoon man now slipping blithely into middle age. He has a shiny bald head, a compensatory mustache, and is being chased by a cheerful lion. MY GOODNESS, MY GUINNESS!

"It's kind of weird that Mom never drank the black stuff," Noelle says. "Don't you think? That's what they call it here. The black stuff."

"Why?"

"Because the color's kind of—"

"No," Claire interjects. "Why is it *weird*?"

"Because, I don't know. Mom was so into all things Irish."

"But she always drank her—what was it again?" Claire says, and is immediately annoyed with herself for not admitting she remembers. She and Noelle spent their entire lives navigating those golden cans, picking them off the coffee table and bending their metal tabs until they snapped off at the first letter of their future husband's name. They filled the blue recycling tubs Gene dragged to the curb late every Sunday night. On Monday morning, the trucks came early and Claire would listen from her bed, flinching at the telltale cascades of metal that were the Gallagher tubs being emptied, then feeling relieved at the crunch that meant the evidence had been destroyed.

"Miller High Life," Noelle pronounces.

"Right," Claire says, setting her glass down. "Of course."

"The champagne of bottled beers! Over here they would have killed her for it. Think she would have cared?"

"Probably not."

"Yeah," Noelle says, smiling. "Probably not."

Their words are identical on the outside, but on the inside they could not be less the same. In Claire's linguistics classes, this was an ongoing debate: Is the meaning in a language or in how we use it? In Noelle's tone there is awe, admiration for their mother's dismissiveness, her imperviousness to what anybody thought. But Claire hears in her own voice the edge of criticism, or cynicism, or both.

"So you still haven't even told me what happened," Noelle says. She folds her hands on the table. "Speak, my child. So the sex was bad?"

Claire reaches for her glass again. "I already told you we're not getting into that."

"Why not?"

"Because it's private."

"So it wasn't bad?"

"It's fine," Claire says. "Good, actually," she adds, which is more or less true. Compared to conversation, sex with Bob had always been an easy exchange; they understood each other's bodies better than their minds. In bed, Bob was sweet and attentive, focused. It never became less good, just less. During those bitter winter months, when Claire felt his lips tickle the back of her neck or his fingers graze her breasts, sometimes she just couldn't bear the gentleness of it. It struck her as so mild, so blissfully oblivious to the big picture, to the cold drafts sneaking through the cracks at the bottoms of the windows— drafts too cold for any sane person to take off her clothes.

Noelle leans forward and glances around the room, as if checking for spies. "Listen, if you want a quality shag—that means hookup—those guys at the bar are totally harmless. That dude Simon?" She points to Middle Age, lips pursed over a fresh pint. "Paul's sister shags him sometimes when she comes home from college. She says he knows his way around."

"Not exactly my priority right now, Noe."

"I'm just saying. He's nice, right? And by nice I mean—"

"I know. Cute."

"More like . . ." Noelle squints across the room. "Rugged. A little old for you, but awesome bone structure. That's any Irish guy, though—they're crazy with the bone structure. This whole country is like one giant fucking cheekbone."

EIRE:

One giant fucking cheekbone

Claire sets her glass down. Noelle reaches for the red-streaked hank of hair and winds it tight around her index finger. It's not a natural-looking red, but almost aggressively unnatural, like her botched attempts at redheadedness when she was a little girl.

"All I'm saying," Noelle says, "is a good shift can be thera-peutic. Especially after a bad sex life."

"Noe!"

"Oh, fine," she says, releasing the hair and grabbing their empty glasses. "We need more drinks."

As Claire watches her thread her way back to the bar, she reminds herself that Noelle doesn't mean to be hurtful. Historically, this is how she administers comfort: If there's an uneasy silence, she plunges in and fills it up. When they were little, and Deirdre was in one of her flares, Claire's impulse was always to shrink away, but Noelle assumed the role of entertainer. Standing at the foot of their mother's bed, she would unravel colorful, breathless yarns about the new step she nailed in Irish dancing, her record-breaking bent-arm hang in gym, her daring tumble in the cheerleading routine. Deirdre gobbled up the stories as quickly and, Claire thought, recklessly as the pills above the kitchen sink.

"Hyperbole," Claire once told Noelle.

"Hyperwhat?"

"*Hyperbole*. It's what you do. It's a literary term—it means exaggeration."

"And you," Noelle replied, "are a dork. That's a human term. It means dork."

Looking at her now, standing at the bar and laughing, Claire thinks that their mother would be proud. To be popular and social and even rambunctious was, to Deirdre, a mark of achievement. Noelle had always been the kind of Catholic schoolgirl their mother liked best: the girl with several offers to all the school dances. The girl who modified her uniform to whatever was currently in style; in Noelle's generation, the "phantom skirt," blouse untucked and waistband rolled high enough that the skirt was almost invisible and the men's boxers underneath exposed. If Noelle got caught by the nuns, smoking or cutting classes, Deirdre happily dismissed it. When Deirdre complained about her flaming joints, Noelle would deadpan, "I can get you a flaming joint that's *way* better," and their father would look exasperated while Deirdre just laughed.

Noelle returns, plunking down two full glasses. "Okay," she says, sitting down with new resolve. "Let's get down to business. Skip the juicy stuff, or the not-juicy stuff, or whatever. Tell me what happened before you left."

Claire looks at the table, presses her fingertip into a dark knot in the wood. "It really wasn't that dramatic."

"Did you tell him to bug off?"

"Noelle," she snaps, then feels guilty. This is, after all, why she came. "I told him that I wasn't sure I want to be married anymore."

It doesn't have the impact she had imagined. Noelle responds with only a nod. "Was there another guy?"

"Of course not."

"Was Bob not nice?"

"He was nice. Too nice."

"Was he distant? Smothering? Hard to—"

"He was a good husband," Claire says quickly. Once she admits the negatives, they become officially true. "He was smart."

Noelle rolls her eyes, a perfect impression of Deirdre.

"And kind. And he treated me well."

"You just weren't in love with him?"

Claire looks down at the table. Was it possible it all boiled down to just this?

"So what did he say when you told him? Is that when he brought up the—"

"God, Noelle," Claire says. "Give me a minute. I just got here, okay?" She takes a swallow then sets her glass back down, condensation darkening the cartoon man's face. "Also, I'd appreciate it if you'd stop telling strangers about my problems."

"Sorry?"

"Those guys at the bar—"

"Those guys aren't strangers."

"They're strangers to me. And that's not the point. I'm not comfortable with you telling people why I'm here."

"Why not?"

"Because it's private, Noelle. Plus, Bob and I . . ."

Claire pauses. She doesn't know the last time she used the phrase *Bob and I* and is surprised by how comforting it feels to say. She likes the solidity of it, the ring of exclusivity, those three little words a small but impenetrable matrimonial fort.

"Bob and I aren't definitely divorcing," she concludes.

"I didn't say you were."

"We're just taking time apart."

"I know," Noelle says. "I only brought it up because I thought if people knew—if it was just, you know, out there— you wouldn't feel like it was this big embarrassing thing."

"Why would I feel like—"

"I don't know. Because you never fuck up anything?"

Claire feels like she's been punched. Seeing the look on her face, Noelle rushes to explain. "See, I'm not saying I think you fucked up. I'm just guessing that's how it feels. To you. I just didn't want you to feel like you were doing anything wrong, leaving—if you decide to leave, I mean."

The heat from the fire is making Claire's hair sweat, but her silence gives Noelle license to go on.

"There's nothing wrong with it," she continues. "Especially here. These dudes weren't even allowed to *get* divorced until, like, a decade ago."

"Noelle."

"But isn't that so Middle Ages? And it still takes forever even if they *want*—"

"Stop," Claire says. "Just, please, shut up."

"Sorry." Noelle falls silent. She trails a finger around the rim of her glass. "Paul's always saying I act like his therapist, but I'm like, *someone* has to. I tell him in the States everyone analyzes everything, but here people just don't deal that way. They go to church, or they drink. Or both." She smiles. "Sounds like Mom, right?"

Claire feels her body tense. She picks up her glass. "Can we not do this now?"

Noelle closes her mouth, smile tightening. "Oh," she says. "Right."

"What?"

"You pretend she doesn't exist."

Claire sets the glass down carefully. Her father's condo, the empty house, a motel on the interstate—anything is better than this. "I don't think I'm going to stay here after all."

Noelle nods. "Because that's what you do."

"What is?"

"You leave."

"I stayed with Bob for almost two—"

"I'm not talking about Bob," Noelle says.

In the silence, the bustle of the pub is louder, the clinking of bowls and throaty laughter. Noelle presses a fingertip against the side of her glass, tracing it down one side. "What should we talk about?"

"Anything," Claire says. "I don't know."

She lifts her glass, finds it empty, and feels a sharp, sudden longing for the life she left behind.

Then Noelle says, "Can I tell you a secret?" and when Claire looks up, she finds Noelle's face a blaze of color: warm pinks flooding her cheeks, artificial red flashing behind her ear. It isn't just the fire. Is it happiness? Joy?

"Sure," Claire says, even though something firm and loud inside tells her she doesn't want to hear it.

"It's sort of off-topic, sort of not."

"Okay."

"I wanted to save it for later, but I've been dying to tell you ever since—"

"Jesus Christ," Claire says. "Why is everything such a melodrama?"

"Fine." Her face glows then bursts, splintering like a suncatcher, as she holds up her left hand. "Last weekend," she says. "Paul asked me. Or, like, I asked him. I guess we asked each other—I mean, this is the new millennium and whatever, right?"

Claire doesn't respond. Noelle has now taken away not only her ability to speak but her ability to breathe.

"It was totally unplanned—well, I mean, not totally. We always talked about getting married, just not specifically, more like 'when we're married I'll still love you even if you're fat' kind of thing. But last Saturday we're driving around, and it was this totally awesome day. I mean, *brilliant*. Blue sky, not a cloud in sight—"

Claire feels the swirl of the words, superlatives mounting around her—*best, most, prettiest, sweetest*—but she is only half-listening. Vaguely, she hears a boat float by. A sunset. The most romantic poem in the world.

"And want to know the best part?" Noelle leans forward, palms flat on the table, and Claire registers the ring for the first time: an intricate silver design with an emerald in the middle. "We're doing it next week."

Practicality reawakens Claire's powers of speech. "Next week?"

"A week from Saturday. Isn't it romantic?"

"Are you kidding?"

"Why not! We want to do it, so why wait a year picking out, like, tablecloths? Paul's uncle is a priest so he can do the ceremony; his cousin's in a band; we'll have the reception here in the pub—I mean, how convenient are these Irish families? They all own pubs and play instruments and have a black sheep uncle who went and got ordained."

But Claire is no longer listening. She is distracted by a movement in the room, a shift that is subtle but familiar, the walls tilting, pictures slanting, all energy and attention sliding toward her sister.

CHAPTER FIVE: } Noelle

Ocean City, New Jersey, had a slogan that inspired confidence: America's Greatest Family Resort. The beaches were crowded with perfect families: babies toddling in sand-logged diapers and ruffled bathing suits, fathers struggling with runaway Frisbees, mothers doling out peanut butter crackers and metallic Capri Sun pouches, pushing tiny straws into open mouths. Maybe this aura of healthy family values was the reason Gene always insisted they go there; if this was a vacation town for sober happy families, theirs must be one too.

It was a dry town, distinguishing it from much of the rest

of the Jersey shore, where bars thrummed with college students tossing back electric Jell-O shots and splitting the rent of three-bedroom houses with twenty of their closest friends. This was a rite of passage that would elude Claire, or Claire would elude it, spending every summer of her twenties at jobs or internships away from home. Noelle, on the other hand, would be exactly the kind of girl to split a run-down party house in Sea Isle, find an odd job selling soft pretzels or water ice, and return home the Tuesday after Labor Day with a deep tan and elaborate tales of bars, boys, and illegal beach parties. It would be at one of these parties that she would meet Paul, a bartender, an Irish summer import, and decide he was *the one*. But when Claire and Noelle were children, that other shore was still swathed in mystery, and Ocean City exuded an air of innocence, of wholesomeness; it also meant that Deirdre packed two cases of Miller High Life in the trunk.

Gene rented a different place each year, trying to right whatever wrong he'd found in the house the previous summer: air-conditioning that was too loud, paint that was starting to bubble from the sea air, furnishings that were oppressively beachy—lamps with buoy bases and seashell shades. Maybe his condo, fifteen years later, was the solution to all those summers spent searching: a place so small and bare there was nothing to dislike, so modern there was nothing to fix. A place he didn't like well enough to truly settle into or dislike enough to trade for something else.

Their vacation rentals were all essentially the same: the top floor of some weathered house in the clogged blocks on the ocean side of Third through Tenth Streets. The houses were front-heavy, puff-chested, with porches wide enough to park a car on. For Claire, being in Ocean City meant sitting on that porch and watching people. They seemed more human, less guarded, than at home. Grown-ups in church wore T-shirts and flip-flops, even Gene, though the creases in his shorts never broke in completely. Claire was startled by the whorls of dark hair on her father's legs, the dimpled fat on her mother's thighs. She felt embarrassed by her own body, by all of their bodies. In shorts and a one-piece, she was the oldest twelve-year-old on the beach.

Naturally, Deirdre had been told numerous times by Dr. Vyron that sun exposure, for her, was especially dangerous. It was a reality she refused to accept. "I'm one hundred percent Irish!" she crowed. "I can't afford to be any whiter than I am."

If the sun provoked a rash, she reasoned, a nice even burn would help conceal it. This was the kind of logic that made Gene extra-vigilant. He bought her floppy sun hats, expensive moisturizers, beach umbrellas covered in polka dots and watermelons—"so the girls can always find us," he maintained, but Deirdre promptly dragged her chair from beneath the umbrella's shadow. Claire slathered on the SPF 15, trying to help her father, but it didn't matter. At most, Deirdre showered on some coconut tanning oil spray, then arranged herself on her chair in her favorite suit, the iridescent green one that looked like mermaid skin and pinched the soft, freckled flesh at the tops of her thighs. She lifted her chin to the sky, as if daring the sun to find her, and smiled her half smile. Claire, hidden behind her sunglasses, would study that smile, how it seemed not a whole smile but a failed attempt at one, as if the lips had started widening then snagged on a burr of some unexpected doubt or sadness and got stuck there, neck arched defiantly backward but corners of the mouth receding into the pinkness suffusing her face. Of all the things exposed at the shore, the most naked was that smile, and the possibility that her mother wasn't as brazen as she pretended to be.

Nights at the shore, Deirdre often felt feverish. No one dared say, "I told you so." She parked herself in front of the TV, in the blast of central air, leaving Gene and the girls to wander along the boardwalk, a long carnival of wide gray planks lined with food stands and arcades and shops where you could buy temporary tattoos or hermit crabs that would be dead by dawn. Each night, Claire and Noelle were allowed one treat. Noelle went for the quickest and biggest—pretzel braids, giant cherry Sno-Kones that stained her mouth like lipstick—while Claire thought carefully about her options, waiting to savor it for the walk home. Her favorite was a Kohr Brothers ice-cream cone, a perfect newel post of vanilla and chocolate rolled in a tub of rainbow sprinkles that melted down her fingers faster than she could lick them. Noelle, stuffed but suddenly empty-handed, would complain that she was hungry. Gene would shoot Claire a quick, pleading look.

"One bite?" he asked.

Claire understood this look, the responsibility it conferred. It wasn't the look an adult gave a child, but the look an adult gave another adult, with its quirked brow of camaraderie, the slight eye roll that meant they were allies in the same tired, affectionate fight. Her father was counting on her and Claire wouldn't let him down. But there was something in his look Claire didn't like seeing—the way he glanced away after asking, looking down at the wooden planks or out to the darkened beach. This shifting of the eyes exposed the kernel of embarrassment at their center: the knowledge he was caving, taking the soft way out rather than standing firm. Though at twelve or thirteen Claire couldn't perceive this in a specific way, it made her nervous and sad.

"One bite," she repeated, holding out her cone. Then she steeled herself for the excruciating moments when Noelle stretched her jaw as wide as it would go and sank in with her cherry-stained lips.

Their final night, Friday night, rain or shine, Gene took them to the amusement rides at Wonderland Pier. The entrance announced itself with a row of colored poles, each topped with a different letter—*W, O, N*—innocent as children's blocks. Behind them was a sweaty ocean of kids and babies, strollers, camcorders. The air was thick and dissonant with jangled merry-go-round music and the ringing of the skee ball lanes. Toddlers were placed gently into ladybugs and fire engines, looking alternately dazed and terrified, while bigger kids clambered onto miniature rocket ships and Safari jeeps, choking the steering wheels and leaning on the horns.

Noelle was unimpressed. She pushed through the mob of wholesomeness, knowing on the other side the ceiling gave way to the real sky, to the cool night air and garish, flashing lights of the real rides: the Salt-N-Pepper Shakers with their menacing black cages and the Tin Lizzy Skooters with their spindly, oily stems and the Golden Galleon pirate ship that crested and dipped on waves of glee and terror.

The only difference more pronounced than indoor and outdoor Wonderlands was the ages of Claire and Noelle. This was a fact of their childhoods, and a fact of their lives beyond their childhoods; given the seven-year age gap, they had never really shared one. Claire got to do what Noelle didn't and Noelle got away with things Claire never could. There was a certain logic to it, Claire thought. She was older; she didn't need to be coddled. And as Gene liked to remind her, she had a "thicker skin," which she knew was supposed to mean that she was less sensitive, though she couldn't help hearing in it some acknowledgment of her sister's rail-thin body and her own slightly thicker frame.

In Wonderland, the age difference meant that just as Noelle was beginning to crave the big rides, Claire was old enough to ride them. Noelle wasn't interested in swings or teacups. She was transfixed by the slithery wrath of the Super Cat, a lightning-fast, tiger-striped monstrosity that always smelled vaguely like an electrical fire and spun around to Top 40 hits by Bon Jovi and INXS. On the inside, it felt something like a self-contained roller rink: loud music, spastic strobe lights, rowdy teenage couples, and the sense of hurtling out of control.

Claire waited in line alone, counting out her crumpled sweaty tickets twice or three times to make sure she had enough. She handed them to the tanned, uninterested teenager at the entrance who stared off over Claire's head, fingering the braided jewelry at his wrist or throat. Taking her seat, Claire made sure her belt was on securely. Then she located her family. It wasn't hard. Noelle would be leaning against the slack belly of the wire fence, spread-eagled, the underside of a belly flop. Her hands were over her head and poked through the fence holes like a listless galley.

The Super Cat started fast, hurling Claire's head back against the seat. She struggled to look happy when she passed her family, a wind-whipped smile frozen to her face, but with every revolution she felt sicker. Her head rattled on her spine. After a minute, the ride slowed down. With a feline hiss, a tiger-striped tarp began cranking over the seats like the top of a covered wagon. The seats were sunk in sudden darkness, trapped under the grimy orange skin. Then they were flying backward, sealed in a blind tunnel of screams and heat and furious makeout sessions. Claire hated that she couldn't see anything, loved that she couldn't be seen. Closing her eyes, she succumbed to the motion, letting the smile blow off her face as she waited for the ride to be over, terrified as much by the proximity of the primal screaming and French kissing as she was by the Super Cat itself.

When it was over, everybody booed. The striped tarp peeled away and they were released back into the world. The other kids rushed the exit, but Claire moved slowly. Her entire body was vibrating, confirming with each step the firmness of the ground beneath her, which was not as solid as she would have liked but was made of loose, pebbled sheet metal that clattered beneath her feet.

"Was it awesome?" Noelle said, waiting by the exit.

Claire looked at her sister's face, imprinted with a map of diamonds. That Noelle envied her being older was to be expected; what Claire wouldn't admit was how much she envied her little sister in return. She was jealous that Noelle didn't have to experience the Super Cat's seamy underbelly, didn't have to feel as though she had been somewhere she shouldn't have, didn't have to feel ashamed—shame made worse by the fact that her family had been on the outside, watching. It was the same feeling Claire had had in fifth grade when her father drove her and two friends to see *Sixteen Candles*. The movie was rated PG-13 but seemed to her the equivalent of porn. When Gene picked them up, she had felt a knot in her stomach: guilty for having seen the movie, guiltier that her father had been implicated in her going.

"Totally," Claire said, looking down at her sister's eager face. "It was awesome." Then she lined up for the roller coaster, not because she wanted to, but because she could.

But Claire's upper hand, she knew, would be gone by night's end. Every year, the ride Gene saved for last was guaranteed to appease Noelle. No matter that Claire was bigger, and older, that all night she had been standing in line for the big rides while Noelle gazed at her through wire fences. This was the ultimate and unfailing magic of Wonderland Pier: Claire always left hurt, Noelle left happy.

The ride was called the Trabant, and it was the only big ride little kids were allowed on if accompanied by someone older. In her head, Claire pronounced the word *trampant*. She had never heard it spoken, but this seemed right, a combination of trampling and trumpets, which was how the ride felt: chaotic, circusy, oblivious to its own strength. It resembled a giant spinning top with tiny, spastic lightbulbs running up and down the middle. Blinking bulbs also spelled out its name—TRABANT—like a larger, more intimidating version of the sign on DANNY'S PIZZA back home.

"Don't forget to take the outside!" Gene would shout to Claire as they scrambled to claim a seat. Claire would nod at him over her shoulder; she wouldn't have forgotten. She was more vigilant about the ride than its attendants, who sauntered around the perimeter tugging at the safety bars as nonchalantly as the zippers on their hooded sweatshirts.

She let Noelle climb in first, then unwrapped a spare hair band from her wrist. "Here," she said. She had heard on the news about a long-haired girl at a different amusement park whose hair got caught in the Free Fall and ripped out of her head.

"I don't want to," Noelle said, shaking her hair loose around her ears. "I want to feel it." She twisted around in her seat. "Hey, Dad!"

From the other side of the fence, Gene was already waving. Only once had Deirdre been standing there beside him. She was blowing kisses when the ride began, but by the time it was over, was parked on a bench with a lap full of funnel cake.

"Hey, Dad, over here!"

The Trabant began slowly, lulling you into a false sense of security, skating on the ground in easy figure eights. Then it slowed, stopped. In the world of rides, nothing was more ominous than a full stop. Noelle screamed with delight. Then, like a spaceship, it rose straight up and tilted dramatically to one side, like a beast cocking its giant head. The slant sent Noelle crashing into Claire's side of the seat. When the ride started again it was in earnest, diving left and right and up and down, and even though Noelle weighed no more than ninety pounds the centrifugal force was strong enough to press her hard into Claire's left shoulder, flattening Claire against the far wall where metal screws and hinges dug into her on the right. Tears sprang to her eyes.

"Dad! Look!" Noelle screamed. "Dad, no hands!"

Claire could see them in her peripheral vision, fluttering like moths. Noelle's hair blew around in the night air, whipping against Claire's cheek. Claire kept both hands on the safety bar as Noelle screamed and waved. Muscles taut, jaw clenched, she bore the pressure of her sister against her.

———

Opening her eyes, Claire has no idea where she is. She does a cursory scan of her surroundings. The room is at once spare and crowded: a wooden desk in one corner, a wooden dresser, curtains that look like they're made of old green tablecloths. She recognizes the signature colors—walls the color of oatmeal, rug the color of dirt—as anxiety starts thrumming faintly in her chest. She is in Ireland, she thinks. *Ireland*. Yesterday, she was in New Hampshire. It seems inconceivable that this world and that one could exist simultaneously, and how easily she traded one for the other.

Claire hears the distant bang of a door. She has only a hazy memory of the rest of Noelle and Paul's house. They had come home last night tired, sullen, eaten a few handfuls of something—were they Taytos? were they pickle-flavored?—and gone to bed. Claire's head pounds. She has a pathetic tolerance for alcohol. She stares up at the ceiling. *Oatmeal*: It had been the color of her favorite sweater in college. She liked the name then, thought it cozy, collegiate, stacked in a fluffy sandwich in one of her Yaffa block towers. It was the sweater she'd worn so long and stretched so well that it engulfed her, made her feel small, cuffs curling to the middles of her palms. When she and Bob first started dating, his arms would get tangled in the sloppy sleeves when he bent to hug her, collapsing like a sigh.

Her chest tightens. She tries to stay in the moment, to concentrate on the falling of the rain, on the throbbing in her head. She imagines the present like a tightrope: veer to the left, plunge into the abyss of memory; teeter off the right, stare into the future's gaping hole. Growing up, she was prone to making such comparisons, like some ongoing internal competition, the impulse to measure today against its predecessor the previous week, the previous year. New Year's Eve was the most stressful, with its subtle undercurrent of pressure, the ominousness of the countdown and the spangled ball hanging literally and metaphorically over everyone's head. As the clock struck midnight, Claire would find herself frantically reflecting in her journal—trying to find the perfect sentiment to end the year, the perfect word—while the rest of Eastern Standard Time was drunk at a party and Deirdre was down on the front porch banging on a wok.

In New Hampshire, the comparisons became too depressing, dangerous. Now Claire tries to focus on the ceiling—*oatmeal, oatmeal, oatmeal*—but soon she's plunging off to the left, back to when she and Bob first met. Mornings, in the graduate dorm, he would stay in Claire's bed while she snuck down the hallway to the communal kitchen and cooked them breakfast. Back then, "cook" meant "boil." Occasionally "toast" or "shake gently." But these limitations were a source of pride. A straight-A student who couldn't make chicken was charmingly paradoxical, although two years later, a wife marinating chicken would be just that: a wife, a marinade, chicken.

CHICKEN:

Cordon bleu

Dance at a wedding reception

Fried, in Kentucky

Nugget

Wimp

"Thank you," Bob would say when she returned. The graduate dorm, it didn't take advanced linguistics to deduce, was oxymoronic. And also, moronic. A cinder-block tower with rooms the size of closets, windows the size of toasters, a place where adults committed to higher learning brushed their teeth in coed bathrooms and hung dry-erase boards on their bedroom doors. The floors were done in the faux-mica tile of high school cafeterias, and in the communal refrigerator, everything was identified by Post-it note: pints of frozen yogurt flagged REBECCA or sandwiches wrapped in grease-spotted paper branded MARK—HANDS OFF!

Bob had an apartment a few miles off campus. It was a grown-up apartment, small and respectably shabby, with a cramped galley kitchen and mostly bare walls. His possessions were so few and so tidy that the place had the feel of an exhibit: a bottle of mouthwash, a single family photo, one limp blue towel hooked to a nail on the back of the bathroom door. Lying in his bed at night, Claire found herself missing the dorm. Sometimes, as she knelt on the floor of her room packing a few clothes, or rode the elevator down to the dorm lobby, she felt a twist of nostalgia for a place she hadn't even left, that she didn't even like. She began suggesting they sleep in the dorm more often; from a practical standpoint, it was closer to campus. And even though they kept mostly to themselves, somehow just the presence of nearby dorm life—the annoying neighbors down the hall, the TV blaring in the lounge—made Claire like Bob more. It reinforced the core belief all couples want to maintain about themselves: how different they are from the people on the other side of the door.

"This is good," Bob would say, spooning up the oatmeal. Claire appreciated the sentiment, even though it wasn't. It was instant. The good part was the trivia on the backs of the ripped paper packages that Claire tucked in her pocket and read out loud back in the room.

"Name the only U.S. president who was a bachelor."

"What is the only one-syllable U.S. state?"

"Where does the phrase 'dog days of summer' come from?"

"The Dog Star," Bob would answer, with endearing fervor. "Sirius. The, ah, Dog Star. In the summer it appears on the horizon just before dawn."

There was something romantic about it, the frugality and seclusion, the sense that they were partners in this small, shared universe in which even instant oatmeal could be made exciting. It was easy for a thing to seem romantic when it was temporary. No matter what, the present was touched with the certainty of a different future, in which they would eat real breakfasts, and have multiple rooms filled with affectionate clutter, and make love noisily in a giant bed, not having to whisper so Claire's floormates wouldn't hear.

Claire closes her eyes. She concentrates on breathing. She isn't sure if it's Bob she is missing, or Bob In The Beginning, or herself in love or herself in school or just the feeling of knowing where she is and that she belongs there.

Another door slams. She hears the distant sound of voices. Maybe Paul and Noelle have friends here. She imagines their house a surrogate pub, the living room darkened with pulled shades, littered with empty pint glasses, and pale, skinny lads waking up in various states of hangover. She wonders how long she could get away with staying in bed. Noelle's announcement returns: *engaged*. The word, like Claire's headache, seems concentrated between her eyes. She hates the term. Even when she herself was engaged, she never used it, preferring the straightforwardness of "getting married." After the wedding, she was even partial to "newlywed," at least in theory. To be *engaged*, though, felt less like a hard fact than a state of being, swampy and dramatic, a condition prone to exactly the sort of distractedness and self-absorption that so often seemed to overtake brides-to-be.

ENGAGED:

Engrossed

Occupied

Fascinated

Entered, as in combat

Claire hears a knock. "You awake?"

"No," Claire says, closing her eyes.

She hears Noelle enter and shut the door, pausing by the foot of the bed. "Are you hungover?"

"No," Claire says. "Just tired."

"So, listen. I told Paul that I brought up the wedding stuff yesterday and he said that I was an insensitive cakehole and I should apologize."

Claire listens for the apology in her voice, hears none.

"I know it was shitty timing," Noelle continues. Claire feels the foot of the bed sag under her weight. "I was just really psyched about the wedding, and I was psyched you're going to be here for it. You're going to stay now, right?"

Claire opens her eyes. Noelle is not sitting on the end of the bed, but standing. She's wearing jeans and a thick brown sweater, chewing on a cuticle. When she sees Claire looking, she drops her hand to her side. "You're the whole reason we decided to do it next week."

"Oh, come on. You're lying."

"I'm not lying!"

"You weren't even going to call me if I—"

"Yes, I was!"

Gazing up at her sister standing on the foot of the bed, it occurs to Claire this is the way Noelle used to address Deirdre when she was in one of her flares. Claire struggles up onto her elbows.

"I want you to be in it," Noelle adds.

"What?" Claire says. She is distracted by the corner of the room behind her, plastered with pictures of American celebrities. Jennifer Aniston. George Clooney. Jessica Simpson. P. Diddy. Angelina Jolie. Her head hurts too much to dwell on how weird this is. "The wedding?"

"I mean, don't worry. No bridesmaid shit. Wear whatever you want." She reaches up to touch the ceiling with her fingertips, sweater rising to expose a flat stripe of stomach. "You owe me. Remember that blue fucking shower curtain I had to wear at—" She pauses and drops her arms to her sides. "Shite."

The bed bounces painfully. Claire remembers hearing once, in college, that a hangover is the feeling of your brain rubbing against your skull.

"I'm sorry," Noelle says.

"It's fine." And it is. They were, Claire thinks, blue fucking shower curtains. In retrospect, Claire is amazed she even had bridesmaids. She is amazed she used the term bridesmaid. A bride's *maid*—had she ever thought of that? She pictures the three of them lined up behind her, like mismatched backup singers—Noelle, with metal earlobes flashing; Erica, her college roommate, seven months' pregnant with a child Claire has met once; Bob's sister, Susan, with her big red glasses that covered half her face. Susan—the thought makes Claire's chest fill with a sharp, surprising sense of loss. Claire had always liked her. They'd traded book recommendations. They shared a cigarette behind the garage one Thanksgiving and didn't tell their husbands. She might never see Susan again, and for a moment she veers off to the right, the future gaping before her, a vast and invisible minefield of aftershocks, adjustments, losses she hasn't even begun to calculate.

"So you'll stay, right?" Noelle says.

Claire looks up at her, the question sparking a mixture of gratitude and resentment. Already, it's all about Noelle. She should have known this would happen. She wouldn't even have been invited to this slapdash pub wedding had she not happened to call. She would have heard about it in a frenzied, messy letter a month later—*luv ya! miss ya! Noelle CONNEELY*—and tucked it in a drawer, purchased a gift online, and felt concerned but not surprised by her sister's impulsiveness. Noelle had probably taken this week off before she knew Claire was even coming. Her assertions to the contrary are enough to make Claire want to leave, on principle.

But it is, after all, her only sister's wedding. If not Claire here representing their family, then who?

Noelle stands with both arms outstretched, raising and lowering herself on tiptoe. She is wearing satiny pink slippers that look like Deirdre's old ones. Another look confirms that they are Deirdre's old ones. She used to have Gene buy them in bulk whenever they went on sale: pink because it was girlish, faux-satin because it felt soft against her aching feet.

Claire says, "Have you told Dad?"

Noelle sighs loudly. In one motion, she throws her legs out in front of her, cheerleader-style, dropping to the bed. Claire's brain jostles in her skull.

"Noelle?"

She holds her thumb above her eyes. "What?"

"When's the last time you talked to him? I mean, since . . . last summer?"

"You mean since Mom died?"

"Right," Claire says. "Since Mom died. Dad would want to be here, don't you think?"

"I don't know, would he?"

Noelle crosses one leg over the opposite knee. "My nails are repulsive. Isn't that so, like, unbridal? Aren't you supposed to keep your hands looking perfect for when people ask to see the ring? I can barely—"

"Noe."

"What?" She lets her hand drop to her chest. "He hasn't even called me."

"Have you called him?"

"He probably wouldn't even come."

"Of course he would. He will," Claire says.

"Maybe," Noelle says. "But *you're* staying, right?"

Claire is surprised to hear the hint of anxiety in her voice. The question isn't just a courtesy. She looks at the pink slipper, hovering between them like a shiny bird, and for a moment she's convinced it is the spirit of Deirdre, watching to make sure she does the right thing. How like her mother to reincarnate as a slipper: bright and gaudy, part Sears clearance, part Cinderella. But it works. Noelle is getting married, getting married without her mother. Claire is staying. She has no choice.

"Fine," she says.

"Brilliant." Noelle sits up. "Come on, I'm starving. Let's go meet the fam," she says, the pink slipper diving victoriously to the floor.

———

Claire's first impression of the kitchen is chaos—dogs, babies, children, mothers, screaming kettles, popping toasters. It had never occurred to her that Paul and Noelle might live with Paul's family, but here they are, scads of them, ten or twelve or more children all dressed in identical school uniforms: gray linen pants or skirts with starchy white button-down shirts and dark blue ties under blue V-necked sweaters. Claire had forgotten it was a school day; she had forgotten, for maybe the first time ever, about school.

"This," Noelle says, "is Paul's family. And some random others."

Claire scans the crowd: a girl of eleven or twelve wearing giant yellow headphones, two younger boys battling thumbs over a video game, a teenage girl with a curtain of long dark hair bent over a book. Claire smiles at them. Paul smiles back.

"Tea?"

"Tea?"

"Tea?"

She isn't sure who's asking but gives a pronounced nod, remembering Noelle's warning about tea and rudeness. The table is cluttered with used cups and dishes, off-white, each stamped with a single faded flower. In the middle of the table is a stack of toast, slightly burned, five boxes of cereal, and two embattled, crumb-crusted sticks of butter. The walls are decorated more like a living room than a kitchen, with patterned wallpaper, framed photos, thick curtains draping the windows. There's even a fireplace in one corner. From the front of the house, a door bangs intermittently: people entering and leaving, small interchangeable boys and girls with dogs on leashes, cups in hands. If they wonder who Claire is and why she's there, they don't show it.

"Those are the twins, Sean and Seamus," Noelle is saying, pointing to the boys manhandling the video game. "And that's Graham, and Gilly—he lives down the road—and Lyndsey and Aoife—"

An older woman holds a cup toward Claire.

"And this is Lillian!"

"Thank you," Claire says.

"Mum," Paul says. "That's my new sister-in-law. Pretend to be nice."

Lillian smiles, though not particularly warmly. The smile is a hard, thin tweak of the lips, as if she has no excess emotion to spare. She has a blunt chin, a neat cap of brown hair. There's an air about her that is pretty, but beleaguered; she has the look of a woman who lives in a place where it constantly rains.

"Nice to meet you," Claire says. "I'm sorry, I didn't even realize I was staying—" but Lillian is already busy picking used plates off the table. Claire wonders if she offended her, if Noelle even told her Claire was coming.

Claire lowers herself to a seat and takes a cautious sip of tea. The teenage girl, Aoife, glances at her, then quickly looks away.

"So," Paul asks. "What's on today?"

"We're going to be total tourists," Noelle says, reaching for the box of Frosties. "And I don't want to hear it. We're Americans. We're allowed."

Aoife almost imperceptibly arches an eyebrow. She is wearing the same proper sweater-and-tie combination, but her face is long, languid, as impassive as an Irish dancer's. In America, Claire thinks, she would be cast on a reality show, thrust into the world of high fashion modeling from a bland existence in a rainy small town.

"You should take her to Thoor Ballylee," Paul says, cutting a wedge of butter thick as cheese. "Yeats's tower. Spiraling gyres! You'd love it, Claire, with the writing and all."

Noelle rolls her eyes. Claire half-expects her to say: *Spiraling gyres? Sounds like geezers! Sounds like geysers! Goobers! Boogers!*

Paul rakes the mound of butter across his toast. "Or Sligo! Grave of W. B. Yeats. '*Cast a cold eye on life, on death.*'" He waggles his long fingers, an attempt at looking spooky. "'*Horseman, pass by!*'"

Claire wonders if Noelle recognizes these references, hears in them the teary, drunken echoes of their mother. But Noelle says only, "Are you showing off for my sister?"

"I'm not!" Paul says, sinking his teeth into his toast. He speaks with one balled cheek. "She knows what I'm going on about, isn't that right, Claire?"

"Sort of." Claire decides not to admit that she doesn't like Yeats. It's not just because of Deirdre—all that mysticism, that relentless idealism.

Lillian drops a plate of bacon on the table. "Thank you," Claire says, as it's attacked by a flurry of hands. She looks at Noelle and wonders if she, too, can't help but compare this scene to the family breakfasts they used to endure on Saturday mornings.

Then she notices Aoife looking at her. "You're a writer, like?"

"No, not really. I'm a—"

"We're *not* going to the writer tower," Noelle interrupts. "We're supposed to be having fun. I was thinking, like, the Blarney Stone."

Paul buries his face in his long, webby fingers and groans.

"What?" she demands.

"Like you need any more gift of the gab!"

This provokes a giggle from the other end of the table. From the stove, Lillian cautions, "Paul, don't be bold," but the children all obviously adore him. His face is like a friendly, skinny ox in a children's story: wide blue eyes, flaring nostrils, cheeks suffused with pink.

"Besides," he says, "you don't want to know how many drunk eejits have pissed on that rock. Himself included."

Another round of giggles. Noelle swats him on the shoulder. Suddenly Claire notices that the little boy sitting beside her is staring. He looks both nine and forty-nine: bright eyes and a mischievous smile, enormous forehead and a receding hairline.

"You're sleeping in my room," he tells her. His voice is raspy, either a sniffle or a lifetime of unfiltered cigarettes.

"Oh," Claire says. "Sorry. But thank you. It's a very nice room."

"Are you from New York or Vegas?"

She starts to say, "Neither," when Noelle aswers, "New York." She looks at Claire and shrugs, as if to say, close enough.

"Do you know yer man Eminem?" the boy says.

"Sure."

Aoife speaks without looking up, voice flat as lead. "He means, have you met him. Graham's obsessed with American celebrities."

Claire expects the boy to defend himself, but he just waits for the response.

"No, sorry," Claire says, "I haven't."

"Mariah Carey?"

"Ah, no."

"Jessica Simpson? She's divorced."

"Yes, I know," she says, thinking: *Americans! Aren't we all!* Then she realizes the boy's still waiting for an answer. "No, I don't know her either."

"Buffy the Vampire Slayer?"

Aoife mutters, "Jaysus, Mary, and Joseph."

"Actually," Claire says, "I'm from Philadelphia," as if this might explain her lack of celebrity connections.

"Philadelphia?" Graham repeats, and Claire can't help but smile. In the city, locals pronounce the "phia" like "fyuh," compressing it to one gruff syllable. But in Graham's mouth, the combination of his lilting brogue and romanticism of all things American make "Pheel-a-del-fee-a" sound like the setting of a fairytale.

He pauses, riffling through his mental celebrity files, then looks up. "Where the fighter comes from?"

Claire looks at him, uncomprehending. He slides off his chair, lowers his chin and throws a few punches in the air.

"Oh! You mean Rocky?"

"Rocky! You know him?"

"Yes!"

"Yes?"

"Oh. I mean—not like that. No."

The boy sits back down and stares at his knees. He is wearing hard little shoes, dark blue with dark blue laces. He is part child, part mailman. Part groupie, part hard-boiled detective. Claire can tell that she's disappointed him. She feels she owes him something in exchange for borrowing his room; in a house like this, you must need all the personal space you can get. She mines her past for some minor brush with celebrity—how can she be a U.S. citizen and not have had some minor brush with celebrity?—but comes up with nothing except a few overused crossword puzzle clues (WKRP boss, Woody's ex-wife) and the autograph her mother got when Charlotte Rae came to her jewelry counter. FOR DEIRDRE—A REAL GEM!

The boy looks up at her once more. Claire can tell this is his final effort. Something has stiffened inside him: chin high, back arched. "Fresh Prince?"

Heads around the table pique with interest.

"Who?" Claire asks.

Seamus or Sean shouts: "Will Smith the Fresh Prince of Bel-Air!"

"Oh." Claire's heard of the show but never seen it. "Sorry," she apologizes. "I don't watch much television."

Graham hasn't moved. Claire realizes that he needs to hear her say it. "I don't know the Fresh Prince either."

"But he's from Philadelphia," the boy points out.

Aoife scoops up her books and scrapes back her chair. "Not every country is as fucking small as this one, Graham."

Lillian snaps, "Language!"

Paul says, "Ah, Mum, let her be."

Aoife drops her dishes in the sink with a clatter. Lillian turns the water on. Graham is still looking at Claire. "She's studying for her exam," he explains. "She's allowed to say whatever she wants to." Then, with the world-weariness of an old man, he rises and shuffles out of the kitchen cradling a cup of tea in both hands.

# CHAPTER SIX: ⟩ Blarney

If Sunday mornings belonged to God and Deirdre, Saturday mornings were Gene's domain. In a life otherwise unpredictable, his was a small attempt at order: Each week's breakfast routine was essentially the same as the last. Claire and Gene were always first to the table. They drank coffee, negotiated the paper. Claire started the crossword puzzle and passed it to Gene to finish. They didn't speak; they didn't have to. This silence felt like proof of something. Gene always wore the same thing: plaid flannel robe, pale blue pajamas, bedroom slippers like worn brown canoes. His hair remained the same graying, curly crown with an island of pink in the middle.

Claire loved her father for his steadiness, his mild dorkiness, for acting like a parent should.

"Phooey," Gene would mutter, scrutinizing a stubborn clue. Even his stodgy, old-man vocabulary Claire found reassuring. Her father was smart. He could sweep a board in *Jeopardy!* and finish the crossword any day of the week. He should have been a teacher, she often thought, a librarian maybe. Being a salesman seemed beneath him.

"Ah, hell," he would say when he got stuck, shoving back his chair. He would wander into the living room, returning several minutes later to pick up the puzzle, eyebrows arched over his reading glasses, one hand moving absently over his bald spot, then lean down to scribble in the missing piece. "Sometimes," he would say, settling back into his seat, "if you just walk away from it, it looks different."

Claire's last family breakfast, though she didn't know it at the time, was on a gray Saturday in March. She was home for spring break; the night before, she'd told Deirdre and Gene that she and Bob were getting married. He had offered to tell them with her but she insisted he stay on campus, work on his thesis. What she didn't tell him was that the conversation might be easier without him there.

The night before, Gene had said congratulations, planting a kiss in the middle of her forehead, but Deirdre hadn't spoken to Claire directly since. At breakfast, Claire was savoring her last moments alone with her father, knowing he would stick to the usual script. When he finished the puzzle, he put down his pencil, picked up his coffee, and asked, "What's next?"

It was his signature conversation starter, vague yet oddly immediate. At the breakfast table or on the phone or sometimes apropos of nothing while standing in the middle of the kitchen or buckling into the car—"What's next?" he asked, projecting the question into empty space. Claire would rush to fill it with whatever she happened to be embarking on— a final paper, a summer job, a midterm exam. Gene would pause and look at her, as if resetting his coordinates, relocating himself in the chronology of his own life. This made Claire nervous. She knew, if asked his own question, her father's response would never vary. It couldn't. She always listened carefully for the "s" in the middle; it was the "s" that made his question hopeful, forward-looking, rather than its bitter, thinner stepsister—"What next?"—suggesting some burdensome past and had-it-up-to-hereness with the world.

That morning, Claire answered, "I guess we book a place, for the reception. And put together an invite list."

Gene was smiling mildly, tracing one finger around the rim of his mug. Claire sensed, as she often did, that these weren't the details he was asking for. Sometimes she wondered if his question was meant for her at all.

"For the wedding," she added.

Gene's smile widened and grew firmer. He picked up his mug. "It's great news, honey."

"Don't worry," she said. "It won't be expensive."

"You don't worry either. Get whatever kind of gown you want."

Claire smiled at this, at the wrongness of the word *gown* and the prospect of her wearing one in the first place. She and Bob were going to keep things low-key, simple, and she was about to tell her father so when she heard the slow, muffled thump of Deirdre's cane from the upstairs hallway. Claire listened as the sound traveled across the kitchen ceiling and down the stairs, intervals of carpet and tile, hard tapping and soft silence.

When Deirdre appeared in the kitchen doorway, she looked like an exaggeration of herself. Her hair was too thin, her face too shiny. Even her hips looked wider than usual. She had taken to overemphasizing the parts of her body she still had some control over: slicking White Strips to her teeth and bright paint on her nails, applying makeup in an oily-thick palette, as if this darkening of her eyebrows and defining of her cheekbones might distract from the decimation of other, more vital things.

"How did you sleep?" Gene asked her.

"Lousy," said Deirdre. She headed straight for the counter where, as usual, she dressed a cup of coffee with heaps of sugar, then helped herself to painkillers and anti-inflammatories as if grazing the Roy Rogers fixins bar. She didn't sit. Until Noelle showed up, Deirdre always stayed standing. Normally she occupied herself snorting over Gene's shoulder as he worked the cryptogram or snatching up the advice column and reading aloud—"Want to hear how you know your guy is cheating on you? Want to know how to zap a stain out of suede?"—but this Saturday morning, she didn't say a word.

Claire found herself wishing that Noelle would hurry up. She always dominated breakfast from the moment she arrived—dragging a spoon through her Lucky Charms, tipping her head back to guzzle the pink-stained puddle at the bottom, spinning her latest saga about the awesome party the night before, the boy she met who looked exactly like

Ethan Hawke and the senior who puked all over someone's parents' barbecue grill. Though under normal circumstances Claire found Noelle's antics irritating, today she longed for the loud, busy bluster into which the rest of them could recede.

As if sensing she was needed, Noelle came thumping down the stairs. She was wearing baggy plaid pajama bottoms and a T-shirt that said IRISH WEEKEND WILDWOOD, NJ. Dark makeup was smudged under her eyes and caked on her lashes. When she dropped into her chair, Claire caught a whiff of cigarettes.

"How was the party?" Claire asked her.

"Totally cool," Noelle said. "There was this band, Meg's brother's friends—" but she had just reached for the cereal box when Deirdre slapped a palm against the counter and shouted: "Let's go to L.L.Bean!"

They all looked up. This kind of thing was not without precedent: impromptu midmorning runs to eat bacon cheeseburgers, play the quarter slots in Atlantic City, go shopping at the mall. Armed with Deirdre's employee discount, Noelle and Deirdre would barge into the house hours later weighed down with shopping bags, reeking of free perfume samples, laughing at some inside joke like the popular kids descending on the school dance. Usually, the worse Deirdre had been feeling lately the more extravagant her scheme.

"L.L.Bean!" Deirdre said. "It never closes! Twenty-four hours a day! Three hundred and sixty-five days a year!"

"Mom." Claire kept her voice even. "Do you know it's in Maine?"

Noelle was already on her feet, pulling a coat on over her pajamas and tucking the Froot Loops under her arm.

"That's nine hours away, Dee," Gene said.

"But *honey*." Deirdre's tone was dumbfounded. "Don't you *see*? That doesn't *matter*! It never *closes*!"

Gene looked at her quietly. "You shouldn't push it. You know that."

"I know more than you do," Deirdre replied. She kissed the top of his head and hugged the crook of Noelle's arm. "Let's go, Noe."

Claire watched as they headed for the back door, arm in arm, when suddenly Noelle turned and looked at her. She was holding one hand up to her forehead, two fingers splayed in the shape of an *L* for Lame. Or, Lupus. Or who knows, maybe L.L.Bean. But underneath the smugness of that *L*, Claire detected a glimmer of something else, there and gone so fast she wasn't sure she'd really seen it. Noelle dropped her hand to open the door for Deirdre. As they started down the back stairs, a process more tedious than the spontaneity of the trip required—the scuffing of the slippers, thumping of the cane—Claire was seized with guilt. She looked at Gene, but he was looking at the paper. The car doors slammed, the engine revved. Claire tried not to picture Noelle in her pajamas behind the wheel. As the car radio came on blasting, Claire reminded herself that she wasn't invited to go. Deirdre wouldn't want her there. She focused on Bob, on her pending wedding, on a future more rational and less ridiculous than this one. As the car tore away, she and Gene returned to their breakfasts, so convinced of their rightness that they didn't need to speak.

"Today," Noelle proclaims, slamming the car door, "we will have great craic."

GREAT CRAIC:

Fun time!

No writer towers!

No mention of Dad!

*Girl, loosen up!*

"So where are we going?" Claire asks, pulling on her seat belt.

"The Blarney Stone," Noelle replies.

"You were serious?"

"Why not?"

Claire tries to think of a reason besides the obvious, that you don't drag a person to a cheesy tourist trap when they're still recovering from jet lag, but she defaults to Bob mode: "Do you know how to get there?"

"Basically," Noelle says, pulling away from the curb.

Claire waits until they are back on the highway, heading south, before saying, "I wish you'd told me you lived with Paul's family."

Noelle smiles. "If I had, would you have come?"

"That's *why* you should have told me. I think I should stay in a hotel."

"Don't be an arse."

"I just—" Claire expels an exasperated breath. "I didn't get the feeling I was welcome there."

Noelle glances at her. "What, you mean Lillian? That's just how she is. She'll love you, but she'll never say she loves you."

Claire wonders if Noelle has relied on a similar rationale to convince herself that Lillian loves her. What must Lillian have thought when Noelle arrived on her doorstep—a young, loud American girl with metal holes in her ears claiming her son was "the one."

"Wait," Claire says. "Do you and Paul sleep in the same room?"

"Of course not," Noelle says. "We're good Catholics. I share a room with Aoife. Me and Paul find creative places to snog."

Claire ignores this.

"Paul sleeps in Roisin's room," Noelle adds.

"Which one was he?"

"She. She's away in college, in Dublin."

Claire pauses. "You're not living there once you're married, are you?"

Noelle cuts a corner too sharply. "Claire, we just got engaged last week."

Which is another version of yes. It occurs to Claire then how much Noelle should not be getting married. She's too young, Paul's too young—or at least, acts too young. How old is Paul anyway? Nineteen? Thirty-four?

"Paul's family is brilliant," Noelle says. "Don't you think?"

"I guess," Claire says, then feels guilty. "How many of them live there?"

"The kids, you mean? There are seven total. Six at home, plus Roisin."

"Where was the father? Opening up the pub?"

"Dead."

Claire glances at her. "Oh."

"Liver disease," she says. "Five years ago. Isn't that such

an Irish cliché? Paul says he wasn't even that big a drinker. I mean, it's all relative, I guess."

At least Claire thinks this might help explain why Paul still lives at home. She recalls how he acted at Deirdre's funeral, his sympathy blunt, impassioned, angrier than Claire ever was. "That's sad," she says.

"Fucking tragic," says Noelle.

Claire turns to the window. Somehow, knowing about the father, she feels more inclined to stay. It makes her presence in the house matter less. Maybe if she did something for Lillian to show her appreciation. Make a puzzle? Cook a chicken? Do they have crockpots in this place? The thought awakens a friction that is becoming familiar, the impulse to place this world next to that one. Subtract five hours: almost 7:00 a.m. in New Hampshire. The snow must have taken root by now, hard, heavy and sparkling. Bob would have already shoveled and salted the sidewalks, the driveway, a clean path from the house to the garage.

Then the car is slowing down. They are approaching some kind of roadblock. As they draw closer, Claire sees a herd of sheep. Fat, wet, marked with blue haunches and melancholy faces. A shepherd dressed in blue jeans is weaving among them and shouting, but the sheep are in no hurry. One of them is flopped, sunbathing, in the middle of the road.

"Yes!" Noelle says. "I was hoping this would happen."

"Is this normal?"

"Totally." She puts the car in neutral and pulls a cigarette from her pocket, like popcorn for a movie. "You don't have a light, do you?"

"No," Claire says, as Noelle starts groping around the floor. Claire rolls down her window and lets the rain freckle her arm.

She can hear the sheep's unconcerned *baa*s. As the shepherd waves his arms, Claire recalls Noelle's story about the farmer-husband she met on her way to the airport. "This isn't like that matchmaker thing, is it?"

"Aha!" Noelle says, surfacing with a lighter. "What isn't like what matchmaker thing?"

"What you told me yesterday. How Irish people get married based on a feeling—is that why you and Paul got engaged?"

"Because of a feeling?" Noelle feigns a shudder.

"That's not what I mean. You know, the impulsive—"

"We've been together almost two years, Claire," Noelle says, flicking the lighter in brisk, annoyed snaps. "He's not, like, some random guy I bumped into on a farm."

"I'm just concerned," Claire says.

"Well, don't be."

The sheep are shuffling grudgingly to the side of the road. After the shepherd collects the last few stragglers, he motions their car forward. Noelle rolls her window down, gives him a wave then falls silent, smoking. Claire rolls her window back up. She tries to distract herself with the scenery, endless variations on a theme—loose stone walls, green squares, limestone mazes—but the unruly acres remind her of New Hampshire. She focuses instead on the road signs. They don't appear often, but when they do, the immediacy of the old Irish language gets her attention. Each word is like a miniature artifact: defiant in its construction, in its very existence—knotty combinations of consonants, vowels flecked with accents like breath marks in music. The ends of some words are softened with *h*'s, which seems a dubious softness, a sigh with a hook on the end. *Eachdhroim. Gaillimh.*

*Béal Átha na Slua.* It is several miles before it occurs to Claire the signs are in Irish only.

"Wait," she says. "There's no English."

"Sorry?"

"These road signs. They're all in Irish."

"Yeah." This Noelle delivers as nonchalantly as if Claire had observed, *Sure got a lot of sheep!* "They just changed them."

"They did?" Claire is surprised she didn't know this. But then, she hasn't been staying on the cutting edge of linguistic theory. "Are you sure?"

"Yes, I'm sure." Noelle sounds annoyed. She starts digging in her jacket pocket, as if for evidence, and emerges with another cigarette. "Only in certain parts, where people seriously speak it. Like this section around here, it's part of this thing—"

"The Gaeltacht," Claire says, and feels a stirring of excitement. Her first year of grad school, she took a course on historical linguistics, about places in the world where ancient languages have survived. In Ireland, she recalls, native speakers live mostly in pockets along the West Coast. "Do you ever run into people speaking it?"

"Like, old guys in the middle of nowhere. When Paul and I went to the Aran Islands—oh my *God* they are fecking *amazing*—and we ran into this old guy on a beach going a mile a minute. We didn't understand a word he said, but we all sat down and had a pint."

Claire sees a lone sheep standing by the road. They exchange a look of what feels like empathy.

"But the language," Claire says. "The kids are all required to take it in school, right?"

"I know." Noelle blows smoke out the window. "It's so cute, isn't it?"

*Cute* denotes smallness and preciousness, bunnies and babies and buttons. To Claire, this loyalty to an old, endangered language is grand. Romantic. "Is that part of what Aoife's studying for her exam?"

"Oh my God, do you *ever* stop thinking about school?"

Claire is startled. For a second Noelle seems surprised too, then summons a laugh. Claire turns back to the window. She remembers when Noelle was applying to college and was dead set on following her friends to New York City: Hunter, Columbia, NYU. "You're aiming too high," Claire told her. It was harsh, but true. Noelle's grades and SATs weren't good enough. She had always fluttered around a C average, with the occasional B in gym or music, D in chem or calc. She insisted her activities would make the difference, hunt-and-pecking IRISH DANCING in a crooked line on the application form.

"That isn't even a school activity, Noe," Claire told her.

"So?"

"So it shouldn't be there."

"That's your opinion," Noelle said.

"It's not my opinion. It's just the way it is. College admissions boards don't have the same priorities Mom does."

Noelle stopped typing, one finger frozen above the keys.

"I'm just trying to help," Claire said, but Noelle wouldn't look at her again. Only when Claire left the room and was halfway upstairs did the sounds of typing resume, the rhythm of long pauses and hard clacking as painstakingly slow and intermittently fierce as Deirdre's cane navigating the geography of carpets and floorboards.

"You've *got* to try this," Noelle says, slamming the glove compartment shut.

Something lands in Claire's lap. A peace offering, disguised as chocolate: thin, wrapped in yellow, called a Flake.

FLAKE:

Airhead

*Frosted* cereal

Erode

Forget

Claire feels vaguely insulted. "Thanks," she says, but doesn't open it.

Noelle takes a drag from her cigarette. "So, the exam," she says. "It's called the Leaving Cert. It's this major test the whole country has to take to get into college, where you have to remember everything you've ever learned in your life. Gross, right?"

Claire makes a noncommittal sound. She recalls Noelle's college rejection letters arriving one by one, all of them thin, officially regretful, postmarked New York.

"And the more points you get, the better college you can go to. Roisin took it last year and was a total head case for, like, months. Studying, praying—"

Claire looks at her. "Praying?"

"Totally. Like, Mom times a hundred."

Deirdre had torn up those rejection letters as they arrived, pushing them down the mouth of the garbage disposal and letting them churn with the onion skins and coffee grounds. Noelle had ended up filling out an application to a state school, starting late admission the following spring.

"But the best part is," Noelle says, "the night the results

get printed in the paper, the whole country goes out and gets *twisted*."

Always, it comes back to this. Claire feels her jaw hardening. Noelle keeps talking.

"Irish names are great, don't you think? I told Paul we have to have at least fourteen kids because there's too many names I like."

"Sounds healthy," Claire murmurs, picking at the edge of the candy wrapper.

"My favorite name is *Aisling*." She overpronounces it, as if for a nonnative speaker. "You can spell it different ways. A-i-s-l-i-n-n. A-s-h-l-i-n-g. A-i-s-l—"

Claire had forgotten how this annoyed her, the way Noelle took liberties with spellings. Growing up she was alternately Noel, Noëlle, even briefly nOel. She'd probably been one of those students in English classes who peppered her essays with made-up words like *assimilize* and *sociate*, the ones Claire resented almost as much as the teachers who sang, "Well, if it's *not* a word, it *should* be!"

"You must be relieved you didn't have kids, right?" Noelle goes on. She flicks a glowing ash out the window. "I mean, things would be so much messier. Plus, you'd have to explain what's going on, like 'it's not about you' and all that gobshite, even though you totally know they'll think it is anyway, right?"

"I guess."

"Did you, like, plan it this way?"

"No," Claire says. "I mean, we thought we would have kids."

Noelle waits for the explanation, but Claire doesn't have

one. She and Bob had talked about it, hypothetically, as couples do, splicing together their most flattering characteristics. But in reality, it would have been Claire's decision to initiate, and something in her resisted. Maybe she saw having a baby as the last frontier of domesticity. Maybe it was her aversion to the phrase "we're trying," so clinically intimate it made her skin crawl. Maybe she was clinging to the notion that she should make more of herself *because* of herself, not by virtue of having a baby. Or maybe she sensed it was unfair to bring a child into a home with a mother who was unhappy, with a father who would one day say, "If you want, we can have a baby." Really, was there a lonelier proposition in the world?

"Well," Noelle says. "Probably better now."

"Probably." The headache has reawakened between Claire's eyes. She surveys the naked chocolate in her lap: It looks like a piece of driftwood, a fossilized twig.

"The thing I love most about the Irish names," Noelle says, "is how the most common ones over here seem totally exotic anywhere else. Like, Liam Neeson. In the States, it's the hottest name ever, but here that's like any dude at the sausage shop."

From the top, the chocolate looks like collapsed ribbons. Claire takes a huge bite. A crumb melts on her tongue and the rest flurries in an extravagant hail onto her lap. "Are you kidding me?"

Noelle glances over and laughs. "Isn't it ﹍ ﹍me? It's so fucking flaky! That's why it's called a—"

Claire stares down at the broken cho﹍ used party trick, the whoopie cushion of ﹍ her lap a furious swipe and chocolate dr﹍

"Aisling has an awesome meaning to﹍

already told Paul, if he picks some random Irish name, even if it's cool, I get to veto if it means, like, potato or death." She pauses. "Are you going to name one of your kids after her?"

"Who?"

Noelle flicks ash in the wind. "Mom."

"No," Claire says. "I wasn't planning on it. Why?"

"Just checking," Noelle says. "Because I am. Even though it has, like, the most depressing meaning in the world."

It was one of the first things Claire knew about her mother, though she can't remember the being-told, only the knowing, as if she were born with the definition under her skin. "Of course I'm sick," Deirdre liked to say. "Name a kid sadness, what do you expect?"

Sadness was not only the meaning of Deirdre's name, it was the cornerstone of her relationship with the world: permission to chalk up every small misfortune—from a busted oil burner to a burned bag of popcorn to a near-miss lottery ticket—to another comma in a long, tragic sentence.

"It's the sadness!" she would crow, after accidentally dropping an earring down the drain, then twist open a High Life with a consolatory hiss.

This was why, when Claire learned her mother was sick, it hadn't felt surprising. Not unimportant, but inevitable. It was late August; she and her father were heading to Kmart for school supplies. Claire was content, alone in the car with her father, envisioning her new lunch box and Trapper Keeper, way from the house with its constant baby noise and baby nd baby smell, a mixture of talcum and dampness and bananas. They were stopped at the red light next to the Roy Rogers. Since leaving the house, she had been thinking about how she might ask if they could stop there, when: "Your mom is sick," her father said.

It was not unlike his trademark "What's next?"—the words dissolving in a vague mist around his face. Claire looked up at him, waiting for more, but he only nodded, almost impercep- tibly, a secret signal exchanged between baseball players or spies. Claire turned back to face the road. She asked no spe- cifics, not so much because she felt she couldn't as because it didn't occur to her there were any. In her mind, her mother was *sick* in the same way she had always been *sad*, less a tan- gible condition than an abstract state.

When the light changed, so did the subject. It was as if the sickness existed only in the space behind them, the wrinkle in the universe between the red light and the green. Years later, whenever Claire found herself sitting at that intersection, she felt the revelation rumbling beneath her, a downed wire ready to sizzle if touched. When she was old enough to drive, she would speed up or slow down to avoid getting trapped at that light. She never went back to that Roy Rogers. The place struck her as laughably naïve, the kind of thing she once had the luxury of worrying about.

For most of Claire's childhood, everything she understood *sick* to mean was in the associations. The orange bottles that began appearing on the kitchen windowsill. The hush that darkened the house, sudden and lightless, like a wet towel. The thin yellow lamplight that leaked from beneath her par- ents' bedroom door and the rash that periodically spread, silent and defiant, across her mother's face.

But most of her mother's symptoms were on the inside. This, too, made a certain sense. Like the Lord's name, the workings of the body fell within the realm of Deirdre's selective sanctity; they were not discussed. Claire was alert to evidence of her mother's body—damp cotton balls, toenails like slivered moons, and once, a long gummy fake nail that looked like a purplish fang. *I know more than you do*, said Deirdre's clutter in the medicine cabinet, said the clicks and plinks of her makeup kit, said the pillowy packs of maxi pads stockpiled in the bathroom closet as if for some female war. Claire scrutinized the words on those packages like a cryptic adult language—*carefree thin super slender stayfree*—so incongruously light and airy, so unlike her mother. "Ultra thin overnight with wings," she read, picturing Tinkerbell from *Peter Pan.*

As she got older, Claire began to suspect that as much as Deirdre moaned and complained about "the sadness," deep down she enjoyed it. She relied on it, reveled in its tragic certainty, the fact that it had predisposed her to suffering. After a while, the combination of her invisible pains and tragic name gave her a martyrish glow. Deirdre prayed for her family, ailed for them, rigged their house like a Catholic home security system. When the word *God* dropped from their mouths, she corrected them so fast they could snatch it back like a crumb of food that hit the floor. At some upper echelon, she was cleansing her family's slate, getting them in good with the man upstairs. Her piousness would trickle down and benefit them someday, like children with fathers in high places who pulled strings to get them into good colleges or erase their DUIs.

"My work is done!" she would announce, returning from

a bout of confession or an impromptu weeknight Mass. "You can all thank me later." Then she would sink onto the couch, High Life in hand, Sears name tag flashing in the light from the television. DEIRDRE: 15 YEARS OF SERVICE.

Dierdre's name—and by extension, her suffering—was also yet another nod to her Irish heritage: Deirdre of the Sorrows, tragic heroine of Irish myth. Secretly, Claire suspected it was the real reason her mother cozied up to Yeats. He'd written a play called *Deirdre*, based on the old story. It sat under the coffee table, in one of the *Collected Works*, though Deirdre preferred her own version.

"Once upon a time, there was a beautiful baby named Deirdre . . ." she began, and no matter where Claire was, she heard it, ear tuned to that first line like the radar she would later develop for pills tipping from a bottle.

"Girl was ravishing!" Deirdre said. "Such a knockout they had to raise her in a cave."

Her rendition fell somewhere between a fairytale, a sermon, and a Harlequin romance; it was also the only bedtime story Claire's mother ever told. Though Claire may have heard the story as a baby, her only memories of it were as an older child, eavesdropping on Deirdre telling Noelle. As a newborn, Noelle was as she would be always: loud, skinny, and demanding, with a wild thatch of dark hair. "A matchstick in a crib," Deirdre called her. During the long hot afternoons the summer she was born, whenever Noelle cried, Deirdre launched into another telling. Claire would creep into the living room and hide in a corner, unseen.

"Had to have her sequestered!" Deirdre would shout. She delivered the lines with a hint of a brogue and heavy dose of fatigue, as if she, too, had inherited some of this ancient burden. "Too hard on people to be amongst good looks like that."

She always used the same words in the telling, words Claire otherwise never knew were in her repertoire. The heroine Deirdre was raised by King Conchobar (Claire pictured some crunchy, mythical candy bar) and when she was "of age," was "betrothed" to the king. "Like bringing up a cow to make a burger," Deirdre remarked; in retrospect, one of her more feminist insights.

"Problem was," Deirdre said, lowering her voice suspensefully, "she was smitten with the king's nephew, Noise."

His name was Naoise, but Deirdre preferred "noise," which permitted her to insert some wolf-whistling, catcalling sound effect. As the story went, Deirdre and Naoise "fled" and "fell head over heels," but Conchobar sent Naoise's brothers to "fetch" him and had him "slain!"

Claire knew Noelle was too young to understand the story, but that it wasn't about the meaning. It was a matter of rhythm, of melody, a lullaby. Her mother was a good storyteller: adding a low-breathed tension to the scary parts and letting the word *slain* slice the air like a blade. Even her word choice was an oddly appropriate blend of the raw and the regal, the elegant and the uncouth. *Uncouth*—later, it would be one of Claire's favorite words to describe her mother, some combination of *couch* and *mouth* and *tooth*, all of which were accurate predictors of Deirdre ten and twenty years later, nightgown billowing like a lily pad on the couch beneath her, voice screaming with laughter and teeth screaming with bleach.

"Poor Noise never stood a chance," she would add, sighing. "The good-looking ones never do."

Eventually, Noelle's crying would grow quiet. Claire stayed in the corner, holding still and watching as her mother pushed the swing with her thick, pink-slippered foot. Only once did she dare edge closer. The house had fallen into a gentle hush, mesmerized by the creaking of the swing and the chugging of the window air conditioner and the rise and fall of Deirdre's voice. It was the part when Conchobar, "unbeknownst" to the lovers, "doth send" someone to kill "the poor, hot bastard." Claire crept toward the couch and sat on the edge. Then, quietly, she eased onto her mother's knee. Deirdre stopped talking midsentence and Claire jumped off her, thinking she had hurt her, by leaning on her knee or interrupting her story or coming near her uninvited or all three.

For what felt like minutes, they were snagged in each other's stares. Her mother's face was somewhere between surprised and indignant, mouth partway open and brows arched. Claire stood still, waiting, hands balled at her sides. Because the story wasn't over. She hadn't gotten to the best part yet, to the word *slain!* and the devastated Deirdre throwing herself from the king's carriage. *It wasn't the fall that did her in*—Claire had the ending memorized, her favorite part—*it was a broken heart. Deirdre died of sorrow.*

Her mother's face began to close: eyebrows lowering, wrinkles smoothing, mouth firming into a wet red line. Excitement leaped in Claire's chest: Here it came. But when her mother spoke again, the brogue was gone. "The end," she said. Then she tucked her feet up onto the couch and cut her eyes toward the crib. "Don't wake the baby."

It was a moment that would dictate a million other moments: Claire left the room, shut her bedroom door, opened a bo and crawled inside it. She was crushed, but not the kind of crushed that makes you break. The kind that compresses you, gives you a harder shape.

———

Claire had imagined the Blarney Stone displayed for maximum tourist accessibility—like a Liberty Bell, a Plymouth Rock— a gently sloping boulder dropped in the middle of an open field. Instead she is waiting in a labyrinth of damp umbrellas and newly purchased Aran sweaters, inching around the spiral stairwell to the top of Blarney Castle and the magic stone she trusts is waiting somewhere at the end.

Claire peers back over her shoulder, at a carnival of bright, squeaky rain gear. It's easy to tell the tourists by their colors: coats in cheerful pinks and yellows, umbrellas with polka dots and stripes. For visitors, the rain has a kind of Irish kitsch value, while the Irish people seem to address the weather with a tired practicality, so accustomed to the landscape they blend right in.

"So," Claire says, as she and Noelle advance a step. Noelle is wearing a hooded gray sweatshirt over her brown sweater, squinting toward the top of the stairs. "Shouldn't you be spending every minute getting ready for the wedding?"

"I am ready," Noelle says. "Band, food, pub, priest, church. Done. I just have one fitting this week."

"You're getting married in a church?"

"C

s Claire, but it shouldn't. Not only are they in
Catholic, but also this entire wedding seems
n of Noelle's desire to take Irish dancing at
eir mother proud. At Claire's wedding, fifty

guests and a justice of the peace, Deirdre had grabbed the mike and brogued the cliché Irish blessing: "May the road rise to meet you . . ."

"There's actually something I was thinking you could help me with," Noelle says.

Claire has a horrific flash—taffeta, line dances, spoons banging glasses, appetizers wrapped in bacon. "What?"

"Paul wants us to write our own vows." Noelle tugs at her sweatshirt cords, hood tightening around her face. "And you know his are going to be all amazing and poetic. Mine can't suck. You have to help. You're the writer."

Claire listens for a note of derision, but the request sounds sincere.

"Maybe I'm not the best person to ask about vows," Claire says, as they advance another step. "You know, considering."

"Why? Did you and Bob write your own?"

At the time, this possibility hadn't even occurred to her. Her main concern had been getting through the ceremony without Bob saying, "I, ah, do." Now she wonders if this should have been a red flag: Never marry a man you don't trust to write his own vows.

"We just said the usual ones," Claire says. "You know, to have and to hold."

"Oh, right. I remember."

Does she? Claire has only the vaguest memory of saying them herself; what she remembers is how the words came back to haunt her during those early, empty months in New Hampshire. Some, like *forever*, had been fairly straightforward—but what about *have*? Or *hold*? Or *cherish*? She had mined the lyrics of that sixties song: *Cherish is a word I use to describe . . .*

which was sweet in the beginning, but was no one paying attention a few beats later? *You don't know how many times I've wished that I could mold you into* . . . Mold? *Mold?* Speaking of which: *Have?*

Claire wondered if her parents *cherished* each other. The word implied some recognition of value, of good luck. She had never sensed that between them, but maybe in any marriage, over time, certain vows emerged with more relevance. Her parents' marriage seemed less about words like *love* and *cherish* than *honor, sickness, health.*

They step to the top of the castle. The stone here is liverspotted, barnacled, something dredged up from the bottom of the sea. From this height, the acres of grass below look soft, spongy, mythical, the edges smudged like a watercolor. The grass is an unnatural, almost chemically bright green against the stark brown tangles of tree branches and still ponds.

"Maybe some of the blarney will kick in and rub off on us," Noelle says. She is looking ahead, toward the stone. "For the vows, I mean."

She sounds so fervent, Claire thinks, so earnest. Something about Noelle has always been so fundamentally youthful— not just her rosy skin and her loping walk but this unflagging absoluteness, this sureness about the world. It's the kind of certainty Claire has always viewed as suspect, the product of an unexamined life, but now she feels a dash of envy.

The group shuffles forward. They are next, behind a husband and wife with three small boys. Claire peers ahead, but the stone isn't visible; apparently it's on the underside of the supporting wall. She is beginning to realize the kind of maneuvering that is required here. To reach the stone, you lie on the ground and arch backward into a hole. A short, thick, leprechaunish man stands beside it like the troll guarding the pot of gold.

"Are you seeing this?" Claire says.

One by one, the boys are dropping to the ground, heads disappearing, legs sprawled. The parents feverishly snap pictures.

"I'm not sure I can do this."

"Yes, you can."

"I'm hungover."

"Too bad," Noelle says. "You're doing it."

The wife is less nimble, confirming Claire's fears. She lowers herself to the ground inch by awkward inch: crunchy new raincoat, stiff boots, stiff knees. "Hold my glasses," she tells the husband, then folds backward at the waist. Her hands grip the metal rungs, legs splay like a rag doll. The legs are reliable barometers of panic, Claire decides, as the wife's left foot flops inward. The leprechaun grabs her at the waist, right above her thick hips. Her Aran sweater rides up to reveal a roll of pale flesh.

"Oh God," Claire says.

"So you'll help, right?"

The wife's arms are visibly trembling. The leprechaun shouts something Claire can't make out. Then the woman resurfaces, tugging down her sweater. Her face is flushed, hair wild, but she manages a small, triumphant fist-pump.

"Will you?" Noelle is saying.

Claire looks at her. Noelle's eyes are bright, expectant, and the slightest bit nervous. It occurs to her these wedding vows might be the reason Noelle was so determined they come here. Most of these people are after the photo op; Noelle is here for the magic.

"What about this," Claire says. She glances at the husband, now lowering himself to the ground, knees and watch akimbo. "I'll help you with the vows if you invite Dad to the wedding."

Noelle folds her arms across her chest.

"You have to," Claire says. "He would want to be there."

"He'll be all, like, worried and disapproving, Claire. And he'll say I'm too young."

"No, he—"

"Or, okay. He won't say it but he'll totally be thinking it and he'll look all nervous and freaked out the whole time."

Claire checks the husband's legs. The bottom of the left trouser has risen to expose a black sock, a hairy shin.

"I mean, honestly?" Noelle says, getting louder. "I'd like it better if he just, like, *said* it. Just say: Noelle, I think you're too young. And then I say: Funny, Gene, I don't agree. But at least we're *saying* it. We never *said* anything."

"Maybe we didn't have to. Do people have to spell out every little thing?"

"Yes," Noelle says. "They do." She yanks her sweatshirt hood down to cover her eyes. "I wish Mom was going to be there."

Claire wishes she were one of those people for whom words soothing and vaguely spiritual just slip off the tongue, like yawns and sneezes—*Don't worry, she'll be there in spirit*—but she can't say these things; she's not sure she even believes these things. Plus, they would sound corny. Even Deirdre would agree. *Oh I will, will I? Then save me some wedding cake. A big corner piece.*

Now the husband is struggling to his feet. The wife is applauding. Noelle brushes a sleeve roughly across her eyes as the family assembles for the leprechaun to take their picture, puckering their lips. *Say Blarney!*

"I'll help you," Claire says. "Okay? With the vows?"

"Sláinte!"

Enter the leprechaun: falsely cheerful, feasting on the two of them with his glinting green eyes.

"Sláinte," Noelle replies.

"Top o' the mornin'!" he says.

Is it still the top o' the mornin'? It can't be. The leprechaun probably says that all day. In his requisite plaid tweed cap and olive-colored coat, he could be in costume; on the other hand, he looks like most of the Irish men Claire has encountered so far.

"Who's first?"

The voice isn't what Claire expected. She imagined it chipper, extra-broguey, but he sounds like any sarcastic Irishman bellied up at the pub. Claire suddenly notices his boots, black rubber, knee-high, the kind she associates with deep-sea fishing and dragging rivers for dead bodies.

He grins at Claire and singsongs: "This one here, with the fiery Irish hair?"

Are they paid extra for rhyming? Claire feels nauseated: the leftover hangover, the height, all that black rubber. She looks in the direction of the stone and remembers what Paul said about it being peed on. The hole looks like a mouth.

"Go ahead, Claire," Noelle says.

"You go."

Noelle sighs, but steps forward. "Fine. But you're next." She drops to a folded wool blanket. It must be there to prevent people from catching pneumonia, lying like fools on the cold wet stone. Claire wonders if during the off-hours the leprechaun keeps it in his trunk.

Noelle arches backward and her head disappears. Claire checks her legs: crossed at the ankle, as casually as if she were lying in a hammock.

"Bit more!" calls the leprechaun.

So that's what he was yelling. It's almost demeaning. It also means that even Noelle, scorer of an eighty-eight on the how-daring-are-you quiz, isn't in kissing range yet. Her arms are gripping the metal bars, tendons standing on her wrists and neck.

Then she pops up, dusting off the seat of her jeans. "I'm inspired already!"

"Next," deadpans the leprechaun.

Noelle looks at her. "Go," she says, with a firmness that leaves no room for debate. If Claire chickens out now, she'll be hearing about it the rest of her life. "You *need* this."

"Need what?"

"Step up, step up," says the leprechaun.

"The blarney," says Noelle, giving her shoulder a shove.

Claire steps forward, propelled by indignation. She is amazed Noelle actually believes in this crap. Why would any sane person do this? Hang upside down, subject themselves to public humiliation? As she approaches the hole, the mixture of dread and resentment is familiar, an echo of many ends of many lines, the moment she was faced with doing something she didn't want to do in the first place: get her school picture taken, attempt the pommel horse in gym class, sit on Santa Claus's lap at the mall. Here, at least, her face is hidden. She clings to this modicum of dignity as she lowers herself to the blanket. Next to her chest is a sign—KISSING THE BLARNEY STONE—that looks like it was made of posterboard and glue.

"Make it a good one!" yells Noelle.

Claire clutches the metal bars and leans back. As the blood rushes to her head, she reminds herself that millions of people have done this. Millions of out-of-shape tourists from around the world. It's a rationale she's used before to comfort herself in the face of painful but necessary rites of passage: losing her virginity, having her wisdom teeth pulled.

Once inverted, Claire had figured the stone would be right in front of her, but she can't find it. How perfectly, maddeningly Irish—the Blarney Stone just a ruse to make tourists embarrass themselves, only to discover it isn't even there! Once you're upside down, a scheming little elf says "sshh!" and makes you swear on everything Catholic to never tell, has you sign a contract with a feather pen stuck between your teeth.

"Where is it!" Claire calls up. She is panicking, imagining the little elf.

"Bit more!" the leprechaun sings.

Then she sees it. It seems amazingly, ridiculously far down—more convenient for peeing on than kissing. It's not really even a stone. She'd expected it to look more magical, some naturally existing, rough-hewn chunk of an ancient boulder, but it's more like a flat slab: a merit certificate, a stone diploma.

"Not quite!" shouts the leprechaun, stating the obvious.

Claire wonders if she can fake it, but this leprechaun sees everything. Her nose fills with the smell of old stone and wet sweater. Inching backward, she sinks lower into the castle's damp throat. She feels her left ankle go cold, realizes her jeans are rising up, wonders fleetingly when she last shaved her legs. The leprechaun's hands wrap around her waist. Blood storms her brain. Her stomach muscles are quivering, the leprechaun's grip tightening. Her necklace falls forward, smacking her in the teeth, the chain tightening around her chin. The stone is just inches from her face, a breeding ground of germs and magic, and she smacks her lips against it—not so much a gentle peck as a challenge. Then she kicks one leg, signaling she's ready to come back up.

———

Claire stands in front of the phone in the Conneelys' upstairs hallway. It's nearly 4:00 in Ireland. 11:00 in New Hampshire. On a Friday, Bob would be leaving for the institute at noon. She can't call him there and risk making small talk with Margie. Claire can only imagine what's being said about her at the institute—the gossip scurrying through the department, the sympathetic looks Bob must be attracting from secretaries and faculty wives and female researchers who don't know how to turn their ovens on.

She stares at the phone, black with a thick cord and rotary dial. From downstairs, she hears the Conneelys' after-school scrambling, a kettle whistling, the barking of a dog and backdrop of the TV. Logic would dictate the distance should make this call more manageable, Bob just a speck in a far-off time zone, but it is the opposite; in the distance Bob is abstract, intimidating. When he answers, what will she say? She just needs to let him know she arrived safely. She should have done it sooner; she promised, in the note. Bob has probably been calculating time differences and flight times and the thought makes her feel guilty, but more than that, vaguely repelled, the image so raw and sad.

Claire stares at a wall of built-in shelves; it is the wall she always dreamed of having. The books are messy and disorganized, genuinely slipshod, their spines seamed and bindings sprouting white threads. Behind her is Lillian's bedroom, the door closed. To her right, a grandfather clock supplies an ominous ticking. Claire thinks of how many conversations she and Bob should have had, all the practice they needed leading up this one. It's no wonder, in New Hampshire, she was diagnosed a tooth grinder. "We've got a grinder here!" Dr. Howarth had shouted to his assistant, as if alerting her to a feisty fish on his line. Dr. Howarth was a "rural dentist," which meant his assistant was his wife and his office was on the first floor of their two-story home. The office was often permeated by the sounds of kids playing and the smells of dinners cooking, ham hanks and video games and the front screen door slapping. He recommended that Claire try sleeping with her mouth hanging open—before they resorted to anything "trickier"—but, she thinks, had he been a real dentist, he would have peered in there and seen the true culprits, extracted the little rabble-rousers one by one: The unhad conversation the morning Claire blew the tire. The evening of the dinner party. The day Bob told her he was offered the institute job.

It was a January afternoon, snow-crusted and freezing, the kind Claire would grow to dread in New Hampshire but in school—and maybe, in the course of one's life, this could be true only in school—made her feel brainy, cozy, and content. She was curled up on her bed studying when Bob arrived at her door. "I have news," he said.

He must have been running. He was slightly out of breath, snowflakes still melting into his hair. His red parka hung open over a green rollneck sweater, the one he hadn't worn since Claire told him it was scratchy.

She stood up, waited, and finally asked, "What is it?" Bob was like this in conversation, needing permission to go on.

"I got it," he said. "I got the, ah, the job."

"Which job?"

"At the, ah, Institute for Biological Sciences."

Claire registered this news with a faint alarm. It wasn't the job itself. There had been many applications, many jobs; she hadn't kept track. But there was a science to Bob's "ah's" that she was beginning to understand. When he was nervous, they were markedly more frequent. This made her nervous.

"What does that mean?" she asked.

"It means, if I accept, it would mean—" He pushed a hand through his hair, a trickle of melted snow escaping and streaking down the side of his face. "It means I would have to move to New Hampshire." He paused, looking back and forth between her eyes. "Claire, would you move with me to, ah, New Hampshire?"

It was the way Bob phrased every stage of their relationship, like a miniature proposal, a question with a yes-or-no response. "Can I call you?" he had said on the quad, that first afternoon. "Claire, would it be all right if I kissed you?" he asked after their first date, and she decided, as she climbed in bed alone ten minutes later, that what the moment lacked in spontaneity it made up for in old-fashioned charm. Even if it was ultimately Bob's career steering their lives together, he was the one asking and she was the one agreeing; ostensibly, she was calling the shots.

As their relationship progressed, so did Bob's questions, giving even fairly innocuous moments unexpected emphasis. "Claire, may I shovel your walkway?" "Can I pick you up some ibuprofen?" "Can I hold the remote?" Depending on her mood, Claire found his questions sweet or irritating or fraught with unintended sexual innuendo. But more often than not, there was a weightiness about them that struck her as sensitive and well earned; for each of these seemingly ordinary gestures *did* mean something, had an everyday significance, nudging them closer in tiny increments: *yes, I will let you decide what we watch at night; yes, I will let you see me feeling sick and ugly; yes, I will let you let me need you.*

The Q&A also permeated their sex life, not stopping with the first kiss but unfolding as a series of permissions asked and granted. Ironic that, for all their more flagrant lapses in communication, during sex Bob was comfortable talking. Had Claire ever tried explaining this to anyone, it would have sounded like some kinky game, but he was earnest in his questions, pausing and speaking so clearly they might have been filming the central plot point of an after-school special about sex and self-respect. Eventually it would become tiresome, but in the beginning, it was sweet and flattering. Bob was concerned with her, with only her: what she wanted, what felt good, where she wanted him to go next.

But that afternoon, Claire's answer didn't come easily. She

had assumed, of course, that Bob would get hired somewhere. They had never talked about what would happen next; until it was happening, it hadn't seemed necessary. Claire had imagined they would manage long-distance for a year while she stayed on campus and finished her dissertation.

"But—I'm not done," she said. Bob was hovering just inside the doorway. Claire was standing in the middle of the room, holding her elbows in her hands. "I have to write my dissertation."

"I know." Bob opened his mouth, then paused. "But could you work on it there?"

Claire felt nervous, vaguely defensive. The truth was, she didn't want to have to give up her last year on campus. Why should she have to go because he was going? It struck her as caving, as embarrassingly traditional. Though facts were facts: Bob had to move, and she didn't have to stay.

"When would we have to go?" she asked him.

Bob took a step toward her, as if the prospect of their future propelled him forward. "End of, ah, the summer. I would start in September."

He pulled her to his chest. His sweater smelled like wet wool.

"We could find a little house," he said, and began tracing his fingers lightly up and down her spine. "We could have a big kitchen. A fireplace, maybe."

Claire closed her eyes. The vision began, reluctantly, to assemble itself: old pine floors, exposed beams, a backyard with trees.

"What's the area like?" she asked. "Is it rural?"

"It's, ah, sylvan," Bob said, or so she heard.

Then his fingers stopped moving, somewhere in the middle of her spine. Claire could feel his heart pounding through his sweater. "I defend my dissertation in May," he said. "So we could get married in, ah, August."

Her eyes flew open, cheek still pressed to his chest. Her first instinct was a hardwired joy, followed quickly by surprise and panic and crushing disappointment. Had Bob just proposed, or had it been a hypothetical? Wasn't a proposal the one thing that was *supposed* to be a question? And shouldn't the man asking it be gazing into your eyes?

And then, he was. Bob got down on both knees on the dusty tiles, looking up at Claire like he had the afternoon they met. He reached in his pocket and pulled out a ring with a diamond so tiny it was endearing. "Claire," he asked, "would you marry me?"

Now Claire looks at the phone, pulse pounding. She wipes her sweaty palms on her jeans. *I just wanted to let you know I'm here*, she will say. It is all she has to say, for now. She lifts the phone to her ear and blinks back angry tears. Angry at herself, for being so spineless. Angry at the Blarney Stone, for clearly being a sham. She finds herself staring right at *The Collected Works of W. B. Yeats*. Of course. The play *Deirdre*, staring at her with an air of mild reproach. Its appearance doesn't surprise her. It seems inevitable, a prop in a play, and a reminder of the most pronounced silence, the one that took hold after the funeral and didn't let up for weeks. When Claire returned to New Hampshire, she got on the couch and stayed there. Bob came to check her now and then, hovering, as if unsure whether to sit or stand. He brought her things: a pint of ice cream, a giant puzzle book, or once, an extravagantly tacky bunch of chrysanthemums. Claire thanked him, but stayed put. She let the empty hours unspool before her, challenging anyone to stop her. Every day was another long defiant stretch of nothing. She could skip the potlucks, ignore her dissertation, watch TV all day, and no one could say a word. Maybe her mother had been on to something all along: Sadness was the ultimate excuse.

One night, Bob found her curled up on the couch in the dark. "I'm sick," Claire said. "I have a fever."

He lowered himself gingerly to her side. "How high?" he asked, a tinge of relief in his voice. This problem, at least, was tangible.

"I didn't check it."

"Let me get—"

"I don't need to check it. I just know."

Tentatively, Bob reached down and smoothed her hair from her face.

"I'm tired all the time," Claire said. "And I have headaches. And my hands are freezing."

"It's probably just—"

"I have a fever!" she snapped, and began to cry.

"It could be the flu," he said. "It could be just a cold." It was perfectly reasonable. Nothing Claire described was out of the ordinary, nothing that couldn't be chalked up to symptoms of a drafty house in New Hampshire, but Bob's attempts to convince her otherwise made her cry harder, not because she really thought she had her mother's illness but because she wanted him to indulge the possibility that she might.

Claire's mouth is dry as she dials, a long series of numbers concluding with her own familiar seven digits. The first ring she can hardly hear through the blood rushing in her ears. On the third, Bob still isn't answering. When the answering machine clicks on, it is surreal: that this machine on the other side of the ocean could still be functioning, still perched on her old phone stand in her old kitchen in her old life; that her own voice could be saying, "You have reached the Wells residence, we can't take your"—had she ever felt as calm, as upbeat, as this woman sounds?—"get back to you as soon as we can." After the beep, Claire says nothing, just holds the phone to her ear and listens, as if the sounds of the house might permeate the receiver from the other side.

---

"Hurry up! It's almost on!"

The shouts are coming from the living room. Claire hurries down the stairs, wiping at her eyes. From the entryway, she discovers the breakfast crew and then some. School-uniformed kids of all sizes are crowding the floor, straddling the back of the beige couch like bleachers at a football game. Their braids are loose, shirts untucked, floor strewn with book bags and teacups and hard blue school shoes. Lillian is seated toward the back, in a brown wing chair. At the head of the room, an enormous console TV dominates the floor like a shrine.

Everyone is gazing toward it, faces cast in a greenish glow. Claire spots Noelle on the carpet, lost among the other skinny bodies and tousled heads of hair. When she sees Claire, she pats the floor beside her. Then one of the little boys cries, "Would you be guilty!"

Claire looks at the set: the opening credits of *The Fresh Prince of Bel-Air*.

"Would you be guilty!"

All at once, the room is a collective shout of laughter. Every one of them, from the weary mother to the edgy teenage daughter to the multiple little-old-man-boys, whoops unabashedly as Will Smith spray-paints a brick wall and gets reprimanded by a woman in a hairnet.

"Look at yer man! The shame!"

Their laughter is infectious, outrageous, as uninhibited as any laughter Claire has ever heard. Even Lillian is howling. As Claire scans the room, she finds herself smiling, even as her brain is working to decipher what the phrase means: *Would you be guilty? Would you ever? Would you be caught dead?* On the surface the words are condemning, but there is a juiciness about them, a wicked, vicarious delight in the antics of the Fresh Prince. And of course, there's the inevitable Catholic overtone—a dash of guilt for good measure—but it, too, has a twinkle in its eye.

"Would you be guilty!" the room hollers, as the Fresh Prince is tossed to the curb in front of his new mansion in L.A. "The shame! The shame!"

# CHAPTER SEVEN: } Smart

Saturday's rain is hard and relentless, slashing against the window-panes. In a country of signs and omens, this one feels clear: permission to spend a lazy day at home. Which isn't the same as spending a lazy day at *your* home. This, Claire thinks, is why she should have stayed in a hotel. She may not be an imposition, but is she even capable of relaxing? When she offers to help with the breakfast dishes, Lillian waves her away. She folds her clothes, makes her bed, then stares down at the nubbly brown comforter. What she wouldn't give to be tucked inside her own house: invisible, alone.

"Sit," Noelle commands, when Claire returns to the living room. Noelle is sitting cross-legged on the couch, Lyndsey kneeling on the floor before her as Noelle braids her hair. They are watching an Australian soap, trading off explanations of the characters as they appear on screen.

"They snogged two weeks ago."

"That one's a right bastard."

When Lillian walks through carrying a basket of laundry, she asks, "Are she and yer man back together yet?"

"Not yet," Noelle says.

The house, Claire begins to notice, moves in cycles: The kids run in and out, arriving in a small damp mob every so often to shed their wet shoes and slickers by the front door. The kettle whistles. People call over constantly, front door opening and slamming, though the phone rarely rings. The TV show changes, but the set never goes off. Claire finds herself consuming a ridiculous number of sweets and dunking them in a ridiculous number of teacups; somehow, being in a foreign country, the calories feel imaginary.

The living room, like much of the house, has a sense of orderly disarray. Two flat-cushioned couches, a loveseat, and a wing chair are stuffed in close quarters, all of them inconspicuous shades of beige and dull gold. The walls and rug are patterned in competing brown stripes and dense gold flowers. On the wall above the fireplace hangs a photo of a man Claire thinks must be the Conneelys' father. He has Paul's long face and narrow shoulders. He is standing in front of a fence with his hands stuffed in his pockets and hair moving slightly in a breeze. His expression is warm but his eyes are squinting; it could be the wind, but looks like he's peering at his children from inside the frame.

When there is a lull in the action—the kids outside, Lillian busy with laundry, Noelle reading *Hello* magazine—Claire goes into the kitchen and surveys the cabinets: canisters of sugar, flour, eggs, whole milk.

"Hungry?" Lillian asks.

Claire turns, startled. "Oh—God, no," she says. "I feel like I'm going to explode," she adds, then regrets it. She has a suspicion women in Ireland don't stand around complaining about how fat they feel. "I was just . . . I was thinking I might make something."

Lillian shifts her laundry basket to the opposite hip.

"As a thank-you for letting me stay," Claire explains. "Chocolate chip cookies, maybe."

"Ah!" Lillian smiles. "Lovely."

Alone in the kitchen, Claire goes blank. It occurs to her she doesn't know for sure how to make chocolate chip cookies. She must be able to improvise, but she is not a cook-by-gut person, and Lillian's rare smile feels like added pressure to make these cookies good.

"Is there a store nearby?" she whispers to Noelle, still on the living room couch. "I need chocolate chips."

"They don't have chocolate chips."

"I know. That's—"

"No. I mean, they don't, like, exist here."

Claire pauses. "But I need them. I'm making cookies."

Noelle tosses her magazine on the floor. "What about we get a big bar of chocolate and hammer it?" Before Claire can protest, she is yelling for Graham. "Go to the store and buy us a big bar of Hershey's," she instructs. "Don't eat it. And don't let anybody have it. Here, buy yourself a sweet with the change."

Back in the kitchen, Claire finds Lyndsey sitting at the table, her new braid already starting to unravel and yellow headphones clamped firmly on her ears. "Hello," Claire says awkwardly.

The girl removes the headphones. "I'm helping," she says, then proceeds to point Claire toward the cooking trays and mixing bowls. Together, they slather the trays with Crisco, Lyndsey humming lightly. When the pans are greased, Claire reviews their ingredients. "We're missing vanilla extract," she says.

Lyndsey drags her chair to the counter and spins the rack on the top shelf. "Don't have that," she says, plucking out a small bottle. "Use this."

Lemon extract. "No vanilla?"

"It's the same," Lyndsey says, with such assurance that Claire can't bring herself to double-check, and almost convinces herself that in Ireland lemon and vanilla are in fact the same thing.

Graham returns with a pound of Hershey's and a small battalion of boys and twins in tow. They gather around the table, strip the bar of its wrapper and start pounding at it gleefully with dull kitchen knives. "Careful," Claire says, as chocolate shavings start flying. "Not too big."

She feels like she's conducting an ill-advised arts-and-crafts project, but the kids seem to be having fun, licking flecks of chocolate off their forearms. As Claire and Lindsey make the batter, approximating the measurements, Claire finds herself smiling. It feels good to be in a home so teeming with life, the good kind of life. Good to be in a kitchen that acts like a kitchen, with no ulterior motive: no army of medicine bottles on the windowsill, no minefield of bug traps on the floor. The racket has attracted Noelle, who jumps in and starts pounding. Claire watches Noelle laughing, Seamus leaning against her knees. What had Claire expected Noelle's life in Ireland to be? She had never stopped to envision it— not beyond a vague sense of irreverence, immaturity—but if she had, it would never have resembled this. Noelle may have run off with the abrupt drama of an angry teenager, but she had run to a new family, a better family. Suddenly she misses her, her sister who is sitting in the same room.

The cookies turn out just as Claire feared: lemon-flavored with chunks of chocolate hard enough to break a tooth. The lemon extract also has an unexpected shrinky-dinklike effect, making them expand until they are flat, wide, oddly spongy. They taste a little like dish detergent.

"Gorgeous!" they shout. "Splendid!"

"They're not supposed to taste exactly like this," Claire says. "I didn't have a recipe—" but the Conneelys are devouring them with such guiltless, vigorous delight that Claire stops protesting, lest she ruin it.

After the crowd has dispersed and the cookies have disappeared, Claire insists on doing the dishes. Her ears are buzzing lightly, all her senses pleasantly exhausted. She feels comfortably sick from the chocolate. Looking out the window, she realizes it's been hours since Bob crossed her mind. Homesickness, she thinks, can be deceiving: The first rush is pure reflex, the comfort of the known. Right now, at least for now, she would rather be here.

For dinner, Lillian makes soup and grilled cheeses—

"toasties," she calls them, with her usual bluntness, busy-ing herself around the stove. The tea water whistles, and she snaps off the burner, shifts the kettle. The kitchen windows are fogged with steam. To Claire, this mealtime bluster is beginning to feel familiar; same spirit, minor variations. Paul is there or not there, depending on his pub schedule. The neighbor kids are replaced with new neighbor kids, the dog might be a different size and color. Tonight Paul is missing, and Aoife. She's been out of sight all day.

"Where's Aoife?" Claire asks. "Studying?"

She takes a bite of her sandwich. It's the most indulgent kind of grilled cheese—greasy, oozing, toast so drenched in butter you could wring it dry. *Cheesy:* There's an implicit con-nection, there must be, between the impulse to be melodra-matic and the sandwich in her hands.

"She's at church," answers Lyndsey.

"By herself?"

"Novena."

"Oh," Claire says. She has never been to a novena, but Deirdre used to say them on occasion, leaving every night for nine days straight with a tight-lipped, sacrificial calm. Claire knew you went to novenas with specific intentions, though she never found out what it was her mother prayed for. Deir-dre treated her intentions like wishes on a birthday cake; if divulged, they wouldn't come true.

Graham offers, "It's for the exam."

"What else?" adds Lindsey.

"Hush," Lillian says. Though her back is turned, she doesn't miss a word. "She'll be along any minute."

Claire senses not to ask more, even though she's intrigued. To her, the combination of academics and prayer is a fundamental contradiction. It's one of the things she loved about academia: the reliable cause-and-effect of it. Study hard, do well. It's hard to imagine the sharp, wary teenager who went storming out of here yesterday morning believing anything different.

Lyndsey clamps her headphones on. "Not at supper," Lillian tells her, and the girl sighs as she pries them from her ears. Lillian slides a sandwich onto Lyndsey's plate, then pauses for a moment to fuss with her braid, ostensibly to neaten it but really, Claire sees, to touch her daughter's hair.

Then a small voice from the other side of the table says, "Someone phoned."

Claire looks up and is surprised to find one of the twins pointing a small finger in her direction.

"Me?"

"Bob," the boy says. He glances at Lillian. "You were busy. With the cookies."

Claire feels her last bite of sandwich lodge in her throat.

"What did he say?" Noelle asks.

Graham pipes up, "Is he your boyfriend?"

"Hush," says Lillian. "Sean."

The boy shakes his head.

"You're sure?"

He nods, and Claire is sure he's sure. Bob wouldn't leave any more message than that. He must have seen that she called yesterday, on the Caller ID. Since when does Bob check the Caller ID? Since, she realizes, she left him.

Claire looks down at the half-eaten sandwich. She can feel Noelle's eyes from across the table but can't look in her direction. She can't bear the expression, anxious but eager, that she knows will be waiting on her face.

Graham is still looking up at her. "He's not my boyfriend," Claire tells him. "He's my husband."

"Graham," Lillian interjects. "Go get my jumper."

"But—"

"Now, please."

Graham sighs and slides off his chair. Lillian turns back to the skillet. Claire feels a surge of affection for this mother, this mother so unlike her own.

"Where is it!" Graham calls.

"Back of the chair," says Lillian.

Claire subtracts five hours: Bob is probably at the institute. He likes to go in on Saturday afternoons, when it's quiet. To catch him at home, she should call late.

"I can't see it!" Graham shouts.

From the front of the house, a door slams. Footsteps move quickly down the front hall and a moment later, Aoife appears. Her wet hair is plastered to her cheeks and forehead and her face is white, frozen, the stripes of eyeshadow as pronounced as bruises. Her expression is so still and damp that it takes Claire a moment to register the tears slipping down her face.

"One magpie," she says.

Lillian sets her spatula down. Graham appears behind Aoife's left hip, clutching a thick pile of sweater.

"Leaving Mass," Aoife says. "I saw one."

The response in the kitchen is immediate, a collective shifting of energy and concern. Aoife is lowered to an empty chair, as the rest of the room rises. A cup of tea is placed in Aoife's hands. A toastie on a plate appears, a cookie, a bloom of tissues. Graham hands the sweater to Lillian, whose face has gone slack, admitting a deep V of concern between her eyes. But she stays in motion, tucking the sweater around Aoife's shoulders, stirring sugar in her tea. There are no words.

Claire is standing too. She looks at Noelle, who hangs back. Claire realizes Graham has reappeared by her elbow. He is already looking up at her, waiting to be consulted.

"One magpie," he says, but delivers the word softly, soberly, as you would offering condolences. Then he lapses into what sounds like a nursery rhyme: "One is for sorrow, two is for joy, three is for a girl, four is for a boy, five is for silver, six is for gold, seven is for a secret never to be told." The words sound innocuous, but the little boy's voice contains the sadness of the ages. "One magpie," he repeats, a doctor confirming an unwanted diagnosis.

Claire nods. His message is clear.

———

During her course work in linguistics, Claire came across a theory that suggested word games—cryptograms, tongue twisters, puns, jumbles, word finds, crossword puzzles—can breed skepticism. Over time, the game-player becomes so conditioned to distrust the surface of things, to anticipate being manipulated, that she begins to doubt anything is really as it seems. This theorist speculated that such skepticism is a healthy development; it keeps a person from being gullible, taking things at face value. But when does skeptical turn cynical? When does questioning whether something is authentic escalate into assuming that it never is?

When Claire was in fourth grade, she announced that she didn't know if she believed in God. "There isn't any proof," she said plainly.

They were eating dinner, roast beef and oily, orange scalloped potatoes. Claire was nine; she wasn't being rebellious. But Deirdre stopped chewing and stared at her hard. "Don't be smart," she said, then slapped her, a quick, bright sting. Noelle, in her high chair, started crying. When Deirdre drew back, she looked as surprised as Claire felt. "Go to your room," she said quietly, and Claire went upstairs with half her dinner uneaten on her plate.

Sitting on her bed, Claire felt like she should feel guilty, but the truth was, alone in her room was the place she most liked to be. She fingered her cheek. It stung a little, but more than anything, the pain was fascinating, the fact that she could provoke this reaction from her mother, especially since Noelle was born. Claire went to the mirror and examined the mark that was emerging. She could see the individual fingers, blazing red stripes. *Don't be smart*, her mother said. Claire knew this *smart* wasn't the usual kind, not the smart that scored hundreds on spelling tests or brought home A's on report cards or even the *smart* that Deirdre meant when she eyeballed the clothes in the Sears catalog—"isn't *that* smart-looking?"—she would say, poking a finger at the models in their pencil skirts and tailored dresses. That night, her mother's *don't be smart* meant *don't be fresh*. But not fresh like laundry or lettuce. It meant *don't be bad*.

From that night on, Claire kept her doubts about God to

herself. This wasn't hard; there was no place else to put them. It wasn't until she went to college that her skepticism would be given free rein. Here, finally, was a place where questions were allowed—rewarded! A place where, though the climate of PC-sensitivity was almost ominous, Catholicism was an easy, permissible punch line. When one of Claire's floormates asked her religion (she found that in college people asked these things—religion, sexuality, political affiliation—in a way that managed to sound entirely impersonal) and she replied that she was Catholic, his response was "Still?"

"Raised Catholic," Claire amended, and felt pleased when he gave her a sympathetic nod. While other daughters might rebel by dating the wrong boys or piercing the wrong body parts, hers was a different sort of rebellion: quiet, theoretical.

*I know more than you do,* said her mother, said the holy snippets of straw and thumbprints of ash and saltwater glinting in soda bottles on the kitchen counter.

*Oh yeah?* Claire said back. *I know more than you do too.*

But from time to time, Claire had doubts about her own capacity for doubtfulness, like during her poetry elective sophomore year. The class was Theory & Appreciation of Poetry— the T&A seminars, they were called. The T&A's approached their subjects as both writing and literature: Words were savored, but with a cool academic eye. When introducing a poem to the class, the professor would first seduce them with the A—read it slowly, deliciously—then sit back and blast them with the T: "So, did the poet pull it off?"

At first, this approach caught Claire off guard. Not that she didn't realize poems were crafted; of course they were crafted, but that they might be so *calculated*—and that she might be an innocent player in their design.

"Did the poet convince you?" the professor said. "Did he break your heart?"

Claire scribbled in the margin of her notebook: *If we can analyze whether something breaks our hearts can we really be heartbroken?* She didn't like thinking about poems this way. It was so strategic, so cat-and-mousy. She was accustomed to distrusting the abstracts—but language! Language was the one thing she could trust. In retrospect, maybe this was the appeal of becoming a cruciverbalist: satisfying the impulse to chop down words at the root, to intellectualize them before they can affect you. To have the meaning of things, albeit briefly, in your control.

The first paper assignment was this: In no more than three pages, choose a poem you love and argue why. It sounded simple enough, but all week, Claire couldn't bring herself to start writing. It wasn't the kind of resistance she would one day feel about her dissertation. She cared *too* much. This was more than writing a paper: It was making a case for her feelings. The night before it was due, she reread the assignment: a poem you love. *Love.* She wrote the entire thing in one sitting, one to five in the morning, the hours when it's near impossible to distinguish whether a thought is brilliant or absurd. As the sunlight was just starting to drag itself across her wooden floor, she typed the exhausted, uncertain ending: *I fear these are unsophisticated reasons. Or maybe I am simply afraid to admit to being romantic.*

Then she returned to the top of the paper and titled it: "An Apology."

Throughout the day, whenever Claire thought of the paper tucked in her binder, she alternately swelled and recoiled, filled with confidence and doubt. She wouldn't let herself look at it, knowing it was too late to change it. But in class, when they were assigned small groups to read aloud, she felt her stomach tighten.

"'An Apology,'" Claire said to her group, wiping her hands on her jeans. As she began reading, she kept her head down and her eyes on the page. She felt both terrified and oddly detached, listening to her words from the night before gradually returning: the acknowledgment of the poem's "rawness," its "easy meter" and "mainstream popularity." The lines sounded familiar but distant, like diary entries from high school; you can tell you wrote them, but they feel like the product of a different heart.

"But it is the very qualities that make the poem unsophisticated that affect me most—" Claire read on. She felt her face burning, tried not to think about how awkward she looked blushing, how her red cheeks clashed with her hair. "In a romantic tradition that is steeped in sadness, that validates misery, is writing about the miserable truly brave? Maybe it is the so-called mush, the sentimentality, that is, in fact, the greater risk . . ."

It all sounded so convinced, so embarrassingly impassioned, the words soaring and redoubling. The romantic sheen these lines had taken on the night before evaporated abruptly in the presence of the fluorescent gray-green light strips and the smell of grape gum, which the girl beside her was chewing in long, tensile crackles.

Claire was nearing the halfway point when she felt her professor pause behind her. She cleared her throat, tried to swallow. She was staring down the barrel of the poem itself. She couldn't just read it; she had to deliver it, *sell* it. She considered skipping it altogether, but it was so visible, an indented island in the middle of the page. She flew through it without stopping to breathe. "May the road rise to meet you may the wind be always at your back may"—in her head, she could hear her mother fake-broguing it, leaning on this syllable and that one, like notes in a song, but Claire's reading was flat and fast, squashing any feeling she claimed the poem evoked— "and God hold you in the hollow of his hand."

A few words later, her professor moved on, and by the time Claire reached the end of her paper her neck was hot, her armpits damp. "Maybe I am simply afraid to admit I am a romantic," she said, recognizing her conclusion with a kind of defeat.

The following week, when the papers were returned, Claire held hers close to her face as she unfurled it. Across the top was written: *Not the kind of "poem" I had in mind. Unusual ideas, though.* Underneath was scrawled a B-minus. Claire shoved the paper in her notebook. Her body was one hot, humiliated pulse. She hadn't gotten a B-minus since her junior year of high school when she ill-advisedly took jewelry making and mangled one rusted pair of earrings for an entire semester. She shoved her books in her bag, furious at herself for choosing such a stupid poem, at her mother for not raising her on something more highbrow than sentimental Irish toasts.

———

"It's the cruciverbalist!"

The shout comes from Middle Age, seated on the same stool he was on two days ago.

"And look who she's got with her," Paul says.

"How's she cuttin'?" Middle asks Aoife, and Paul adds, "Taking a break from the books?"

"Fuck off," Aoife says. It had been Noelle's idea to bring her, which struck Claire as rather big-sisterly and sweet. The girl had been almost silent since the magpie sighting but brightened at the invitation, disappearing for twenty minutes to apply black eye makeup and brush out her hair. In the States, Claire thought, she would have traded in her drab church clothes for a tight skirt or tank top, but she emerged with only her head radically made over on top of the original gray sweater and dark blue skirt.

Noelle is leaning over the bar, probably telling Paul what happened at the house. If Aoife notices, she doesn't let on. Leaning against the bar, she scans the room slowly, her gaze steady as a searchlight and her expression impressively aloof. It's hard to believe this is the same stricken face that entered the kitchen just a few hours earlier. She exudes the aura of a bouncer, or a kid whose family owns the place. Then Claire hears her breath catch.

"Jaysus," Aoife whispers. Her eye seems to have snagged on something at the end of the bar.

"What?" Claire resists the impulse to turn around.

Aoife swivels so she's facing the bar, where three pints are settling. "Fergus," she says.

Noelle whips around. "Who?"

"*Whisht!*" Aoife shushes her. "*Fergus.*"

"What about him?"

Paul leans forward on his elbows. "What's this?"

"Fuck off," Aoife says, and waits until he disappears. Then, calmly: "I shifted him last weekend."

Claire feels vaguely concerned. The word *shifted*—it sounds so literal, so mechanical. It evokes the physical maneuverings of sex, the skin and bones of it: elbows knocking sternums, hands adjusting hips.

"So was he a good kisser?" Noelle asks.

Aoife's face is already closed over, like a pond that swallowed a skipped stone. "It was nothing."

"Oh, come on!" Noelle says. "I bet he was."

Claire manages a quick glance at Youth, who looks to have aged dramatically in the last few seconds.

"Sweet, right?" Noelle persists. "Sweet, but a little too much tongue?"

But Aoife has already resumed her composure and picked up her pint, effectively ending the conversation.

"Fine," Noelle says petulantly. "Just as long as you two didn't do *the bold thing*." She flashes Claire a smile. "Sex."

Aoife mutters, "No one says it anymore, except your aoul won over there." She glances at Old Age, hunched over a pint.

"I don't care," Noelle says. "I like it. *The bold thing*. It's brilliant!"

How like Noelle, Claire thinks, to not only adopt a vocabulary that isn't hers but fling it around any way she sees fit. From a linguistic standpoint, *the bold thing* is amusing; there's an inherent drama in that definite article *the*, as if of all the acts of courage, having sex with another person is the pinnacle of brave. Claire prefers *shifting*. To shift—and to be shifted. Isn't this what all intimacy is?

SHIFT:

Hook up

Move

Alter

Change

Her first time with Bob, they were in his office, in the beginning of winter. It was near midnight and the building was deserted, the lamplight outside the window illuminating the falling snow. They had all their clothes off, wrapped in a nest of blankets on the floor, when Bob asked, "Are you sure?" Claire nodded, pressing her face into his neck. "I love you," he whispered, and she whispered it back, and meant it, feeling the pounding of his heart through his chest. The next morning, when she stepped out of the building and onto the quad, wrapped up in her boots and winter coat, she blinked into the sharpness of the sunlight and ordinariness of people rushing to the library, talking on their phones; she felt like she was in some secret, parallel universe: lucky, guilty, relieved. She had been shifted, and shifted. She had had sex with a man and was a slightly altered woman as a result.

Now she thinks of Bob's call and feels a tightening in her lungs, the beginnings of panic, but can't seem to follow through with it; this pub is like a sedative, keeping her from mustering the effort true panic would require. From an unseen corner, music starts. The floor begins to pulse, the rhythm of flute and fiddle so all-encompassing it could be seeping from the walls. The beat is in her spine and in the soles of her feet. Aoife's left foot starts stomping. It seems at odds with her usual reserve, though even the stomp has a kind of reserve about it. The rest of her body remains inert, while just the one leg dances, all her emotion caught in a single limb.

As Claire drinks, she feels her body soften. *Wherever you go, there you are.* Bob had meant this as a warning but at the moment, pint in hand, fire flushing her cheeks, it sounds like a comfort. Like permission to just *be* here—forget her old life for a night and melt into this one. Its wit and warmth are so unlike the bars she knew in college, the relentless shouts and bad jukeboxes, drinks chugged and slammed on tables. Here, drinking is steady but casual, congenial; appreciative, somehow. Here, the women haven't come to outdo each other with tiny clothes and bar banter; they are crowded into tables and laughing, clutching pints and digging into heaping plates of sausages and fries. There seems something rather fearless about them, their genuineness, their willingness to tear into a sausage in public, to go into a pub without makeup on, their faces bright, hair damp and corkscrewed with rain.

Claire closes her eyes. Tangled, colorful blossoms of conversation unfold around her, women chatting and laughing, men delivering boisterous tales or toasts or jokes. The Irish voices are like music, lingering on this note or that one, as if performing each sentence.

"To Paul!"

She opens her eyes in time to see a small crowd raise a shot behind her, just as the song ends. Claire assumes they're toasting Paul the bartender—she can't bring herself to call him brother-in-law yet—but it occurs to her they probably mean Paul's father. She glances at Aoife, looking for a flicker of sadness, but the toast doesn't seem to register. It probably happens ten times a night.

Aoife catches Claire's eye then looks away, tucking her hair behind her ear. There's something about the girl Claire finds fascinating, if a bit intimidating. She is the girl Claire never would have been friends with in high school (too cool) but Aoife doesn't seem to fit in with the other girls in the pub either. Her heavy, deliberate makeup betrays her youth, yet her air of knowingness makes her seem older. Like Lillian, she doesn't miss a trick. Claire suspects that behind Aoife's cool exterior there are many, probably accurate, impressions about her stored away, but occasionally, like now, something darts across Aoife's face that is pure child, as if curious about Claire but reluctant to admit it.

"Well," Claire says, and sighs deeply, as if some previous conversation between them were winding down. "So do you think you like Fergus?"

"Don't know," Aoife says, with a shrug. "Might. He fancies me." She manages to add this with no arrogance whatsoever, just matter-of-factness, another one of life's burdens.

"Well," Claire says. "That's nice, I guess. To be fancied."

"I suppose."

Claire takes a drink. She is starting to feel gently buzzed.

"Your husband, then," Aoife says. "Is it for good?"

Coming from someone else, the question might have rattled her, but Claire finds herself answering the girl honestly. "I'm not totally sure," she says. "But it might be."

Aoife keeps her eyes on the crowd, but Claire can tell by her stillness that she is listening. It occurs to her that she should try to dispel the sort of negative impression Lillian might frown upon—a flighty American woman dropping her life to "find herself."

"This whole thing, though," Claire says. "Leaving. It really isn't like me."

Aoife just nods, and Claire thinks it's also possible this teenage girl would see her leaving differently—as modern, independent, savvy about men and the world.

"I just mean," Claire says, "I never planned to leave my husband. We never even had a fight."

"Never?" Aoife turns, raising her eyebrows. "Jaysus," she says, and Claire can't tell if she thinks it's impressive or bizarre. "Why'd you leave, then?"

Claire pauses. Then, with a flourish, she turns and slaps the palm of her left hand on the bar top. "See this?" she says, fanning her fingers wide. "The other morning, I was in the kitchen, and all of a sudden I looked down . . . and this hand had just blended in."

Aoife squints at the hand, the effect of it weakened by the fact that against the dark wood of the bar Claire's skin practically glows. "To the kitchen counter, like?"

"Yes. But the counter was pale," Claire explains. "And kind of freckled."

At this, Aoife laughs. "Looking for a way out, were you?" she says. Claire quickly withdraws the hand. Her palm is wet and stinging. She wipes it briskly on her jeans and wraps it around her glass. Could she really have been so simple? So susceptible to the trickery of her own mind?

Then Aoife asks, "Is he nice?"

"You mean . . ." Claire pauses. "Yes. At least, I think he is."

Aoife nods. "Right," she says. "Fergus too." She raises her glass to her lips, and for a moment the two of them are in helpless cahoots, prey to the Achilles heel of women everywhere: a man who's nice.

"Shots!" Noelle shouts.

She is back and cradling what look like three enormous tumblers in her hands. Her face is flushed. Claire wonders how much Noelle drank when she wasn't paying attention. "Ladies," she says, "it's time."

"None for me," Claire says.

"Oh my God," she blurts, "you need a shot more than anyone I know."

Her words only nick Claire's thick skin before pinging off, caught in the eddy of the pub. The shot glasses are the size of teacups, alcohol the color of ginger ale. The only shots Claire has ever known are tidy and taste like candy, but these look like the kinds ordered by gangsters in movies.

"What is that?" Claire says.

"Whiskey."

"I'm not drinking that."

"Oh, yes you are. We all are." Noelle lifts hers. "Sláinte!"

Noelle and Aoife drink theirs in one swallow. Claire grudgingly tries to mind-over-matter it, like the first pint of Guinness, but it feels like her throat is being ripped out. She comes up coughing.

Aoife hands her a fresh pint. Noelle waits and then says, "Let's teach Aoife an American drinking game."

Claire doesn't like the sound of this but Aoife, to her chagrin and mild disappointment, seems tentatively interested. "How's it go?"

"It's called Two Truths and a Lie," Noelle explains. "You have to say three things about yourself. Like, wild, made-up-sounding things. And the other people have to guess which one is the lie. And if they're wrong, they drink."

Aoife looks dubious.

"It's fun!" Noelle says. "Trust me. Okay, this one's a practice round. I'll make it easy." She presses a finger to her bottom lip. "So Aoif, you could say . . . I'm studying for my exam, and I'm an only child, and I have a huge crush on Ferg over there."

"That last bit's the lie," Aoife says.

"Drink!" Noelle points at her like a sorority pledge master. "Which one's the lie, Claire?"

"Only child," Claire says, feeling like she's five.

"That's right!" Noelle takes a giant swallow, even though the rules don't require it. "Now let's play for real."

Paul leans across the bar. "What's this?"

"Make up two truths about yourself and one lie," Noelle instructs.

"Truth: I am frighteningly good-looking. Truth—"

"No, don't *tell* us! We're supposed to guess which is which. And they should be extreme," Noelle adds. "Like, you know, hard to believe."

"Right, then." Paul squares his bony shoulders. "I, Paul Conneely, have skinny-dipped in the Corrib, pissed on the Blarney Stone, and filched fourteen candy bars from the corner store."

"You're a pig," Aoife says, but she is almost smiling.

"Candy bars!" shouts Noelle.

"I will break the law," Paul intones, making the sign of the cross. "But never the Ten Commandments."

"Now Claire," says Noelle. "You go."

Claire can feel the whiskey warming her veins, the Guinness fuzzing her brain. She takes another sip to clear her head and tries to think of something even mildly outlandish, to recall those few yes boxes she checked on that quiz they took so long ago. Surely she's done something adventurous since then. But her mind feels blank, hazy, and she hears herself say: "I left my husband on Wednesday."

The oddest part, as the words come out, is that they do not sound ridiculous. In fact, they feel surprisingly important—

like an introduction to a support group, a declaration of self. But Noelle is impatient. "We already *know* that," she says.

Claire stares into the murk of her pint, her brief surge of empowerment draining away. "I got a perfect score on the logic section of the GRE," she says. "I once scratched a freckle till my skin turned black. And . . ." She is terrible at lying. "I . . . I once jumped out of an airplane."

"Airplane?" Aoife guesses; rather sweetly, considering.

"That's way too easy," Noelle says. "She would never do something like that."

Claire looks at her little sister and feels a mix of embarrassment and outrage and the urge to burst into tears. She left her husband, she flew to Ireland. She kissed the Blarney Stone. Isn't that *enough*? The edges of the room begin blurring. She hears Middle Age asking, "Perfect score on the exam, eh?" and Paul saying, "Different exam," and Noelle saying, "I told you already, she's the smartest person in the world," but her tone has changed since yesterday. This time it isn't proud, but bitter, and Claire's skin isn't thick, but softened by whiskey and exhaustion. The comment doesn't bounce off but burrows straight inside. *Smart, shmart*, she hears her mother saying, and Claire realizes, with the kind of insight that comes with being almost but not quite drunk, which isn't insight at all but just honesty and weakened defenses, that there is one more kind of smart. Not the kind that questions God, or gets straight A's, or models pencil skirts in the Sears catalog. It's *smart* as in the verb, and it means *to hurt*. Technically: *to hurt, slightly*. It's not the pain itself, but the pain's aftershock, the reminder that it once was there. It is the way her head will smart when she wakes up tomorrow. The way her mother's slap smarted when she was nine. It is the way the Trabant smarted as it dug into her side, and the way Noelle's punches smarted as they fell against her arm, and the way, even years later, when you think it must be healed over, the memory of being belittled by your mother smarts, and even being called smart smarts when you fear it is all you are, because if it turns out that you're not, what are you?

## CHAPTER EIGHT:  } Bold

**M**y turn," Noelle says.

"No," Claire says, too loudly. "Let Aoife go."

Noelle's look lingers on her an extra beat. "Fine. Your turn, Aoif."

"Don't be bold," Paul warns, and Aoife gives him a blank look. He wiggles his eyebrows, and it's comical on the surface, but the face underneath is firm.

Aoife sits thinking, facing the bar. Noelle waves to someone across the room. Scanning the crowd, Claire says, "Who are you waving to?"

"What are you doing?" Noelle says.

"I'm not doing anything."

"What, are you spying?"

"I'm not *spying*, I'm just standing here. I can see there's no one waving back."

"You don't know them, Claire."

"What does that matter?"

"You can't *see* them."

"Okay," Aoife says. "I've got it." She stands. "I'm Jewish, British, and ambidextrous."

Middle Age unleashes a laugh that sounds like a sneeze.

"British!" says Noelle.

"Better hope that one's a lie," says Middle.

Aoife points at Noelle. "Drink."

"Paul," Middle calls over the bar. "Your sister write with her right or her left?"

"Don't think she can write at all, can she?"

"Here." Middle hands Aoife a fresh pint. "Do something ambidextrous. Drink this with both hands."

Aoife smirks, but it looks like she's enjoying herself. Then Youth appears beside her, looking pale and sheepish. Fuzzily, Claire recalls the bleating piles of wool she saw yesterday in the middle of the road. Another thin boy is collapsed against Youth's right shoulder, lips curled into a drowsy smile. His body is pasty and colorless, seemingly boneless, like a strand of overcooked vermicelli.

Aoife raises her eyebrows as Youth catches his friend midsway. "Motherless," he explains, with an apologetic smile. The boy staggers a bit, forcing Youth to stumble backward, not altogether steady himself.

Aoife doesn't return the smile. She watches after them as they lurch toward the exit, the expression on her face a mix of annoyance and affection.

Claire gazes after the motherless boy's narrow, rubbery back. "What happened to his mother?" she asks.

Aoife looks at her for a moment, then smiles. It might be the first genuine smile from her Claire has seen. "Not what you think," she says.

"Why? What?"

"No, the word, like. The mother's fine. *Motherless*—" Aoife shrugs. "Means he's drunk."

In Claire's soft, overly generous head nothing has ever made more perfect sense. She feels her limbs grow warm. She is in love with words, in love with the world. She is in love with drinking, which makes the world so much more logical than when she is sober. To be drunk and to be motherless—the equation is genius. She is motherless too.

"My turn," says Noelle.

The game has by now attracted a small audience. Paul is leaning his elbows on the bar, Middle tipping forward on his stool. A vague crowd of pints and cheekbones has gathered behind them. Noelle sits on the bar top, waiting until she has the group's full attention. Then she pronounces: "Senior year of high school, I cut class forty-five times. I was captain of the cheerleading squad. And I shagged in an elevator."

"Elevator, hope to God," says Aoife.

"Drink!" Noelle says. She is grinning, but Claire flinches for her.

Aoife guesses again. "Cutting?"

"Nope."

"Head of the squad, then," Aoife says, dutifully taking her two swallows.

"Wrong again!" Noelle pauses, then smiles broadly. She scans the crowd, pausing for effect, and says, "It was a trick. They were all true!"

Aoife mutters, "Not fucking fair," as Claire says, "No, they weren't."

No one hears her.

She repeats, louder, "They weren't all true, Noelle."

Noelle looks down from her perch and says, "Yes, they were."

"Captain of the cheerleading squad. You were never captain."

"Yes, I *was*."

"No," Claire says, her voice getting louder, the rightness of it coursing through her veins. "You weren't."

A few heads are turning in their direction.

"Maybe not technically," Noelle says, smiling tightly. She rakes a hand through her hair, red streak flashing like a tongue. "But everybody treated me like I was. Everyone knew—"

"That's not the same. You weren't the captain. You couldn't be because your grades weren't good enough, remember?"

Any trace of amusement in Noelle's face disappears. She jumps down on the other side of the bar and grabs the tap, pouring herself another drink. "Of course you would remember that."

"I'm just saying—"

"You're saying that I'm dumb."

Claire shakes her head quickly. Fuzziness rises like a swarm of bees, settles in her ears. "No. You lie, Noelle. You lie all the time."

"All depends what you call a lie, doesn't it?" says a voice beside her. Claire turns to see Middle looming too close, his face like a prickly crimson moon. "Sometimes lies are truer than fact." He is smiling. Does he think this is funny? His awesome fucking bone structure looks as if it's made of rubber.

"That's such a . . ." Claire is groping for *rationalization* but can think of only *resuscitation*. She pictures fish gills gasping, feels thirsty.

But Middle now has the crowd's attention. "All you need to know about the Irish language," he says. "Mostly bullshit, but sounds like poetry!"

This provokes a flurry of a toast. Claire concentrates on speaking, placing her tongue in the proper grooves behind the proper teeth. "I know about Irish language," she says, carefully. "I *know* about language. I *study* language."

"Can't learn Irish by studying," Middle chuckles.

"No formula to learning Irish!" Aoife pitches in, her voice resentfully perky, like she's quoting something she was taught in school. "Repetition and experience!" she chirps, to a general murmur of recognition.

But that's wrong, Claire thinks. They're both wrong. You *can* learn language by study, and facts *are* truer than lies. She wishes there were an academic in the house—someone sober, sensible, with whom she could see eye to eye. If this is the Irish language, you can have it. She's sick of all the slipperiness and duplicity, the gnarled words with their cryptic accents and double meanings, the chortling, chuckling drunks in tweed caps parked on stools like Irish props, ready to offer the perfect nut of a proverb to put her in her place.

"I'm just saying"—she can hear herself slurring and

despises the sound—"Noelle *cheated*." She pauses, for emphasis, hitting the *t* hard. "She *cheats*." Claire has a flash of her young self in the backseat of their Datsun, hands pressed to the window, looking for the chubby back ends of the Volkswagens Noelle had just claimed to have seen.

"She's a shanachie," Paul says, leaning down to place a light kiss on top of Noelle's head.

For the first time, Claire knows what Deirdre felt when faced with all those obscure words and references. *Shanty? Stinky? Skanky?*

She looks up at Paul's friendly, flaring face. "A what?"

"Shanachie," he repeats, smiling. "Storyteller. She's a natural. Tells a windup with the best of them." He winks at Noelle. "Keeps us out of trouble. Right, love? I'd rather hear about a proposal from a shepherd than another fucking boring excuse for being late."

Claire blinks. The equation sinks in slowly, one sluggish synapse grasping at the next. "The sheepherder?" she says, looking at Noelle, whose eyes are aimed somewhere over Claire's head. "On the way to the airport? You made that up?"

"Not really." Noelle shrugs. "I got lost, and this woman invited me inside and told me all about her son."

"But, but did she—did she say you were the daughter she never had?"

A laugh bubbles through the crowd. If Claire were sober, she might have felt humiliated but she's too drunk, and too angry. "Did she, Noelle?"

"Maybe not in those exact words. But that's what she meant."

"But she didn't cry?"

Another laugh. Noelle's head snaps around quickly, as if trying to suppress it, and Claire realizes then that it's Noelle who's being laughed at. Suddenly she senses the crowd behind her, anticipating her next line.

"What about the son?" she says. "Was he really cut like a rock?"

This provokes a wolf whistle from somewhere in the back, another surge of laughter.

"If you really have to know," Noelle says, "he was." She clutches Paul's elbow as he rushes by with drinks in both hands. "But not as cut as my husband-to-be here."

Paul gives a little bow with his head and keeps moving. But the crowd will not be so easily diverted. Claire can feel them, perched and waiting, smiles ready to crack.

"So you mean, he looked exactly like"—Claire manages what sounds, in her mind, like a perfectly timed comic pause—"Colin Farrell?"

She couldn't have written a better punch line. It scores a room-size guffaw. A girl Claire's never seen before slings an arm around her shoulders like a long-lost friend.

"You weren't there, Claire," Noelle says tightly.

"But that's what you told me!"

"You didn't *see* him."

"Because he wasn't real!"

Laugh score: eight out of ten!

Claire is on a roll. She is out of material but intoxicated by the crowd. "Maybe you and Colin can go cheerleading together! You can travel around the country doing cheers and—and having sex in elevators!"

Noelle turns and pushes through the swinging door

behind the bar. The crowd sends her off with good-natured boos. Paul slings a bar towel over his shoulder, gives the crowd a just-a-minute finger, and ducks after her. Claire laughs, then stumbles backward. The room is spinning. She feels a hand gripping her arm and it takes a moment to connect the hand to the arm of Aoife. As Claire is guided toward the door, the crowd is a blur of teeth and laughing mouths, and for a moment she sees Deirdre, the flash of fiery hair and flinty blue eyes, and imagines the brief, proud weight of her hand against her cheek.

It was Christmas, the first Christmas after Claire's wedding, that she last saw her. Deirdre had not seemed well. This wasn't an easy distinction, as Deirdre had spent two decades complaining about this pain or that one, her migraines and fevers and swollen feet. But this time she seemed uncharacteristically quiet, weakened on the inside. Every visible feature was frantic, insistent, too bright.

Claire, now a married woman, was capitalizing on the new freedom this allowed. Being half a "we" gave her license to control her comings and goings, to claim "they" were needed elsewhere, part of a tangled, busy married life she was not obligated to divulge. She and Bob had spent Christmas Day with his family and came to Philadelphia two days later. The plan enabled Claire to sidestep the Gallagher Christmas traditions—she was no longer a Gallagher, so she could refer to them this way—like Midnight Mass at St. Cecilia's, after which Deirdre plucked hay from the crèche to tuck inside their wallets and Father Mike clasped her thick hands in his thin ones, leaning forward to offer holiday wishes that were extra-sincere, his eyes wide and unblinking in acknowledgment of Deirdre's devotion to the church and long history of suffering.

Claire always felt uncomfortable around her mother's piousness, which seemed such a contradiction to her personality at home. Two days later, Deirdre lay across the couch in one of her new Christmas presents: a silky, eggplant-colored bathrobe, the sash knotted around the bubble of her stomach and purple clashing with her hair. The pocket on the front was probably intended to be decorative but Deirdre had packed it like a purse—a rosary, a wad of Kleenex, an emergency tube of lipstick (just in case, lounging around her own home, she needed to reapply). Gene was wearing his red cable-knit sweater. His "Santa sweater," Deirdre called it. He occupied his usual spot, in the most uncomfortable chair in the room.

Claire, Noelle, and Bob assumed the role of children, sitting on the floor among the strewn ribbons, ripped wrapping, and Deirdre's swollen, pink-slippered feet.

"Your family celebrates Christmas, right?" Deirdre asked.

The question was directed at Bob, though it lacked its usual sharpness; like everything about Deirdre that day, the words seemed dulled.

"Of course they do," Claire answered for him. "We were just there. Remember?" She felt a flash of panic, wondering if her mother's memory might be slipping—"cognitive dysfunction," it was called, common in the later stages of lupus, though Deirdre had never shown any signs of it. "We just came from there, remember?"

"Of course I remember," Deirdre snapped. "I just thought they might be—what's it called?"

"Dee," Gene cautioned.

"Agnostic," Bob said. "But my family's, ah, Presbyterian."

Deirdre made a small noise in her throat, condescending but vaguely conciliatory, the combined effect of her deep-seeded Catholic-Protestant one-upmanship and grudging approval that at least the parents weren't agnostics too.

"My turn," Noelle said, picking up her next gift. They were rotating, opening presents one at a time. Claire had always hated this system, all the slow pomp and performance of it, but it was the kind of focused attention Noelle liked, and Deirdre insisted on.

The gift was from Claire and Bob, a thick gray wool scarf Noelle seemed to not hate—or at least think Paul would not hate. "I can totally see Paul stealing this," she said. Noelle and Paul hadn't seen each other since August at the Jersey shore but, to Claire's surprise, were still going strong. They called and wrote letters; he was coming to visit for New Year's. Noelle, it seemed, was in love, Paul occupying the front room of her brain like a filter coloring her every thought.

Gene opened next: a wool sweater, solid brown. More dignified, Claire thought, than the red one.

"Thank you, honey," Gene said.

"Made by local craftsmen," Claire explained. It sounded stupid, but she had taken special care with her gifts that year, chosen them to evoke her new life in New Hampshire. Wool and flannel, hand-dipped candles that smelled like pine and cedar, and all the traditional foods of New England: pancake mixes, clam chowders, maple syrup, maple candies shaped

like leaves and bathed in sugar. Her family had never suggested coming to visit, but neither had she. It was just as well.
The accoutrements of their life—like the moving announcements and perky, annotated cookbooks—had more charm
than the life.

Bob was next. So far, his gift pile amounted to a stack of
slippery gift cards: Barnes & Noble, Sam Goody, The Gap. But
this last gift, from Deirdre, was large and awkward. Deirdre
perked up as he started to tear it open, pushing up on her
elbows to get a better look. When he saw what was inside, Bob
laughed out loud, something he almost never did—the sound
was abrupt, as if his lungs had been caught off guard.

"What is it?" Noelle asked.

He held it up. It was one of those music-activated dancing salmon, probably purchased at a mall kiosk. The fish was
wearing black sunglasses and mounted on a wooden plaque.
Claire was suspicious: Had her mother deliberately given Bob
something tacky to undermine his smart-shmartness?

But one look at Deirdre revealed that she was genuinely
enamored with the dancing fish. She laughed and laughed
as it wiggled and pelvic-thrusted to a throaty Elvis impression of "Heartbreak Hotel." Bob seemed to enjoy it as much
as she did; his eyes were wet, the laughter like a dry whistle
in his throat.

"It's funny, isn't it?" Deirdre kept saying. "Isn't it funny?"

They ran through the salmon's entire repertoire—"Rock
Around the Clock" and "Blue Moon" and "Heartbreak Hotel"
again—and Deirdre's enjoyment never waned. Claire was surprised, even touched, that her mother had bought it. Maybe
she was beginning to like Bob more. But as she watched her,

Claire felt a sadness build in her chest like swallowed water, filling her until it was a solid, stunning ache. Her mother seemed suddenly old: one of those women who delighted in silly television commercials or moving displays in store windows, who watched other people's puppies or babies with a joy so disproportionate it only reinforced what their own lives were not.

After the torn wrapping was shoved into garbage bags and hauled to the curb, Bob went to get their suitcases. Claire went upstairs, where she could be alone. Unlike Noelle's room, which she had lived in off and on during college, Claire's room had hardly been touched since high school. Her old desk still faced the window, where she'd preferred it. She'd liked being able to tilt her eyes toward the sky when she was writing in her diary, imagining herself one of those girls in the movies who crawled onto her roof to smoke cigarettes or, at the very least, gaze at the stars while thoughtfully tapping a pen against her cheek. Above the desk hung the red bulletin board that had seen all her awards; unlike athletic trophies, most academic prizes were subtle, just a piece of paper destined for a brief life under a thumbtack or a magnet on a refrigerator door. A few still remained: a faded second-place ribbon, some merit certificates, and a dead wrist corsage from her senior prom; in a certain way, a mark of achievement itself.

In the middle of the room sat her bed, mattress sagging where the springs had begun poking through the bottom. The bedside table was empty except for a chubby, spiral notebook with a lightbulb on the cover. BRIGHT IDEAS! She had bought it for herself once at a school book fair, enamored with the possibility of scribbling down half-remembered ideas that struck her in the middle of the night. Turned out, she rarely had any. Along the far wall stood her two bookcases: pale, bulging towers made of cheap, assemble-yourself wood, both of them listing slightly to the left. Her books were all still there, organized by size: soft paperbacks on the topmost shelves and heavy books along the bottom—her old sticker collection, the *Children's Illustrated Bible, Acing the SAT*, the dictionary she'd received as what seemed a backhanded consolation prize for being runner-up in the spelling bee.

Claire knew the geography of this room by heart, every physical inch of it, but what struck her most every time she returned was the memory of how it felt: a combination of coziness and claustrophobia, like suffocating in a cloud. This room had been her escape, an island of order and comfort, but it was a tense comfort, made necessary by the pressure of the house on the other side.

She heard Bob's footsteps shuffling up the stairs. When he appeared in the doorway, with a suitcase in each hand and Claire's purse slung gracelessly around his neck, the sight of him triggered a rush of—was it love? Was it gratitude?

"Hi, darling," Bob said, and Claire's love for him exploded in her chest.

It wasn't fair, but wasn't uncommon, for Claire's feelings for Bob to be a product of context. It had been true that first afternoon on the quad; it was true when she was in Bob's natural habitat, buffeted by his admiring colleagues. Watching him deliver a lecture, his wrinkled clothes and gangly limbs never looked more attractive, evidence of his intellect, his "ah's" no longer a nervous affectation but the necessary punctuation in a long, complicated equation. Sometimes, at home, Claire tried to conjure up those moments, and if she tried hard enough the world's perception of her husband would infuse, briefly, her own.

Around her family, her feelings for Bob were at their most unpredictable. If he said the wrong thing she winced deeply, knowing the potential damage done. But if he elicited a laugh from her father or a smile from her mother, affection leaped inside her, as it did now, watching him disentangle the bags from his fingers and lower himself to the edge of her child-hood bed. This man was the buffer between her old life and her new. Whatever sadness had filled her downstairs with her family, Claire knew her responsibility had shifted: to her *own* family. She was married now, and wife trumped daughter.

Bob wrapped his hands around his kneecaps. He looked like a blond giant in a dollhouse, trying to take up as little space as possible out of respect for this young girl's room. Suddenly, Claire could picture Bob a father. How awkwardly gentle he would be holding a baby, how patiently he would explain things, how seriously he would puzzle over algebra problems, butter toast, and bandage knees. How uncomfortable he would be around his daughter's moods and changes from ages twelve to eighteen.

Claire closed the door and locked it. She slid off Bob's glasses, placed them on the bedside table, and pressed her finger to his lips. He smiled. This was not unfamiliar; it felt like the old days, hiding in Bob's office or Claire's dorm room and struggling to stay quiet. At the institute, he was far too busy, too visible. And in their own bed, where they could be as loud as they wanted, they rarely made a sound.

Now Claire was biting her lip as Bob pulled off her sweater and unclasped her bra. It was the first time she had ever been alone in her room with a boy. She tugged off his pants, cringing a little at the sound of the belt buckle hitting the floor. When Bob started to peel back the comforter, she pushed him down on top of the covers instead. As she straddled his hips with her knees, the sound of footsteps came bouncing up the stairs. They stopped and stared at each other, with the wide, caught eyes of high school kids in a backseat.

"Dinner," Noelle called up, sounding bored.

Claire's response was a too sprightly: "Be right down!"

At dinner Claire felt satisfied, and self-satisfied. She felt a rush of guilty pleasure when she took in Bob's rumpled appearance, hair still mussed in the back and neck flushed a telltale pink. When she felt his hand brush her leg under the table, she looked at him and smiled. She thought of the quiz she and Noelle had taken the last time she was in this house: *Are You Settling Down—or Just Settling?* She hadn't had sex in her parents' bedroom, but she'd come close.

"Did I tell you what Paul said about Christmas in Ireland?" Noelle was saying. "When he was little it was the one day a year they got to eat American fast food."

It was the age-old dynamic: Noelle talking, everybody listening. The difference tonight was, Deirdre was not her usual captive audience. She was mumbling, the words soft and muddled, mostly indistinguishable, but the undertone was defiant; it sounded as if she was arguing with someone, though it wasn't clear whom.

"Here we eat McDonalds every *day*, but over there it was like this big annual *road* trip," Noelle went on, a fork piled with mashed potatoes hovering over her plate. "They drove an hour to get a Big Mac. Isn't that so funny and, like, gross?"

Without her sidekick, Noelle's words felt too big, too much.

Finally she stopped talking and looked at Deirdre. "You feel like shit, huh, Mom?"

In the pause, a few of Deirdre's words became discernible: *hot, foot, chest.*

"Your chest?" Gene said. For Deirdre to have chest pains was not unheard of; like every symptom, they flared and faded, but always sounded more ominous than the symptoms they could see. "Dee, what about your chest?" he said.

Deirdre looked up and enunciated, quite clearly: "I have chest pains." Then she looked at the spread on the table and with equal firmness said: "I'll have more meat."

Claire's guilty pleasure was eroding, whittled down to guilt alone. It was the guilt she'd felt as a child after riding the Super Cat in Ocean City: knowledge she'd been somewhere she shouldn't, done something she shouldn't, and worse, that her family had been right there, oblivious on the other side. Or tonight, in her mother's case, oblivious and in pain. Sitting between her mother in her garish bathrobe and her husband with his warm hand and his pink neck, Claire felt like screaming, like shrugging off her skin. When Bob touched her knee again, she twitched away, wishing he were more sensitive, more attuned to her feelings—wasn't that part of being a husband, to home in on your wife's foot tapping or vein bulging in her left temple and know exactly what that meant?

After dinner, Claire excused herself and went upstairs. She closed her bedroom door, covered her mouth with one hand, and cried. The bedcovers were wrinkled and sliding onto the carpet. BRIGHT IDEAS! was knocked upside down on the floor. This room didn't belong to her anymore, but to some younger, better her. Claire caught her reflection in the long mirror, the

same mirror where she used to survey her outfits and analyze her facial expressions—*Exuberance, Studiousness, Thought-
fulness*—trying to look at herself objectively, to see what the
world saw. Now twenty-six, a married woman, she felt like more
than an older version of herself; she felt like a separate person.
She had been kinder then, she thought, happier. Inclined to
love things. She had loved her room and loved her books and
loved, Claire thought, herself, the realization so swollen with
sadness that it only revealed, like those lonely old women with
the babies and puppies, everything she was not now.

Then she heard it: from one staircase three rooms and one
closed door away, the instant her mother's hand moved toward
the kitchen window. As a child, she had memorized the sound
of pills tipping from a bottle—it was deceptively gentle, like
a rain stick, a sun shower—and the sound of nothingness as
pills struck palm. But in the mirror, as Claire watched herself listening, her expression was one she hadn't seen before,
didn't even know she wore: *Despair*.

Suddenly the room felt small and close and Claire felt
huge, swollen with this new feeling. It seemed a terribly sea-
soned, knowing kind of sadness. Despair that her mother took
the pills. Despair that she needed them. Despair that she pretended to be thick-skinned and impervious when really she
was sick and getting sicker and despair that she made Claire
want to leave—though this, at least, was a feeling Claire recognized. And unlike when she was a child, now she could.

"I'm thinking we should go tonight," Claire said. She
had returned to the living room, where everyone was sitting
around the TV. Her hands were shaking, her face washed and
lipstick reapplied.

Gene looked up. "What, honey?"

"I said, I think we might leave tonight after all," she said.

"Wow," Noelle said. "Happy to see us, huh?"

"Tonight?" Gene said. "Why?"

Claire would avoid her father's eyes. She would pretend not to have seen the makings of tomorrow's breakfast in the fridge. "It's just . . ." Her eyes alighted on the TV screen: onyx earrings on a bed of puffy fake snow. "The roads at night are so much emptier. It's just easier." She knew how hollow it sounded, and knew they knew it, but the need to leave was almost physical. She could not stay.

Then Deirdre said, "You're not staying over?"

Claire forced her eyes to meet her mother's. The combination of her purples and oranges, her rash and her makeup, was at once so comic and tragic that Claire felt like breaking down in tears at her feet, hating and loving her as strongly and simultaneously as she ever had.

"We really need to," Claire said, but her voice sounded strained. "We need to get back."

For a moment the room was caught in her pause, waiting to see if she would change her mind. But she didn't have to, she told herself: It was the royal, marital "we." She would leave because she could. She wouldn't look at her father, or her mother, or even Bob, who she knew would be unable to disguise his confusion. She opted for Noelle, which might have been the worst choice of all: clear-eyed knowing.

"Bob has a meeting tomorrow afternoon," Claire said, the words tumbling out before she could stop them. "He forgot."

Upstairs, she apologized. "I don't know why I said that."

Bob was collecting their things from the guest bathroom:

tiny mouthwash, tiny toothpaste, Claire's contacts swimming in saline solution. She stood just inside the doorway. The room smelled like the green bricks of Irish Spring that anchored the ledges in the sink and shower.

"I just can't stay tonight," Claire said. "I can't explain it. I couldn't think of a better excuse."

Bob sealed the toiletry bag with a brisk zip. His hair was still mussed in the back and she resisted the urge to smooth it.

"I can help with the driving," she offered.

Bob looked up, into the mirror above the sink, and stood perfectly still. Claire stepped between her husband and his reflection. She leaned into his long chest. When she felt his arms encircle her back, she felt relieved, though the gesture could have meant anything; maybe he understood her, maybe he forgave her. Maybe he was just being polite.

Seven months later, Claire would try to reassure herself she could not have known that night that her mother was dying. That they all knew lupus did not travel in a logical arc. A bad day could be followed by a prolonged period of good days. Rarely was the disease fatal. Dr. Vyron would explain that the kidney failure was the result of a combination of factors—Deirdre's predispositions and lack of precaution and what he called her "irreverence," which Claire found almost hilariously unscientific, not to mention ironic, considering Deirdre was buried with a shoebox full of trinkets to ease the transition to the afterlife. And yet, the word was perfect; they all knew what Dr. Vyron meant. He added several times that he'd told her to go easy on the drinking, to take the pills in moderation. But these reassurances were unnecessary. No one blamed Dr.

Vyron. If anything, it was a greater affront for him to assume the Gallaghers would think anyone capable of stopping Deirdre from doing exactly what she wanted.

When Claire and Bob left that night, it was windy and bitterly cold. A thin crust of snow crunched under their feet as they moved down the front walk. They made an ungainly procession, the shuffling of five pairs of shoes and dull squeaking of Deirdre's rubber-tipped cane on the snow. At the curb, when Claire leaned in to kiss her mother, her cheek was freezing. "You shouldn't be out in this cold," Claire said, then climbed into the car.

From the passenger seat, she looked at the shadowy figures that were her family. Gene held one palm in the air. Noelle was already hugging her shoulders and heading back inside. Deirdre looked like some kind of suburban sorceress, leaning forward on her cane, her silky purple robe flapping behind her in the wind.

When Bob started the car, Deirdre stepped forward. She pulled the plastic spritzer from the pocket of her robe and doused the windshield with miraculous water—an extra dose, probably proportionate to the lateness of the hour and the intensity of her worry. "May the road rise to meet you!" Claire heard her shout, but faintly, the sound flattened by the tight windows and the running engine. When Deirdre stepped back to the curb, and Bob pulled away, the image of her parents looked watery and distorted. As soon as they turned the corner, Bob flicked the windshield wipers on.

"What are you doing?" Claire snapped.

"I couldn't see," Bob said, reasonably.

Claire fell silent, rigid. Her eyes filled with tears. When Bob glanced at her, she turned to the window. "What?" he asked.

And again, a block later: "What?"

By two in the morning, Bob was so exhausted he was veering in and out of the lanes on 84. They switched near Worcester, where Claire got a large coffee and drove the last leg herself. She felt almost maniacally alert as she sped along the empty highways, needing to prove this drive had been doable, the foam coffee cup squeaking in and out of the cup holder's plastic claw. When she got off the highway it was four in the morning. The streets of New Hampshire were quiet, forgiving. When a rare pair of oncoming headlights—a truck usually, or tractor trailer—splashed against the windshield, the reflection of the miraculous water flashed for an instant, then receded into dark.

# CHAPTER NINE: Clare

Surely it's no accident that Noelle would choose this morning to bring Claire to a seven-hundred-foot cliff. As she trudges up the cliff path, Claire's head is throbbing. The wind is fierce and freezing. Her loose hair blows wildly, stinging her cheeks. She can't remember every detail of the night before, but she remembers the feeling: being the center of attention, and seeing Noelle shaken. In the car, Noelle had barely spoken, jabbing the radio and smoking. Claire thought about apologizing, but decided against it. Noelle had been making fun of Claire her entire life.

Claire keeps her chin down, concentrating on putting one foot in front of the other, feeling like she's wading through chest-high water. She's convinced that if she lifted both feet she would tumble backward like a dry leaf. Lifting her head, Claire squints into the distance. Her eyes fill instantly with water. Noelle is a good twenty feet ahead, maintaining a determined pace. Only a few brave souls are walking the path beyond her. One is a group of women, all of them bent forward at ninety-degree angles, yelping and laughing. "This wind is crazy!" Claire ventures once, but Noelle doesn't hear her or pretends not to.

She keeps pushing until they reach a "fence" made of large slate slabs. It resembles a row of large headstones, leaning against a bank of tufted, wheat-colored grass. Some are a solid gray, others mottled black and white, like cattle flanks. The cluster of signs is almost comical in its number and urgency. It looks like what a disaster-prone, thick-headed cartoon character might see right before he seals his fate:

VISITORS ARE WARNED TO STAY INSIDE THE FENCE

KEEP ON LAND SIDE OF CLIFF FENCES

UNSTABLE CLIFF EDGE

THE PATHS OUTSIDE THE FENCE ARE EXTREMELY DANGEROUS

A white one with red letters begins: CLARE COUNTY COUNCIL . . .

"Is this Clare County?" Claire asks, trying to catch her breath.

"Yeah." Noelle lowers her chin into her windbreaker. Her eyes are wet. "So you're, like, obligated to love it here."

They follow the safe side of the fence in silence. The wind is too strong for you to open your mouth. It occurs to Claire that the destinations of Ireland all require some commitment from the tourist—to brave the elements, actively participate, leave exhausted, and head to the nearest pub for beer and soup.

On a makeshift bench made of stone, a lone flutist plays, his tune getting whipped and tossed and swallowed. The few other visitors have migrated to the other side of the fence, droplets of color dotting the surfaces where the cliffs plateau like landings on an enormous staircase. Though forbidden, access is almost humorously easy. At home, Claire thinks, they would never simply trust the tourists to obey the rules. There would be guardrails, security officers, waivers to sign upon entering, and on your way out, bumper stickers that said: I SURVIVED THE CLIFFS OF MOHER! But like much of Ireland, this place seems an inherent contradiction: an urgent flurry of warnings paired with a rough semblance of a fence. When Noelle veers to the other side, Claire hesitates only a moment. Those signs must be a formality, not truly intended to keep anyone from the brink, because—just *look* at it.

The cliffs look like the elbows of giants, craggy and muscular, bigger-than-life. These are the backdrops of shipwrecks and fables, of lovers ripped asunder, the jagged perforation where the rest of the world floated away. Here, Claire thinks, the Irish penchant for exaggeration is qualified. The sight is breathtaking—both kinds.

Without a word, Noelle heads toward the drop-off. Halfway there, Claire pauses to watch a man on a nearby plateau. He is standing right at the edge, sticking one foot forward and bowing deeply. Claire thinks that he's honoring the view, then realizes he's taking a picture of his boot.

She makes her way to the edge and, following Noelle's

lead, gets down on her belly and squirms forward to gaze over the craggy stone lip. For a moment, they are silent, just breathing.

"It's awesome, isn't it," Noelle says. Her tone is hushed, whatever grudge she was carrying at least temporarily suspended.

"It is," Claire says. Below them, the inner walls plunge for what look like miles, striped with the layers of centuries, the physical memory of the world.

She and Noelle are quiet, but the earth is loud. Wind rushes past their ears. At least it is cooperating now, pushing the hair back away from their faces. Scraps of flute music drift by, clear and bright and disconnected, then disappear.

"So I called Dad," Noelle says, the edge returned to her voice.

Claire resists the urge to look at her. "When?"

"After the pub last night."

There it is: last night. Much as she doesn't want to pursue it, Claire has to ask, "Weren't you still drunk?"

"Not at all."

She's lying; she must be.

"I mean, I was drunk at the bar," Noelle says.

"Right," Claire says, then adds, "Me too."

It is as close to an apology as either of them will come, at least for now.

"So?" Claire asks. She focuses on the foaming waves, a fury so far away it looks harmless. "What did he say?"

"He's coming."

"I knew he would," Claire says, but feels a touch of relief.

"Like, Tuesday or Wednesday."

"How did he sound?"

"I don't know."

"What did he say?"

"Nothing. I mean, nothing important."

"Well," Claire says. "Good."

Noelle doesn't respond. Claire stares down into the windy, frothing bowl of the Atlantic. The white whorls of the ocean swirl like a sorcerer's beard. Then Noelle offers, "I didn't say anything about you and Bob, if you're wondering."

Claire wasn't wondering, though she probably should have been. She's been the one insisting Gene be here for the wedding, but the fact that she'll have to tell him about her own marriage has yet to sink in. "Nothing?"

"Just that you were here."

Claire pictures her father's face when she delivers the news: the crumpling of his brow, the palm of his hand reaching for his bald spot. He won't ask for details, but what he will ask will be worse: *What's next?* The words awaken a low panic in her chest. It's a valid question, and she has no answer.

"I have to figure out what I'm going to do next," Claire announces. Has she ever made a statement so open-ended? "I guess"—and as she says it, the plan becomes obvious—"I'll finish my dissertation."

Of course. The dissertation. Thank God for the dissertation! Maybe there was a reason she avoided it in New Hampshire after all, saving it for a time she would need it more.

"Your dissertation?" Noelle asks.

"For my doctorate," Claire says. "You know, the big paper at the end."

"Yes, I know what a dissertation is. My God, how dumb do you think I am?" For a moment, the night before rears up again. Claire waits for it to subside.

"I don't think you're dumb," she says.

"I just figured you already finished it."

"I meant to," Claire says. "After I got married. It just sort of got put on hold."

Noelle props herself onto her elbows and looks at her curiously. "How come?"

"I just didn't really have the time. First I had to plan the wedding, then we were moving . . . " Claire struggles onto her elbows too. "And once we got to New Hampshire, things got busy."

"I thought there was, like, nothing to do there."

"Bob's job was very demanding. There were social obligations. Then I got busy with the crossword puzzles." It sounds unconvincing, even to herself. "It was just harder to work on, not being at school." This, at least, was true.

"So why are you going to write it now?"

"Because," Claire says. "It makes sense. Professionally."

"Oh, ew."

Claire feels the defiance from the pub returning. *Not everyone runs around doing whatever they want to! This is the real world, the adult world, not our deranged dead mother's version of it!* The words begin stirring, hoping for an encore.

"I mean, it would look strange," Claire says. "On a résumé. To have an unfinished degree just sitting there."

"It didn't matter for me."

*But it did*, Claire thinks. The response is automatic, and feels mean but true.

"Sooner or later, I'll have to apply for jobs. I can't just put my life on hold and go running around and doing whatever I want."

"I didn't finish college. Mom didn't finish college."

"This is different."

"How?"

*Because I don't want to be working at the same jewelry counter at Sears for twenty years. I don't want to be a college drop-out working in a bar. I want my life to be more than this.*

"I mean," Noelle continues, "do you really love this—what's it called again?"

This time she isn't joking. She is simply doing what they do in their family: Whether it's a detail, like Deirdre's Miller High Life, or a word—*linguistics, shanachie, agnostic*—if it makes them feel uncomfortable, they pretend to have forgotten it.

"Linguistics," Claire says tightly.

"Right. Linguistics. I mean, you love it, right?"

"Of course."

Does she? All she knows is that she used to, that right now she has no choice but to claim to. She had loved language— was it even possible to love linguistic theory?

Then Noelle is standing, feet spread like an athlete. "Well, good," she says, the words flattening as they drift down, battered by the wind. "Because I can't imagine going back to school if I didn't have to."

In a clumsy single motion, Claire pushes herself to her feet. "Good thing you don't then," she says.

Noelle holds her eyes for a moment, then leans forward to

dust off the front of her jeans. "Seriously. I think I'd die. It's so much time, and it's so *boring*—"

"We're different, Noelle."

"Clearly."

Claire senses she shouldn't push it. But her jaw feels tired, loosened by the night before, emboldened by the sheer size of the world. "Because you always got to do whatever you wanted," she says, as Noelle straightens.

"Seriously, Claire. What happened to you? When did you get like this? You're, like, this angry person."

But Claire's voice feels thick, juicy with righteousness. "You did whatever you wanted, and there were never any consequences. And that's not how the real world works."

"Really? Let's review. I dropped out of college—which I know is like a cardinal sin to you—and it turns out it was a degree I totally didn't need because I came to Ireland, to be with the guy I wanted to marry, and I'm marrying him, and I'm happy."

It is frustratingly simple, but essentially true. Noelle didn't follow the rules and got exactly what she wanted. To belabor the specifics would sound condescending.

"I guess I don't live in the real world, huh?" Noelle says.

"No," Claire says. "You don't. Because in the real world, people have responsibilities."

Noelle rakes a hand angrily through her hair. "Claire, oh my God."

"Have you ever once done something because you had to? You always had Mom to back you up so you could screw around and do whatever you felt like."

Noelle's eyes fill with bright tears. "You don't know what you're talking about."

"She always let you off the hook! You could fuck up anything and she laughed it off."

"At least my fuckups were out in the open."

"What fuckups?" Claire says. "I never did anything wrong!"

Noelle laughs, so bitter it's a near shriek.

"What?" Claire says. "Tell me one time I got in trouble. I didn't *do* anything! "

"Exactly. You left when I was, what, ten? You never even lived there."

Indignation hardens like a fist in Claire's chest. "I lived there."

"Not when it got bad you didn't."

"It was always bad."

Noelle shakes her head quickly, hair whipping across her face. "Not like it was in the end. You don't know. You weren't there."

Claire grips her blowing hair in one fist. "Mom didn't want me there."

"Probably because you were so hard on her!"

"She was hard on me. She was hard on *me*, Noelle."

"Why couldn't you just be nice?" Noelle's voice is shaking. "You always had to disagree with her about everything. It was like you didn't even want to be around her, like you were afraid of catching it. And the really shitty part? You got to have her when she was, like, a normal mother. I was always the kid with the *sick mother*—and I was the reason—"

When Noelle turns into the wind, Claire sees her little sister with a sad clarity. Noelle hadn't escaped the fog of guilt in their family; it was here, all along, at the root of her intense loyalty to their sick mother. She believed she'd made her that way.

Claire longs for the perfect words to wash up at her feet. The lover of language, the language *scholar*—she can study and dissect words, but when it really matters, words fail her. The wind is so loud Claire can't hear Noelle crying but sees the tears on her cheeks. Noelle's face looks serene, unsurprised, as if she's cried these tears many times, and this is the most tragic part, her familiarity with her own sadness.

Noelle takes a step toward the edge. Claire lunges forward, grabbing her roughly by the arm.

"Jesus!" Noelle says. "What do you think you're doing?"

She turns on her with wet, accusing eyes.

"I don't know," Claire says.

"What did you think I was going to do? Jump?"

"I don't know," Claire says again. Their faces are just inches apart and Claire is riveted by the sight of her. Her lips are swollen, cheeks wet with tears, the aftermath of rage and sadness splashed all over her face. Claire is amazed by it, by how hard she must work to hide it.

Claire is still gripping her arm. Under all the soft layers, she can feel the bone. She lets go of Noelle and they stand there, silent at the edge of the world.

It was one more thing for Deirdre to love about Noelle—her fiery Irish temper. She threw her first offic[...] Christmastime, the year she was eleven.

"Why do they think my birthday's in Dec[...] complained. She did so each December, [...]

someone assumed her birthday was just around the corner. Noelle, after all, meant Christmas and Birthday—though she was born at the height of summer, mid-July. The meaning of Claire was only slightly less contradictory, and would get more so during those bleak New Hampshire winters: distinct, famous, bright, clear.

Every summer, to drive her point home, Noelle became a mild megalomaniac. She chose whatever party was in vogue that season—roller skating, swimming, wading through tubs of plastic balls at Chuck E. Cheese's—cool but unoriginal, which in elementary school and junior high, made them cool. Claire couldn't have felt more differently about her own birthday. In college, it often coincided with final papers and exams. "I *want* to go out, I just can't afford to *stop*," she would say. It was sometimes true.

But Noelle's birthday parties were proof of her status: She drew a crowd. There were the girls from St. Cecilia's, plus boys from their brother school, St. Mark's. The crew from Irish dancing showed up, freed of their costumes, freckled arms and faces unfrozen and ready to cut loose. Noelle's birthday was the pinnacle of not only her year but, presumably, everybody else's. The parties would start in the afternoon and conclude back at the house in a finale of fireflies and Slip-N-Slides, red-white-and-blue popsicles, and spitting sparklers obviously bought at a post–Fourth of July blowout sale. As Noelle's birthday took on the magnitude of a national holiday, the questions about her name each December caused greater offense.

"It's prejudice!" she shouted. This was in sixth grade, the combined result of her tendency to exaggerate and her recent unit on the Civil Rights Movement.

"It's not prejudice," Claire said, reading at the dining room table. She was home from college for the first time—freshman year, winter break—and already she missed being at school. She missed the thick, chalky smells of the classrooms. She missed the cozy accoutrements of late-night study sessions: sweatshirts and pajamas and fuzzy slippers, flash cards, mugs of powdery hot chocolate and Ziploc bags of chocolate-covered coffee beans. She missed the feeling of exam time and every-body piled in the dorm lounge, hair tousled and faces bare. She missed the library in the week before finals, filled with the hushed sounds of a thousand book pages turning, pens scratching, hordes of students with a shared sense of panic and purpose, heads so filled with facts and figures they leaned periodically against their chairs or sagged onto their arms. But she had not missed being here.

"You shouldn't throw that word around, Noelle," she said. "You don't know what it means."

"Yes, I do." Noelle was belly-down on the living room floor, still in her plaid school uniform, leaning her home-work directly on the carpet so the pencil tip kept tearing through. "Dad."

Gene was in his rocking chair, reading the paper. Deirdre was lying on the couch with eyes glued to HSN. The Christ-mas tree was splattered with blinking lights, school pictures with paper clips stabbed through them, limp icicles dripping from the branches like silver spaghetti.

"Dad, what does prejudice mean?" Noelle said.

Gene didn't respond. He had on the cable-knit red sweater. Deirdre was wearing what she called her "dressing gown," which was a fancy term for staying in your pajamas all day.

"Dad!"

From behind the paper, Gene made a small noise. "What's that, honey?"

"What does prejudice mean!"

Gene finally looked up at his younger daughter. It seemed to take a moment for him to register her question, rewinding to locate its echo and let the words sink in. "It's when . . ." He ran a palm over his bald spot, back then forward, ruffling what little hair he had left. He seemed about to answer, then faltered, as if too weary at the prospect of Noelle's cross-examination. "Don't worry about it tonight," he finally said, adding, "It's Christmas," and shook the newspaper in front of his face.

Claire returned to her book. The TV flashed a cubic zirconia. MAKE HER HOLIDAY DREAMS COME TRUE! Then Noelle threw a temper tantrum. It wasn't just crying, or even sobbing; it was more a high-pitched wailing. She lay on her stomach, face pressed to the carpet, arms and legs splayed like a jumping jack frozen midstride. Her cheeks were bright red and her bony back rose and shuddered with each sloppy cry, but her four limbs just lay there, as if so much energy were concentrated in her face and chest there was none left for the rest of her.

Later, Deirdre would recall the performance with pride. "She's got the black Irish temper," Claire would hear her mother say about one million times. She bragged to the neighbors, to the other mothers at Irish dancing, to the receptionists at Dr. Vyron's. It was as if she had discovered her child was a violin prodigy or could really hit a tennis ball. She's double-jointed—and boy can she misbehave! She trotted it out at home whenever Noelle did something really preco-cious. *What can I say?* her look conveyed, resigned and not-so-secretly delighted. *It's the black Irish!* Finally, Noelle's looks made sense: the signature dark hair, dark eyes, temper like lightning in a jar.

In the moment, though, what was happening had yet to be identified. As Claire watched, she felt fascinated and jeal-ous and a little bit nervous. Her sister seemed half-possessed, Noelle and not Noelle, as if being acted on by some outside force.

"Stop it," Gene said. "Noelle, stop that!"

But it was Deirdre who finally climbed above the clamor. Claire saw this happening before she heard it: her mother, sitting upright, hand pressed against her diaphragm. Her mouth formed a bright red O. Claire thought at first it was some overacted approximation of shock, then realized there was sound coming out:

"... the angels did say ..."

Deirdre was singing. A Christmas carol: "The First Noel." She had a terrible voice, the kind so off tune it could only redeem itself through fearlessness.

"... to certain boy shepherds in fields where they say ... in fields where they say, they are keeping their sheep ..."

Noelle's sobs had turned into a coughing fit. Gene was glancing at the front door, as if expecting to be accosted by the neighbors' association. But Deirdre was almost preter-naturally calm. Her eyebrows had risen skyward, two sharp twin birds.

"Noelle, Noelle, if you stop crying I'll tell you you're swell . . ."

It went on like this for a few more nonsense verses. The tree blinked. A hand fanned across the TV wearing a fat fake ring. But gradually, Noelle's cries quieted, as they had as a baby, soothed by the sound of Deirdre's voice. Eventually she even began giggling, the night of Christ's birth having been denigrated to rhyming mentions of a Snickers bar and *Saved by the Bell*. For all her fear of God, Deirdre must have figured He'd chalk this one up to extenuating circumstances, like people who had to miss Sunday Mass because they were too sick to get out of bed or stuck on a deserted island.

Sitting at the table, watching the twin geysers that were her mother and sister, Claire felt something rise up inside her. It wasn't laughter or anger: It was disdain. She had never envied Noelle's theatrics, not exactly; they were so ridiculous Claire had managed to see them as a measure of her own maturity. But this episode was too unfair. Fling yourself on the floor, throw a fit, and get a song to make you feel better? What was being *rewarded* here? She tucked her chin in her book. She couldn't wait to be back at school.

Deirdre stood and bowed. Noelle applauded, face streaked with tears and a few carpet threads. The two of them headed to the kitchen, arm in arm. When they were gone, Gene stood too. He folded his newspaper, placing it like a dinner napkin on the seat of the rocking chair. When he turned, Claire saw the shadow of some unspoken thought darken his face. She had always wondered about her father's loyalty to Deirdre, whether it arose from guilt or duty or simply passivity, and for a moment, she thought that he might walk right out the door. Then it passed, and he crossed the room, heading toward the kitchen, and paused beside Claire's chair. "On New Year's," he whispered, "we'll sing 'Clair de Lune.'"

Claire forced herself to smile, though in that instant she saw her father in a light that was clear and disappointingly simple: He was whispering because he didn't want Noelle to hear him, because he didn't want her to think he was sharing any of her spotlight, and because ultimately making Noelle happy was more important than making Claire happy—not because it was fair, or because Claire was older, or her skin was thicker, but because it was easier.

——————

Without discussion, Claire and Noelle agree they can't go right back to the Conneelys. They park in Galway City just as the sun is beginning to break through a low, embattled bank of clouds. They walk across a bridge over a choppy gray river, past a majestic cathedral. The water, church, and sky are all slightly different tones of gray. The cathedral presides like a sentinel, a fortress of warmly lit rose windows and solemn stone. Though back at home the sight of a Catholic church makes Claire uneasy, here it is an unexpected comfort, like being in a crowd of strangers and seeing someone you used to know.

They are quiet, mostly, but it's not a strained quiet. Some ancient tension has relented between them; Claire can feel its absence, the new space it's made. They wander down twining cobblestone alleys, past storefronts the colors of taffy, side-walks dotted with fiddlers and flutists, their instrument cases splayed at their feet. They stop for a pint and feel calmed; drink another, feel revived.

By the time they resume walking, Claire is feeling warmer, owing to the Guinness and the sunlight. She follows Noelle south of the city, past a green public square and a sleeping fountain, into a little waterfront town called Salthill. It looks not unlike a miniature Ocean City: a strip of sand and skinny boardwalk peppered with shops and food stands. There's even an amusement park, though it sounds more'like a seedy gentlemen's club: Leisureland.

"Large chips, please," Noelle says, at a stand called Salt 'n' Pepper. She hoists up the paper bag, then leads Claire to a bench facing Galway Bay. With the bag nestled between their hips, they each pull off one glove and drape it across their knees. It is colder by the water. The sky looks like a crazy quilt: swollen gray clouds and scudded pink clouds and swatches of pale sunlight. Through the fog clinging to the top of the bay, distant islands emerge and recede like spongy green shadows.

Claire points toward the Ferris wheel, its top curve obscured by the clouds. "Do you ever go there?" she asks.

Noelle looks up, as if noticing it for the first time. "No," she says. "Weird, huh? I was always dying to go on those stupid rides when I was little."

"You went on the Trabant," Claire reminds her.

"Which one was that? Teacups? Elephants?"

"It was a big ride."

Noelle blows on a fry.

"It was a real ride." Claire looks at her. "We would go on it together. You don't remember?"

"Sorry," Noelle says, and Claire feels surprised, though maybe she shouldn't.

Noelle bites the fry in half. "Paul took me to this 'funpark' once," she says. "That's what they call them here. It was totally small and cheap, but they had this one ride called the Dodgems that was *insane*. Paul wouldn't go on because he gets motion sickness—isn't that funny?—so I said I'd take the boys on because, you know, I want them to like me. So we get on, and before it starts this dude came around with an oil can and greased the joints. I'm not kidding. An old-school oil can, like in *The Wizard of Oz*. We *flew*."

As Noelle reaches into the bag, Claire watches her hand. It is her adult hand, her engaged hand. With her engagement ring on, the hand looks like a grown-up's, but is still abused like a child's: pink and knobby, nails chewed to the quick.

"I like your ring," Claire says.

"Oh, yeah." Noelle holds her hand up, fingers spread wide against the busy sky. "It's a claddagh. You know what that is, right?"

Claire does, but plays along. "I'm not sure."

Noelle points to the design in the middle, a pair of tiny hands. "That means friendship." She indicates, above it, a miniature crown. "And that means loyalty. And the heart in the middle means love. It's supposed to be, like, the three things that are important for a good marriage. There's all these cool stories about where the legend comes from. See that town over there?" She gestures into the mist to their left. "It's called Claddagh. We're practically in it."

Claire is in Clare, the claddagh is in Claddagh. In Ireland, words are bigger than she is, capable of swallowing her whole.

"See how the heart is pointed in, toward me?" Noelle is saying. "That means *my heart is taken*. But if it's facing out—" She pulls the ring off and twists it so the point is aimed at the horizon. "People know you're single. It means *take my heart*."

Claire looks toward the bay, where the heart has offered itself, knotted and bursting. It would require more than being single, she thinks. The heart would need to be willing to be taken. She thinks of her own ring, sitting in the bottom of a jar in a garage on the other side of the ocean. From this distance, the gesture feels ridiculous, the dramatic conclusion to a long and drawn-out fight that never really began.

"You recognize it, don't you?" Noelle says, swiveling the ring back to its rightful position.

"Should I?"

Noelle shrugs. "It was Mom's."

So Deirdre had saved the ring for Noelle. She had so disapproved of Claire's agnostic entomologist of a husband and godless, caution-to-the-wind marriage that she didn't want Claire wearing it.

"Dad gave it to her when they were, like, eighteen," Noelle says.

"She gave it to you?" Claire asks, unable to keep the hurt from her voice.

Noelle licks salt off her thumb. "I asked."

It isn't the answer she feared but somehow it feels worse. Claire had never asked to inherit anything of their mother's, from her genes to her beliefs to her rings and slippers. She can picture the wooden jewelry box that sat on her dresser, chains and bangles drooling from under its lid. Inside was a

cheap tangle of sterling silver and cubic zirconia, knotted like
a ball of metallic yarn and tarnished with black and green
bruises. It never occurred to Claire that anything in that box
might mean something. She feels a pressure in her chest, a
sadness fill her up inside, and realizes she's inherited something from her mother after all.

Claire looks up, blinking, at the mottled, rushing sky. "You
know you can't think that about her, Noelle."

Noelle stops chewing and gathers her hands in her lap.

"It wasn't because of you," Claire says.

"It might have been."

"It wasn't, Noey."

"You don't know that."

Claire opens her mouth to argue, but Noelle is right. They
don't know, and can't. *The only thing predictable about lupus is
its unpredictability*, went the refrain of their childhood, and
it was true. Claire has read all the books and websites; she
knows how much is still unknown. In sixth grade, the day
they learned to use the card catalog, she went to the library
after school to find out what *lupus* really meant. She learned
that from an etymological standpoint it was the Latin word
for *wolf*. That it was named for the rash under the eyes,
thought to look wolflike. That from a medical standpoint, it
was a disease of the autoimmune system, in which the cells
became confused, hyperactive; they sounded like children
on the same sports team who, in the flush of excitement,
began to turn on one another. The more she researched, the
more the ironies mounted and contradictions thickened.
The immune system, designed to protect against attackers,
began to attack itself. These attacks caused inflammation,

which was meant to heal the body, but also meant to set it on fire. Lupus was both the protector and the force that needed protecting against. It sounded not unlike Deirdre: set loose among her family, threatening them and protecting them at the same time.

The bag sits limp between them. "Did you ever ask them?" Claire says. "Mom and Dad?"

"Uh-uh. But one time I asked Dr. Vyron. When I was like, six. We were in the parking lot. I pretended I had to go to the bathroom and ran back inside."

Claire can imagine this: how Noelle would have whined and hopped from foot to foot, making such a scene they would have had to let her go back in. How she would have run full speed through the halls, jabbing at the square orange elevator buttons and announcing herself to the receptionist, demanding to see Dr. Vyron, all untied shoe-laces and flyaway hair.

"So what did he say?"

"He told me it could sometimes be a 'trigger'—"

Claire had forgotten how much she hated that word, so quick and violent.

"—but there was no way to know for sure, blah blah blah. Then he gave me a Tootsie Pop and said not to worry about it anymore."

"Well," Claire says. "He was kind of right about that part, I guess."

Noelle is silent.

"I mean, either way—"

"Yeah."

A cold, wet wind sweeps off the water. Suddenly all Noelle's years of frantic entertaining look different. Claire pictures the exertion on her face as she performed her Irish dances, performed like something depended on them bigger than the coarse VFW hall or tacky local parade. She recalls that last Saturday breakfast, Noelle marching toward the back door with that two-fingered *L* sprawled across her face. Underneath, the look in her eyes had been fearful. Claire had seen it but convinced herself it wasn't there. She is sorry now for not going, for all the ways she avoided her mother that meant Noelle was left alone with her.

"Maybe we should get going," Noelle says.

"Probably," Claire says, but her voice catches. She shakes her head quickly. "I'm fine. I'm just happy for you. About the wedding."

Noelle studies her a moment, then fishes a napkin from her pocket and smoothes it on her knee.

"Thanks," Claire says, taking it.

Noelle sits back, pulling her glove on. Neither of them makes a move to leave.

"Remember that name game we used to play?" Noelle says.

"Which one?"

"The one where I say a name, like a famous person, then you say one that starts with the last letter," Noelle says. "Like, I say Michael Jackson—"

"Natalie Wood," Claire says.

"Daniel Day-Lewis."

"Sally Struthers."

"Steve Winwood."

"Daisy Duke."

"Elton John."

"Neil Diamond."

"Diana Ross."

"Sinéad O'Connor." Noelle pauses. "It doesn't feel as hard as it used to."

# CHAPTER TEN: } Sadness

I t is nearing ten when Claire picks up the phone. The little children are in bed. Lyndsey and Aoife are doing homework in the kitchen. From the living room, Claire hears the faint drone of the TV but no laughter; it sounds like a newscaster, the flat tone signifying something tragic. Claire dials evenly, the numbers grinding under her fingertip—she had forgotten the sound and texture of a rotary phone, how engaged you are with the call as you make it.

One ring. Two.

It's five o'clock on a Sunday. Bob must be at home.

Three. Four.

When the machine clicks on, Claire feels more concern than relief. Then the message begins: "You have reached the Wells residence," Bob says. "We can't come to the phone right now."

They are the exact words as the old message, and this makes it worse. Not only did Bob erase it, he stood there first memorizing it, the impulse only to erase the sound of Claire's voice.

The beep ends and Claire finds herself unprepared again in the cave of static.

"Bob?"

She imagines the sound of the word falling in the empty kitchen, the refrigerator humming in recognition like a trusty pet.

"Bob, it's me," she says, then wonders if this sounds presumptuous. "Me, Claire."

The tape grinds on.

"Well, I guess—I just wanted to let you know I'm—"

She hears a fumbling at the other end. "Hello."

"Bob?"

"Yes."

"You're—you're there?"

She is alarmed by what her heart is doing, the crashing and surging. She is surprised she feels so *much*. It's Bob. *Bob.* Yet she feels as nervous as she did when they first started dating, probably more so, an attack of butterflies so intense it feels more like pain.

"I'm here," he says.

She wonders what he was doing when the machine came on. Eating in the kitchen? Working in the yard? Had he run for the phone or stood beside it, debating whether to answer?

"How are you?" Claire tries to apply just the right amount of pressure: not so much that it sounds patronizing, enough to sound genuinely concerned.

"Fine," Bob says. "How are you?"

She doesn't know how to answer. Anything positive might sound hurtful; anything negative, regretful. Amazing, how much we ask of words. Even in a single conversation, how many opportunities to do damage or kindle false hope.

"I guess I just wanted to say hi," she says.

Bob waits a beat. "All right."

"And to just let you know I'm here."

"Okay."

"I mean, here, in Ireland."

"Yes."

She can hear him breathing, waiting. He is right to wait. She's the one who called, the one who left. She focuses on the bookshelf in front of her, the march of soft spines. What would she tell him if she were brave enough? Had they written their own vows, what would they have said?

"This is my fault," Claire says. "I shouldn't have just left."

The line stays quiet, breath and static.

"I mean," she amends, "not that I shouldn't have left, but I shouldn't have done it like that. So abruptly, with no warning." Pressure rushes behind her eyes.

Then Bob says, "I knew you weren't happy."

Claire feels surprised for a moment before she feels hurt. "You did?"

"It wasn't too hard."

What is this—humor? Sarcasm? The first glimmer of sarcasm in four years and he saves it for now?

"Well, you didn't have to pretend," Claire says. "At least I wasn't pretending."

"I wasn't," he says. "Pretending." He pauses. "You're not an easy person to love, Claire."

And there it is: confirmation of everything Claire has always believed and feared was true. "Then why did you say it? That you—you loved me?" To speak the word is almost more than she bear.

"I'm not saying I don't," Bob says carefully. "That I don't, ah, love you. But you don't make it easy."

Claire closes her eyes. Her heart pounds in her chest. "Bob."

"Yes."

"Are you still there?"

"I'm still here," he says.

Her eyes fill. "I'm sorry that I wasn't a better wife."

Bob is silent. She can't even hear him breathing. Then he replies: "Ah."

But it isn't his old "ah," the product of nerves or excitement. It's not the ornament of the statement, but the statement itself. This "ah" means that he gets her, that he hears what she is saying—what she didn't even realize she was saying: She's cast their marriage in the past tense. She's admitted it's over.

Claire's heart is growing quiet. She pictures Bob on the quad that first afternoon, the bright worm on his finger and the sunlight glancing off his glasses. The memory fills her with a weary kind of sweetness, a return to the hopeful beginnings that is the surest sign of the end.

Then Bob asks, "Is it raining? In, ah, Ireland?" She hears

the strained politeness in his voice. It isn't denial; he is letting her off the hook.

"Not right now." Claire bites down on the inside of her cheek. If he can do this, so can she. "What about New Hampshire? Is it still cold in New Hampshire?"

"Today it was fourteen below. Friday it's supposed to snow."

"How much?"

"Eight to ten inches, they're saying. Up to fourteen in some places."

Eventually there may be resentment, lawyers, papers, but for now there is just this: an exchange of pleasantries, a reversion to how they began.

Then neither of them is speaking. Quiet crackles.

"This call must be expensive," Bob says.

Claire nods, pointlessly.

"We should probably say good-bye."

How many times has she said it? Hundreds? Thousands? Getting off the bus, leaving for school, hanging up the phone. Mornings in grad school when Bob left her dorm room, pulling on a sweater and his winter boots. Nights in college, leaving the dining hall with a friend and branching off on the quad, shuffling contentedly through the snow. At her wedding reception, as guests left one by one, pressing warm, tipsy congratulations to her cheeks. At her dinner party in New Hampshire, as the guests left in an awkward mob of thanks and dumb jokes, the slams of car doors punctuating the night. To Bob's family, last Christmas, having no idea it would be the last time. To her mother, in conversations real and imagined, on the phone, in the hospital, in her mind. How is it possible each moment boils down to the same seven letters? That we return to the same simple construction over and over, expecting it to bear up under all that weight?

Bob says it first, so she doesn't have to. "Good-bye," he says. "Good-bye."

---

The morning is damp and misty, but no actual water falls from the sky. Claire has come to gauge each day in Ireland in degrees of rain. "A soft auld day," Paul called it, at breakfast, assuring Claire it was a perfect morning for a drive: He didn't work until afternoon, Gene arrived tomorrow, and Paul just knew this place would make Claire feel inspired.

"Go," Noelle prodded, as Claire made her bed. Noelle had zero interest in the "writer cemetery." Plus, she thought the idea of the day trip, just the two of them, was endearing. "He wants to bond," she said.

Now Claire and Paul stand side by side in Drumcliff cemetery, a patchwork of grass, gravel, and age-spotted slabs of limestone. "'Under bare Ben Bulben's head, in Drumcliff churchyard Yeats is laid,'" Paul recites from memory. His pelt of long hair is unbound today, lifting slightly in the wind, and he is wearing the gray wool scarf Claire gave Noelle two years ago for Christmas. "'An ancestor was rector there long years ago, a church stands near . . .'"

The air is cold and damp, but Claire can barely feel it. Under normal circumstances she might feel awkward, standing alone with Paul in a graveyard, but today she feels hollow, not quite here, a combination of lack of sleep and the aftershocks of last night's phone call.

She stares at the ground in front of Yeats's grave, a bed of clean white stones strewn with three flowers—two fresh, one withered. In the distance, like the poem says, the Ben Bulben mountain rises in a mighty, shadowy arc. It's an odd shape, like a giant skateboard ramp, the top flat and sides sloped in an exaggerated decline. Like the other Irish landscapes, it seems to have a distinct personality, an emotional specificity—the slope not resigned but protective, as if guarding the town of Sligo and all the living and dead inside.

Paul closes his eyes as he recites the final lines, the ones engraved on the stone itself: "'Cast a cold eye on Life, on Death. Horseman, pass by!'"

Claire has a flash of her mother's grave: LOVING MOTHER & WIFE, and in the lefthand corner, that tacky shamrock. Even in death, Deirdre managed to combine the sacred with the downright secular.

"Published five days after his death," Paul says, shaking his head. "Can you imagine it? Writing your own fucking epitaph?"

Claire watches a brilliant red bird alight on the headstone. Paul notices it too.

"Day my father died," he says, "I opened the window and saw one magpie. He was just sitting there on the grass, the bastard. Sitting there and fucking grinning. I tried to reverse it, but did no good."

She looks at him. "You can reverse it?"

"You say, 'Good morning, Mr. Magpie!' Then you give the damn animal a salute." He jams his hands in his jacket pockets. "Didn't make a difference. I knew the second I saw him. Turned around, went inside, and said my good-byes."

Claire looks at the muddy ground. She hadn't said good-bye. She had arrived at the hospital too late. She hears a flutter and looks up to see the red bird departing in a deep arc, and wonders if maybe she's gone crazy, imagining her mother's spirit in every mundane flash of red and pink.

"You all right?" Paul asks.

"I'm fine," she says, but her voice is shaky. Without a word, Paul pulls a pack of cigarettes from his pocket, lights one, and places it between her lips.

Claire inhales gratefully, waits until she feels steady. She can feel Paul's eyes on her face. "Last night," she says, "I talked to my . . ."

What word is right? *Husband*? *Ex-husband*?

"Bob," she concedes. "And we decided to . . ."

*Break up* is too casual, *divorce* too formal. How insufficient language is. How downright spiteful.

"Oh fuck," Paul says, sounding genuinely stricken. "And you let me drag you to a graveyard this morning?"

"It's okay," Claire says. "It's a distraction."

"Right. Distracted with thoughts of our own fucking mortality. Jaysus, Claire. You might have said something! You should be knee-deep in crap television and fucking Hobnobs right now!"

She laughs.

"Do you want to go back? Hash it out with your sister?"

Claire shakes her head, maybe too quickly. "Noelle doesn't even know yet."

Paul smiles. "Girl's got one channel and no volume control, eh?" Then he lights a cigarette for himself. They smoke in an easy silence.

Paul says, "So you were miserable."

"Yes," Claire replies. "I was miserable." How simple, liberating, to just admit it.

"Did you love him?"

"I'm not sure," Claire says. "I'm not sure I ever loved him." She looks at Paul. "I never admitted that to anyone."

"The man included, eh?"

"We weren't very good at—talking."

"Sins of omission," Paul says. "The flaws of the kindhearted. Hell, if there were no fights, Noelle and me would have nothing to talk about."

Claire smiles at him. "I doubt that's true."

He exhales. "Well, you're right there. We'll always have things to talk about, won't we? Every bloody thing that's on that girl's mind," he says. As he squints into the smoke, deep wrinkles appear around his eyes. Without the lively trappings of the house, the bar, the children, Paul seems older. "You know the only reason my family's not pulling each other's fucking hair out is because the telly is on twenty-four/seven. We turn it off, all hell breaks loose."

"Really? But they seem so—loving."

"Is that what you call it." He expels a dry laugh. "After Da died, Mum was a wreck. She was useless."

Claire can't imagine Lillian this way, and doesn't want to.

"A good year or more it lasted. Mum a zombie, everybody bloody screaming at everybody. I had to kick some arse," he jokes, but Claire can imagine this was far from easy, feeling responsible for not just one person but an entire household. It occurs to her that though the Conneely clan may seem chaotic, really it is governed by a firm, invisible hand. They are a

224 { ELISE JUSKA

family that has lost its father, and everyone in it has absorbed that loss in a different way—become a little too hard, a little too angry, too determinedly funny, too old before his time.

"After she was back on her feet," Paul says, "I got the fuck out."

Mentally, Claire fills in the gaps: a summer in the States, a bartending job, the night he met Noelle. Then Paul says, "How did we get on about this? Aren't you supposed to be weeping on my shoulder?"

Claire looks at the ground, the toes of her boots stained with rain and plastered with wet threads of grass. "My mom and Noelle were closer," she says. "But you probably already know that. She liked Noelle better." It sounds immature but there it is: her childhood boiled down to its raw matter. "She may not have liked me at all."

"Bollix."

"No, it's true. She didn't even want to be near me. And she didn't like my husband either, so this news would probably make her day."

"I know I never met the woman, Claire, but I know she didn't hate you," Paul says, and Claire tries to smile, but suddenly she has to get away from all this, the immediacy of grief and loss. "I'm going to take a walk, okay?" she says, and without waiting for an answer, drops her cigarette on the grass. As she starts toward the mountain, her knees are shaking. The mountain blurs. That July afternoon, when her father called and said, "Deirdre's in the hospital," at first Claire hadn't even recognized his voice. It sounded fragile, splintered. He had never referred to her mother as Deirdre before. As Claire held the phone to her ear, his words increased in seriousness and specificity—*emergency, kidney, failure*—and finally: "You need to come home."

First she called Bob's secretary, sounding near-motherly as she asked Margie to page Bob, please, and send him home. Next she dislodged two suitcases from the basement, filling them up with toothpaste, socks, deodorant, sweaters. She debated packing a dark dress and suit then decided against it, fearing it might jinx things. Then she carried the luggage to the kitchen and stood in the middle of the room. Everything was still, silent. The breakfast dishes were sitting upside down in the drying rack. The only sound was a distant swish of tires, a faint breeze rustling the trees. Already Claire could begin to imagine her life through the lens of what would happen next: how, upon coming back, this kitchen would never look the same, but be a reminder of how innocent she once was.

On the road, she and Bob didn't speak. Claire felt she couldn't drive, or shouldn't. "Go fast," she instructed, and Bob tried his best to oblige. He sped, but awkwardly. Claire's foot came down on an imaginary brake every time he stopped too short or cut a merge too close. She wished she still had her cell phone—one of those modern extras she'd deemed unnecessary in New Hampshire. What had she been trying to prove? No life was simple, no matter how simple the setting. If you have a mother with lupus, you carry a cell phone at all times.

At a rest stop in Connecticut, Bob got in the Burger King line. Claire found a public phone and pressed her forehead against the scratched metal box. Her call went straight to voice mail. There was no point leaving a message, but she listened to the entire outgoing message anyway—"Hey, you've reached Noelle. If you know how much I love to talk on the phone you know how bummed I am that I missed you so please, please, *please* leave me a message"—taking comfort in the healthiness of her sister's voice. In the car, Bob looked at her. "No answer," Claire said. He offered her food but she wasn't hungry. The awkwardness of his driving was intensified by the cheeseburger and fries spread on a napkin across his knees. The smell was nauseating. Claire closed her eyes, felt the detailed topography of the road beneath their wheels, but it brought none of its usual satisfaction. She felt skinless, every movement rattling inside her, the rumble strips racing like scraped fingernails up her spine.

When they reached Philadelphia it was late, and hot, the sun just beginning to slide down the blanched Philadelphia skyline. Bob was pulling into the hospital parking lot slowly, too slowly. Claire could feel every inch of every speed bump. He wound through the aisles, melted ice jostling in his paper cup, sun splintering the windshield and the cheeseburger warmth of the car making Claire bite her tongue to keep from screaming until finally she snapped at him to let her out at the emergency exit—and so it happened that she was alone when the face of a nurse named Kathy told her she was too late.

There were no words. The woman's eyes were bright with sympathy, her lips drawn down tightly on each side. "I'm so sorry," said Kathy, but Claire had already begun to stiffen. She blinked back her tears, aware that they were leftovers from the car and feeling guilty that this nurse would think otherwise. She stared at the woman's earrings, two pink pearl droplets, knowing she would remember them for the rest of her life.

The nurse said they'd kept her mother in the room so Claire could see her, said this with such sweetness Claire heard herself thanking her. She followed the back of the nurse's pink smock through a maze of hallways and doorways, eventually turning into the room that contained Deirdre. The first thing Claire saw was her father and her sister, and her first thought was: How odd. The two of them alone together—how often did that happen? Her father looked small, blank, tamped down somewhere so deep inside himself nothing registered on his face. By contrast, all the rage and sorrow in the world had swept over her sister like a storm across a hayfield, leaving a path of ruin: wet cheeks, red eyes, damp strands of hair stuck to her face. They stepped back, probably to give Claire privacy but making her feel more on display. She moved toward the bed, feeling like she was on stage enacting a play's final moments. After all these years of wishing Deirdre were more accessible, her immediacy now was unbearable. In death, her mother's body was finally real, awful and sudden, and somehow, terribly uncomplicated. It was just a body. The fierceness and the mystery were gone, and Claire felt guilty even looking at her, knowing her mother would have hated to be seen that way.

Was it better or worse, how she looked at the wake? *Wake*: It had to be the most sinister word in the world, the noun and verb in such dramatic, tragic opposition. Was it deliberate, designed to remind the grief-stricken that in death there is new life? The notion struck Claire, like many words she would hear that week, as so overly sensitive it was borderline offensive. Deirdre's friends from Sears said the makeup job was so *professional*, looked so *lifelike*, but it wasn't. *Lifelike*: another word that was trotted out at funerals, that went down easy, rolled in sugar and passed around on a silver tray. It was part of the language of consolation, the soft, soothing, and emotionally correct script. They called Claire "beautiful," even though she had never felt less so. "All grown up," they added, which was not as complimentary at twenty-seven as it had been at thirteen. "Gorgeous," they persisted, the words as untrue as, when congratulating Claire on her wedding—and her first anniversary, right around the corner!—they said, "Your mother was so proud."

The black dress was one she'd found in her bedroom closet, preserved under the slippery sheath of old dry cleaners' plastic. She'd worn it to an awards banquet in college—the color was faded now, the armholes tight—but there was no sense buying a new one she'd never wear again. The nylons were too small; the crotch met midway up her thighs and the waistband dug into her thick hips. The color, sun beige, was the shade of wet teabags, too dark against her skin. She had found them the night before, in an unopened L'Eggs egg stuffed in the back of her top dresser drawer along with a few frayed bras, a button, a small wooden doorknob, and a folded piece of paper—*Are You Settling?*

"My mother was one of a kind," Claire said in her eulogy, or thinks she said. She was the one elected to speak at St. Cecilia's. "You're the writer," Noelle had told her, and Gene nodded, so Claire agreed to write it, while on the inside she thought, *But she wouldn't have wanted me to.* She sat up alone at the kitchen table the night before, staring at the blank pages of BRIGHT IDEAS! Noelle was out with her high school friends, Bob was upstairs asleep. Paul was arriving from Ireland in the morning. Claire stared at the lightbulb on the cover. The second hand on the oven clock stuttered every time it passed the :14. When she began writing, she was hovering over the pages, on them but not in them, smoothing on the sentences like varnish on raw wood. *One of a kind. Unique. Vivacious.* Had she really said these things? She can't remember the words, only the way they felt, like marbles on her tongue. She remembers how hard Noelle was crying, how Claire thought Noelle should have been the one speaking. How when she returned to the pew Gene planted a kiss on her head, and Bob placed his hand on her knee, and later, at the house, well-wishers had murmured "perfect" and Claire had winced inside at how wrong words can be, how they can mean nothing, and how the only opinion that mattered was Deirdre's and for once she didn't have one.

An hour later, she was in Assumption cemetery, the one she'd held her breath in front of in the backseat until she was fourteen. This was the first time she'd actually been inside it. The morning was hot and windless. Claire's nylons stuck to her legs. Noelle looked like a wilted lilac in her shapeless purple dress, her "not-black" dress, as she told anyone who looked at it funny. The color was irreverent but, Noelle reasoned, probably correctly, an irreverence that Deirdre would have liked.

"May the road rise to meet you . . ." Father Mike said. Noelle sobbed and Paul held her with both arms. Father Mike said words like *death, love, forever.* Claire recognized them from her wedding vows. *Eternal rest. A better place.* As ever, her mother was out of Claire's reach, closer to God and the mysteries of the universe than the rest of them. ". . . and may God hold you in the hollow of his hand," Father Mike concluded. Then

Noelle stepped forward. From her dress pocket she drew a plastic spritzer. It was the last of the miraculous water Deirdre had scooped from the ocean the previous summer, probably the same bottle she'd used to douse Claire's windshield at Christmastime. Noelle sprayed the coffin and, one by one, the rest of them followed. When it was Claire's turn her hand shook so much the spray missed the top of the coffin, where it seemed most symbolic, and dribbled weakly down one side.

Back at the house, well-wishers took small, tidy bites of small, tidy foods. Brownies and olives, glistening pink scrolls of lunch meat. They exchanged words like *special* and *strength* and *what doesn't kill you*. They played Deirdre's Irish records and raised toasts with Miller High Life. Noelle's friends from high school were there in full force, many of them having flown in from new lives in new towns and cities. It was like some grown-up version of Noelle's old birthday parties, the cool kids crowded in a corner drinking and laughing and occasionally ducking out back to smoke. Claire resented them, but was grateful to them too, for providing the spark of life that helps lighten a death: the reminder that all is not sadness.

That night, when the house emptied, Gene went straight to bed. Noelle and her friends migrated to the backyard, a scattering of makeshift ashtrays, folding chairs, citronella candles flickering like lightning bugs in glass jars. Claire washed the dishes, Bob dried. She listened to the sounds drift through the open window—Noelle's friends imitating Paul's accent, shouts of "bollix!" and "fockin' brilliant!" cresting upon loose, drunken laughter—and in the background, the natural music of summer, the sweet, sluggish melody of crickets and night wind. She thought of the life she would return to in New

Hampshire, of the crickets' dying chirps. Of her backyard, split down the middle like the set of some absurdist play. She was glad her mother had never seen it. *What the hell? Mower run out of gas?* Claire's house was a joke; it was a caricature of academia. This, here, citronella candles and soggy lasagna, was life. This was real.

"See that?" Claire said, pointing a sudsy finger out the window.

In the glass she saw Bob's face behind her own, above her left shoulder. The window was partly raised, so only the tops of their faces were visible, cut off and off center, like photographs couples take with cameras in their outstretched hands.

"That's how normal people deal with bugs," Claire said flatly, letting her hand fall back in the water with a faint splash. "Citronella candles."

Bob's face, in the window, did not react. Then he disappeared from the frame. Claire listened numbly as he walked upstairs. She heard the distant squeak of the faucet, pipes stirring as Claire's dishwater and their unfinished conversation swirled down the drain. It wouldn't matter. They would carry on as if nothing had been said, and Claire's comment, like every other regret or doubt or misspoken sentence she allowed herself this visit, would be chalked up to her altered state of mind. These are the luxuries of grieving: You can say anything and it won't be held against you. "I didn't mean it," she would say to Bob, and if need be, to herself.

Claire squeezed the excess soap from the sponge and placed it gently on the sink. She walked to the refrigerator, opened up the vegetable bin, and pulled out a High Life, the cans jostling and resettling as she shoved the drawer closed with her foot. She sat down at the table and raised the can to her lips. *This is the real miraculous water,* she could hear Deirdre saying. She forced down another swallow, hating the feel of metal against her mouth but knowing that if she poured it into a glass her mother would roll her eyes from inside the walls. As she sat and drank, she listened to the whoops and laughs outside grow louder, to the rattles of empty cans and bottles as they were pitched into a recycling bin. Some hit the target; others struck the back door and rolled forward, delicately chastised. Claire traced their path as they minced across the concrete landing, plinking down one step, then another, landing on the soft grass as soundlessly as pills in a palm.

# CHAPTER ELEVEN: }Genes

Occasionally, when one constructs a puzzle, the intersection of two words is about more than cosmetics. The mind makes subconscious associations, draws invisible connections. *Ade* needs *ice*. *Levee* sprouts *eau*. Other connections are murkier, less exact. They are the truths you didn't know were inside you but, given the confines of a grid, rise to the top. *Sis* becomes *sad*. *Hubby* and *home* become *bored*. Claire once watched *dad* turn into *cold*, which then spawned *ocean*, *ole*, *gone*, and *alone*. She stared at the resulting tangle, the garish, knotty truth of it. Then she deleted it, leaving just the original *dad*, replacing the words around it with *dip*, *pen*, *den*, *are*, and the slightly more incriminating *ire*.

Every now and then, though, an *ire* is unavoidable. It is meaningless, a matter of coincidence and convenience, the parsley of crossword filler. Claire feels no *ire* when she thinks of her father. If anything she feels sorry for him, protective of him. Still, she can't avoid the irony of where she sits now, alone in the *land* of *ire* waiting for him to arrive.

From the upstairs hallway, Claire watches the road. The sky is the color of pigeon feathers. She listens to the sounds of the house waking: the creak of a floorboard, shudder of a pipe. Behind her loom the bookshelves, the grandfather clock, the telephone, but not a single chair. Claire doesn't feel right poking in Lillian's room to look for one so she kneels on the hard floor by the window, the pose uncomfortably reminiscent of prayer.

The smells of grease and coffee rise from the kitchen. Lillian was up early, preparing a more elaborate breakfast than usual, mixing sausage, egg, and bacon into something unabashedly called "fry." Claire remembers their old Saturday breakfasts, she and her father alone together in that calm pocket of silence before Deirdre and Noelle arrived. Now it's the prospect of Gene's arrival making her feel nervous. The last time the three of them were together was the week of the funeral. Bob had left the day after, but Claire stayed in Philadelphia for the week. She had no specific reason for staying, just a nagging feeling that she should, and a suspicion that if she left she would miss something important.

Noelle and Paul were almost never home. They stayed out late, slept late. Occasionally, Noelle brought friends to the house and they drank to all hours in the backyard. Claire worried about bothering the neighbors, but knew that, this week, no one could complain. When Noelle and Paul weren't there, the house was still saturated with their presence: stale smoke, pungent candles, and the phone ringing as persistently as when Noelle was in high school. In their combined absence, Deirdre and Noelle dominated the house as much as they ever had.

If she was there, Noelle was holed up with Paul in her bedroom but the sadness leaked out from under the door: the slow, depressing music and the haze of pot smoke. Once, Claire knocked to tell Noelle she had a phone call and found them both dazed and red-eyed, the room a mess of magazines and tissues and cupcakes with the tops eaten off. "Cheers," Paul said, smiling faintly at Claire and taking the phone. Behind him, Claire caught a glimpse of Noelle, curled on the bed by the window.

Claire and Gene, though physically present, inhabited the place like ghosts. Claire turned faucets delicately, stepped softly, trying not to make any sudden moves or sounds. The silence was a visceral thing, like cold or heat. Sometimes Claire walked into a room and found everything trembling slightly, as if someone had just run through it. No one dared move anything of Deirdre's, like evidence from a crime scene: the cane propped on the railing, the pink Isotoners curled like soft shrimp on the bottom stair. Claire jumped every time the phone rang, letting the answering machine pick up if Noelle wasn't there—"Noey! How are you! Where are you! I'm worried about you, sweetie! I love you!"—the endearments taunting her as she tended to the tasteful bouquets or marched a knife down the middle of a quiche or received a few kind cards and awkward calls from old friends and made her nightly call to Bob at seven-thirty.

Without discussion, she and Gene avoided situations that made their aloneness too pronounced. Whoever woke first left coffee in the pot and the newspaper on the table. Claire started the crossword, Gene finished it. At night, they ate separately, warming up squares of casserole and eating them alone in front of a book or the TV. Though for Claire's entire life she had lived for moments alone with her father, now she found herself avoiding the living room altogether: the sagging sofa, the birth certificate, the wooden cross above the door. They looked like props on a darkened stage, the set of a play whose run had ended.

On Sunday evening, the house was silent. Paul and Noelle were out; Gene, Claire assumed, was asleep. She nibbled on butter cookies and worked on a new puzzle—JUST DESSERTS, she called it, trying to redeem the sickening number of cakes and pastries jammed in the fridge. By eleven, her eyes were hurting and she felt vaguely sick. As she moved through the down-stairs, turning off the lights, she stopped. Her father was sit-ting in the darkened living room, in the slatted rocking chair. Even with Deirdre gone he didn't feel entitled to the couch.

"Dad?"

He wasn't rocking. He was just sitting there. Maybe he was sleeping, even if the stiffness of his shoulders indicated other-wise. Maybe he was grieving, mired so deep in his sorrow that he couldn't be disturbed.

"Dad," she said, this time more softly, then walked quietly upstairs.

Later, after her father bought the condo, Claire would wonder if what she mistook for numbness that night was actually a state of heightened alertness, a concentration so deep he couldn't hear. If this wasn't a man looking backward, but forward, considering his next move: *Where would you go?*

The next morning, Claire's body woke automatically and early. She sensed the garbage truck from blocks away, the way Deirdre felt rain in her knees. Claire followed the truck's slow grind as it rose from the silence, the hiss as it braked in front of the neighbors' houses, the shouts of the men signaling the driver to inch forward. When the truck paused by her curb, she listened to the crunch of beer cans, an alarming cascade of them, one tub and then another and another. When Claire heard the shout that meant the truck was moving on, she felt a collision of deep sorrow and relief. She waited until the sound had faded completely, melting into the swishes of distant tires and twittering of birds.

Then she got up, got dressed, and began packing. Had she known then that she wouldn't be back, that within a month the house would be locked up and deserted, she might have taken something more. Something of her mother's. She'd like to believe this was true. Instead, she began subtracting. The nylons and black dress she stuffed in the bathroom trash can. Toothbrush, saline solution, shampoo—all of these she would replace with new ones that she didn't associate with being there. She began taking down everything that remained on her bulletin board—the ribbon, a few curling merit certificates, the dead prom corsage—and tossing them into the bin, topped with BRIGHT IDEAS!

Downstairs, Claire found Gene, facing the kitchen window. The coffeepot was empty, the paper still folded. Two pans had soaked overnight in the sink, the islands of suds on top turned an oily orange. Gene held the edge of the counter, lightly, with two hands, the way he held the backs of the pews in church. The window was shut, but over his shoulder Claire could see the detritus on the picnic table in the backyard: the melted stumps of candle wax, an empty pie pan filled with plastic forks, a pile of wrinkled cigarette stubs.

Gene caught her eye in the window glass and asked: "What's next?"

Now kneeling by a different window, Claire's knees are starting to ache. She leans her elbows on the sill, chin on her fists. Framed in the glass, her face must look like a little girl's waiting for a father to come home. When the cab finally appears, it is with impossibly little fanfare: a white and red taxi creeping alongside the curb, tires splashing dully through puddles of stale rain. Claire sits forward, nose nearly pressed to the window. When Gene steps out, the sight of him takes her by surprise. Since Christmas, he's put on weight and grown a beard. As he hoists his suitcase from the trunk and makes his way across the front yard, everything about him suggests a long day at the office: the shoulders soft, the gait beleaguered and slightly lopsided, as if one leg has grown tired of keeping up with the other. His new bulk seems less about adding weight, than simply yielding to gravity's pull. He is wearing a raincoat, sun yellow with wooden toggles, that she cannot imagine him owning. He must have bought it for the trip.

Suddenly he stops and looks up. Claire has to restrain herself from ducking. It's the instinct of having been a shy child:

the moment of alarm when the scene turns inward and the watcher becomes the watched. Her father lifts a hand. He is still wearing his wedding band. By the time Claire collects herself enough to wave back, he's disappeared under the eave. A moment later, she hears the scenes below and behind her merge: the ring of the doorbell, a flurry of footsteps, a barking dog, Paul saying, "Sláinte!"

Claire pushes herself up off the floor, tucks her hair behind her ears, and starts for the stairs. From the top step, she can see feet only: her father's brown loafers, toes darkened with puddles; Paul's dull black boots and Noelle's (Deirdre's) pink slippers; Lillian's sensible brown flats, surrounded by a huddle of small feet in identical blue shoes. She hears the stiff, polite children's chorus: "hello," "hello," "hello," "hello." As she descends, the bodies lengthen, like a curtain rising, feet giving way to knees and torsos, Paul's ropy black sweater and Noelle's folded arms. When Claire reaches the middle stair, necks sprout heads, just as Gene kisses Noelle on the cheek.

"Hey, Dad," Claire says.

Gene turns and smiles. "There she is."

In the crook of his neck, Claire can smell the new rubber of his raincoat and see its sprightly plaid lining and she clings to him for an extra second, filled with a brief, convincing swell of hope.

———

Within minutes, Lillian has deftly relocated the masses to the kitchen, where she moves back and forth between table and stove, ferrying stacks of charred toast. The dishes are nicer than usual, cream-colored with blue stripes around the rims. Claire is touched by the effort. Gene is given the head of the table; it is usually Paul's seat, but was offered without discussion. Even the children seem on unusually good behavior. There are no video games, no books or headphones. They regard this unfamiliar father with something between fear and curiosity, the little ones with wide eyes, the older ones with sidelong glances.

Gene, seated next to his almost-son-in-law and inundated with small round faces, looks as uncomfortable as anyone. Only Graham, stationed at his right elbow, gets down to business. "What's your name?"

Gene looks momentarily taken aback, by the question or the gravelly little voice that asked it or both.

"Mr. Gallagher," Lillian says, as Gene answers, "Gene."

Graham nods, filing away the information. Claire has never liked her father's name. In school, it reminded her of biology, the rubbery cells and chromosomes on the old filmstrip reels shot through with threads of broken light. His full name was even worse: Gene Gallagher. It sounded like a game show host. If the name Deirdre suited Claire's mother perfectly, her father's name suits him in its very unsuitedness, as ill-fitting as everything else about his life.

Her father stirs a heaping teaspoon of sugar into his coffee, unaware that Graham is only warming up. "Like Gene Simmons from KISS?" the boy says.

Gene puts his spoon down, a brown stain spreading across the paper napkin. "What's that?"

"Gene Simmons from KISS. Do you know him?"

Aoife looks up. "Do *you* know Gene Simmons?"

"'Course," Graham says, and matter-of-factly sticks out his tongue.

"Graham!" Lillian barks.

"That's what they do, Mum," he explains. "The lads in the band."

"And are you one of those lads?"

"I don't know," Paul says, lifting his fork and studying Graham over the pile of fry. "I can picture Graham in a rock band." At this, Graham sits up straighter. "Blue hair," Paul muses. "Tattoos on his arms."

"Ring in me brow!"

"By all means." Paul swallows his eggs. "Ring in his brow."

"If Graham gets a ring," Lyndsey pipes up with a soft urgency, "I get a—"

"No one's getting anything," Lillian says, looking pointedly at their guest. "Eat, the lot of you. You'll be late."

They return to their plates in furtive silence. Only Gene chews vigorously, obviously, like a man grown accustomed to eating alone.

"I've got to go," Paul says, scraping back his chair. "The drunks await."

As he stands, Noelle looks sad and vaguely nervous. Paul places both hands on her shoulders. "Good-bye, my love," he says, leaning down to kiss the part in her hair.

Noelle tilts her head back and smiles. They treat each other kindly, Claire thinks. It is not a small thing.

"Come around for a pint later?" Paul asks her, to which Gene replies, "Will do."

Graham waits for the sound of the front door slamming before turning back to Gene. "So do you know him?"

"Jaysus," Aoife says.

"Gene Simmons," Graham reminds him.

"Right." Gene pushes his glasses up his nose. "Gene Simmons. I think I'm familiar."

"But he doesn't *know* him know him," Claire says quickly, provoking a quick smile from Lillian.

Graham changes tactics. "Do you come from Philadelphia?"

"Originally," Gene says.

"Where do you come from now?"

"New Jersey."

"New Jersey?"

Claire prays that Graham doesn't push the issue. She glances at Noelle, stabbing a fork at a stick of butter. "Dad," Claire says. "Have you ever met anyone famous?"

Gene pauses, holding his coffee near his chin. "Anyone famous . . ." he wonders out loud, wrapping both hands around his cup. "Let me think . . ."

Noelle drags a buttered knife across her toast, ripping a hole in the middle.

"I once met Martin Landau," he says finally.

"Who's Martin Landau?" Graham pounces.

"I was in an airport. In Duluth."

"What's Duluth?"

"We were at the same baggage claim," Gene explains, as Graham says, "Was he the chap on *Little House on the Prairie*?"

Aoife sighs, but speaks gently. "That's Michael Landon, Graham."

"Oh." Graham looks down into his plate. "Right."

"Eat your breakfast," Lillian tells him, resting her palm briefly on top of Graham's head, then moving on to refill Gene's cup. Claire gives her father an encouraging smile.

"Wait just a second," he says, "we have a famous person right here."

Graham looks up. "Where?"

Gene points his fork across the table.

"Me?" Claire says.

"The name Claire," Gene says proudly. "Means famous."

Graham picks up his fork. "That's not what I meant."

⌒

Whatever urgent Irishness Noelle possessed in the initial days of Claire's visit is back with a vengeance. She allowed Gene just a brief nap before announcing they were going to the pub. Just past noon on a Tuesday, Conneely's is in full throttle. The place is packed with locals attacking steamy plates with knives and forks, full-cheeked children too young for school darting in between the tables.

Gene looks ill at ease amid the commotion. In these crowded confines, his new girth seems even more apparent; it occurs to Claire that for all their pints and sausages, she has yet to see an Irish person who is seriously overweight.

Noelle takes off for the bar, leaving Claire to hunt for an empty nook. It would be too awkward sitting with her father on bar stools; it's awkward enough sitting with her father in a bar.

"Sláinte!" a young man shouts as Claire passes by. She returns an uncertain smile. Threading her way through the maze of tables, she attracts a number of waves and hellos. "Aye!" shouts a young woman with corkscrewed red hair. "It's the comic!"

The only empty table is wedged in a corner, the wooden seats making a sharp right angle with the wall. Claire slides in on one side, Gene on the other. The seats are hard and straight as pews.

"Friendly place," he says, sounding slightly winded. "People here seem to know you."

"I've been here a couple of days," she says.

Up close, Gene's new raincoat looks even more stiff. It reminds Claire of the summer clothes he used to wear in Ocean City, refusing to wilt even in the heat.

"You got here over the weekend?"

"Last Thursday," she says.

"Thursday," Gene repeats.

Now, she thinks, would be the perfect time to tell him. Maybe Noelle's last-minute invitation will overshadow the real reason Claire came. She imagines the words leaving her mouth: *So, Dad. Listen, Dad—*

"How's your work going?" Gene asks.

Claire hesitates. "You mean—you mean the puzzles?"

"I did the last one."

"You did?"

"It had a winter theme, right?" he says, shifting slightly, pew creaking beneath him. "Was it Snow Time? Snow Fun?"

It was called SNOW DAY and it appeared in Jumbo Puzzle Special, Volume 14, Number 3. Claire isn't sure whether to feel touched or mortified. "You do my puzzles?"

When he lifts his shoulders, the raincoat rises and stays

there, the ghost of a shrug hovering by his ears. "You know I've always liked crossword puzzles," he says.

Yes, but, she wants to say, the *real* ones. The clever ones in the Sunday paper, the ones that require a hotline and a thesaurus and that Claire could never finish on her own. She imagines her father pawing through a magazine rack in an off-season Jersey shore drugstore, looking for the pulpy pink covers next to last season's boogie boards and half-priced suntan lotions.

"They're silly," she says. "I mean, they're just for fun, really."

"Well," he says, the shrug deflating. "I think yours are very well done."

Claire looks at him carefully, the individual beads of sweat standing like raindrops on his brow. In the realm of the EZ crossword, there is no real difference between one puzzle and the next. It occurs to her to wonder if her father's praise has ever been as meaningful as she thought.

"What's your next one about?" he says.

Ordinarily, the answer would come easily: Screen Stars. Citrus Fruit. A Day at the Zoo. "I'm not sure," Claire admits. *See, what happened is, my schedule was kind of thrown off track. I had a change of—*

"How's Bob?" Gene asks.

"Bob?"

"How's his work? His research?"

"His research is going great." The question is so familiar, the response so ingrained, she doesn't even flinch. "He's publishing an article in May."

"He's not coming for the wedding?"

"Who's not coming for the wedding?" Noelle says, appearing with her fingers threaded through a wobbly triangle of glasses. She leans forward to ease them onto the table.

"Bob," Gene says.

Thankfully, Noelle doesn't say anything, doesn't even look at her. Paul must have filled her in the night before. Noelle pushes the glasses across the table, then squeezes into the seat beside Claire, the ends of her red scarf piling in her lap.

Gene lifts his glass and takes a deep draught, licking foam from his top lip. Claire is surprised by how comfortable he looks with a beer in his hand. "So," he says, "getting married."

"I told you I would," Noelle says. She picks up her pint. Claire can feel her leg jiggling under the table. "I told you I would marry Paul, remember?"

"What's that?"

"I told you I would marry Paul. I called it, like, two years ago."

Claire searches their father's face, but he doesn't remember: the night before her own wedding, Noelle's threats to drop out of school and move to Ireland. How could he have forgotten Deirdre's response: *I'd love to see you become an Irish barmaid. Just do it on your own time, not mine.*

Noelle takes a swallow and holds it, cheeks swelling.

"The Conneelys seem like a nice family," Gene says.

Noelle swallows. "They are a nice family."

Gene taps one finger against his glass. Claire is quickly realizing how much they rely on Noelle's voice; without it, they are unmoored.

"So the wedding is on Saturday," Gene says. He pulls his

glasses off, studies them, and pushes them back on. "Well, I'd like to contribute something. Financially."

"That's okay."

"No, I—"

"Seriously," Noelle says. "We don't need it."

Claire knows that they need it, of course they need it, they live with Paul's mother and five children. She wishes Noelle would just accept the offer, if not for her own sake, for his.

"Where are you two going to live?" Gene asks then, and Claire steels herself for the answer. But to her surprise Noelle says, "We're getting our own flat."

"You are?"

"Good for you, honey," Gene says. "Where about?"

"Just a little town," Noelle says. "You don't know it."

Claire looks down at her lap. She reaches for her glass. The room feels too close, too warm. When she lifts her head, Gene is looking at her. Claire knows this look. She's been seeing it her entire life: the quirked mouth, hint of camaraderie, eyebrows arched in mild appeal. It used to feel like proof of their closeness. Now Gene shifts his gaze to the bar, raising his glass to hide his face. They were allies, Claire thinks, but only by default.

"So," she says, "Dad. How's your place?"

Noelle's eyes flick toward him, then away.

"Oh, pretty good. The same."

"Have you been back to the house?" Claire asks.

"Actually," he says. "I have some news."

Claire's heart sinks. Noelle is clueless for another second, then sits up straight. "Oh my God."

"I thought—"

"You sold it," Noelle says. "You sold it without *telling* us?"

"I thought it would be easier," Gene says. "You girls haven't been back in—"

"What did you do with all the stuff?" Noelle demands.

"It's in storage. Most of it."

"Most of it?" Noelle looks like she might burst into tears.

"I have your things. Don't worry."

"I don't care about my things. Where are Mom's things? Did you throw away Mom's things? You didn't give them to some charity, did you?"

"Of course not. They're in storage." He rubs a hand across his beard. "You can get them anytime you want," he says, appealing to Claire.

"You should have at least told us, Dad," she says.

From across the pub, music strikes up. Claire is relieved for a place to fix her eyes, a sound to seep into the spaces where words should be. A moderate jig, flute and fiddle, and within minutes the whole place is stomping, accompanied by whoops and shouts. The pint glasses shiver, jostled by a roomful of pounding feet. When the song ends, the room unfurls in applause.

"Dad?" Claire says.

He doesn't hear.

"Dad!"

This time, Gene and Noelle both turn. "Bob and I—" The words get stuck in her throat. The music is starting up again, a dizzy-fast reel, the sound incongruously joyful as she says, "I left Bob."

For a second she's not sure he heard. Then Gene gives an almost imperceptible nod. "For good?"

"I think so," Claire says. "Yes."

The pub is singing and stomping. Gene touches his glasses. Then, unexpectedly, he smiles. It is not a happy smile; it is resigned, sorry. It is the smile of a person no longer surprised by sad things. As the three of them sit there, floor quaking beneath them, Claire admits there is another meaning of *wake*. Not just where you go to pay respects, not just the act of waking. It is what remains *in the wake* of something, everything that is spared.

CHAPTER TWELVE: } Limerick

It was Gene's decision that they go there, and even though it was entirely out of character, or maybe because it was, neither Claire nor Noelle objected. The specifics of the trip were vague, but the impulse to gravitate toward Deirdre was one each of them understood.

"Where was she from?" Lillian asked at breakfast. "The city?"

"Right," Gene replied, "the city." But he didn't sound sure. None of them were. The Limerick of Deirdre's first thirteen months had always had a fairy-tale quality—the place she cried for on Saint Patrick's Day, wellspring of chocolate and fiddlers. The details were, Claire knows now, probably as true as Noelle's shepherd, the difference being that Noelle knew she was exaggerating while Deirdre believed wholeheartedly in her story.

In the car with their father, the silence is thick and warm. Claire and Noelle sit in the front. Gene, at his insistence, squeezes in the back. The combination of the light rain and their collective breath make the windows fog almost immediately. Noelle cracks hers and lights a cigarette.

Claire rubs a patch of glass clean. She watches the road. It may be the same road she and Noelle traveled before; it may be a different one: a narrow black ribbon threading through vast sweeps of muddy green, a grid of words and stone.

"Dad, see the signs?" Claire says.

Gene leans forward, an orchestra of squeaking rubber. "Well," he says, "would you look at that."

It is nearly an hour later, just as Claire is about to propose they ask for directions, that Noelle announces: "There it is." Sure enough, the word LIMERICK has surfaced on a sign. Claire actually feels a little bit surprised that the place exists.

"Check it out," Noelle says, as the road narrows into a bridge. She is pointing to the other side of a wide, gray river. It's a castle—more than a castle, it looks like a minor medieval city, a larger-than-life child's toy made of formidable pillars and squares. Claire's first thought is that the castle must be King Conchobar's, the place Deirdre and Naoise were tricked into going.

Then the bridge ends, and the myth dissolves, spilling them into a maze of narrow, rain-wet streets. Noelle makes a left, hugging close to the river. Up close, the city looks vaguely industrial, choked with gray-brown buildings. Claire still hears

Bob's words in her head: *Where would you go?* Never would she have guessed the answer would lead her here, or look like this. A yellow crane peeks behind a church spire. Scaffolding climbs up a building's sides. A McDonald's and Burger King square off on a corner.

Noelle drives the streets slowly, near-reverently, as if crossing over someone's grave. She parks the car across from a small park facing the river. The park is round and mostly bare, a pond of muddy grass encircled by low steps and a few bleached, spindly trees. From across the water, a jumble of houses stares back, flat and crowded as a jigsaw puzzle.

"So here we are," Gene says.

Claire stands still, waits to feel something. She had expected to be inundated with Deirdre, swamped with her presence, but instead, nothing. The patter of rain. Swish of car tires through puddles. A shiver, but only from the cold.

"The Cranberries are from here," Noelle says.

"What's that, honey?"

Two little boys run by, hair tousled, kicking muddy divots.

"The Cranberries," she repeats. "Are from Limerick. They're a band."

*Limerick* also surfaced frequently in crossword puzzles, Claire thinks, a useful blend of consonants and vowels. Poetic Irish city. Nantucket man's form. For all that's unknown about Deirdre's thirteen months here, this part seems logical: that her birthplace would be a city best known for a simple, silly rhyme. A poem that is notoriously bawdy, borderline obscene, and composed most eloquently when drunk.

"So, is this, like, all we know?" Noelle says. She pinches a cigarette between two fingers. There is an edge to her voice

that sounds like impatience, or anxiousness thinly disguised.
"That she was born here? I mean, that's it?"

"More or less," Gene says.

"It's not completely it," Claire says. "There was fog, remember?"

"What fog?" Noelle says.

Gene nods slowly. "That's right. The fog."

"What about the fog?" Noelle demands.

Had Noelle never heard this story? Claire glances at her
father, but when he doesn't offer details, she goes on. "Mom
would say the fog out her window, when she was a baby, looked
like yarn. Like those big balls of knitting yarn."

It sounded more special, the way Deirdre told it. They all
look up at the sky: textureless, cloudless. Claire pictures her
mother up there, watching as they hunt for some trace of her
and laughing her face off, sprawled on some giant celestial
couch.

"What else?" Noelle says.

"There was a house," Gene offers, awkwardly.

"Pink with a red door," Claire says.

"It was the reverse."

Claire turns to him. "The house was pink."

"It was a red house, honey," he says. "A pink door."

"But I remember it."

Noelle says, "How could you remember it?"

"I mean—I remember how I pictured it."

"You're probably thinking of the John Cougar song," Noelle
says. Gene says nothing. He turns back to face the water, and
Claire understands then that her version is wrong, and that
he is letting her preserve it.

Noelle holds the cigarette near her chin. "What else?"

"Her uncles played violins." Claire glances at her father; this time, he doesn't contradict her. "Her aunt ate a scrambled egg and a pound of chocolate every morning."

Noelle tosses her cigarette on the grass. "Who the hell were these people? Why didn't we stay in touch with them?"

"We did, for a while," Gene says.

"Why didn't they come visit?"

"I don't know, honey. They lived in Ireland."

"Maybe we should go knock on doors—"

"They wrote letters," Gene cuts her off, as if this long-ago gesture has earned these people the right to be left alone. "It was a long time ago," he adds, apologetically. "They're probably dead now. Come to think of it, I think I remember them dying."

It wouldn't matter. Claire knows that even if they searched, they wouldn't find anything. No relatives, no pink house, no pink door, no evidence Deirdre ever lived here. "Well, did she write them back?" she says, more sharply than she intended.

"Of course," Noelle says, looking at Gene. "She loved writing letters. She wrote good ones. Didn't she, Dad?"

"She used to," Gene says.

"And she hated email."

"That's for sure."

Had Claire known this? If she hadn't, it doesn't surprise her.

"Because letters you can keep," Noelle says. "Because she liked having stuff. She wrote to Dad too. Right, Dad?"

He clears his throat. "A few."

"Love letters, right?"

*Does he write you love letters?* Claire can hear her voice, that long-ago Saint Patrick's Day. *Does he make your heart go pitty-pat?* At the time her mother's questions had seemed old-fashioned, absurd, some bitter symptom of what was missing in her own life.

"She did, didn't she, Dad?" Noelle persists.

"We were young," Gene says, as if this provides some explanation. But this, more than anything, Claire finds impossible to believe: not a medieval Irish city, or fiddlers and pink houses, but her own parents, young and healthy, happy and in love.

"They were funny," he goes on. "And honest. Your mother was the most honest person I ever met."

Claire looks at the water. She feels suddenly nervous.

"There was one she set up like a scavenger hunt. She left little notes all over the house. I'm pretty sure—did they rhyme?" He tips his head back, as if consulting the sky. "I think they did. They rhymed. And I had to follow the trail to the end."

Noelle is watching him closely. "What was the end?"

"Her."

Rain is trickling down the fronts of Gene's glasses. Claire has never heard her father talk this way. How simple it sounds, how clear: how well he seems to have *known* her.

"When we first met, she was different," Gene says. "She was full of life. She was . . . brightness." He shakes his head, smiling. "I don't know any other word for it."

"Kind of ironic, isn't it?" Claire says.

Noelle gives her a sharp look.

"I just meant—because of her name. You know, the sadness."

Gene laughs. "I can just hear her, can't you?" he says, and they listen, as if her voice might be carried on the wind. "*It's the sadness,*" he intones, laughing again. Claire wonders for a moment if he might be losing his mind. Then Noelle laughs, too, and she feels left out, her father and her sister part of some private joke she doesn't understand.

"She always wanted you girls to think the sickness was out of her hands," Gene says, then pauses. "I shouldn't be telling you this." His tone is almost pleasantly surprised, that of a man who hasn't had to censor himself in months. "She wouldn't want me telling you this."

"No," Claire says. "Tell us."

Noelle looks at the ground. Gene rubs one hand over his beard slowly. "Well," he says, "she knew she should have been better with . . . you know. Taking care of herself. But you know your mother."

"She did fine," Noelle says.

"She did the best she could."

Claire looks at the muddy ground. They are sanitizing her, picking out the good qualities and softening the bad. They are treating her like a dead person. "Why are you being so easy on her? She drank too much, she ignored her doctor, she screwed around with her medication, so she died." When she sees the tears in Noelle's eyes, she stops.

"She wasn't a good sick person," Gene says. "She wasn't cut out for it. She used to say—she said it was more important for you to see her go down feisty than go down weak." He clears his throat. "Those are her words."

Of course. Only she would say that, only she would think it. The most infuriating part was, she'd succeeded. Even at her sickest, especially then, she never showed true weakness. Had she ever been soft, mortal, unsure of something, anything, just once—it was the thing Claire had needed from her most.

"She thought doing the right thing was overrated," Gene says, and Claire remembers that night in the living room when she found him alone in the dark. She remembers his question the next morning: "What's next?" He'd been asking it his entire married life, but maybe it had never been a question of resignation. Maybe it wasn't the drudgery of life with his wife he was imagining in those moments, but the prospect of life without her. The possibility leaves Claire speechless. Her mother and her parents' relationship had always been inscrutable, nonsensical, but for all her fruitless analysis she had thought she understood at least this: that her father was a man stuck in a bad marriage. He was duty-bound, caught in the current of a life he couldn't leave. She had always believed this. She had counted on it. But now she sees: Her father loved her mother. The plainness, the purity of it, is staggering.

Gene takes his glasses off and surveys the insides of the wet lenses. "I tried," he says, simply.

Noelle puts her hand on his arm. Gene looks down and for a moment, his mottled face seems to clear. "Her ring," he says.

Noelle withdraws her hand quickly. "She said I could have it."

"No," he says, shaking his head. "I'm just surprised to see it there."

If Claire believed in ghosts, she would have thought her mother the type to come back and haunt the mortal world for sport. Make celebrities trip on the red carpet, birds poop on the heads of politicians. Never would she have predicted Deirdre would show up in the guise of a golden angel—it's so predictable—and yet there she is, soul perched like a bird on the top of a small gray church at the end of a crooked brown street in the town of her birth just as parishioners are filing up the stairs and Claire, Gene, and Noelle are walking by.

The church, St. Michael's, is not much bigger or more conspicuous than any other building on the little winding street. Inside, it is cool and gray. The pale sun spills through the long vertical windows, striping the floors and the floating dust. Claire hasn't been to Mass regularly since she was in high school, but this detail calls up every church she's ever known: dust caught in the light from a stained glass window, moving in a slow, holy daze.

She is seated between her father and sister. Even after all these years, this feels strange; as a child, Claire never sat in the middle. It was Gene who started down the aisle, Deirdre attached to his elbow, and Noelle clinging to Deirdre's hip. Claire brought up the rear, shoes squeaking, tights scratching. She dreaded church, dreaded it as passionately as she loved school. It was only partly the clothes. It was the all-knowing God who could read her every thought, the thorny Jesus that hung above the altar, the uneasiness that prevented her from saying the prayers out loud, compounded by guilt that she wasn't saying them and fear that the all-knowing God would know it. This was the religion cocktail, she would say, years later, at academic parties: fear and guilt, with a dash of fancy shoes.

Sitting in a church again, the uneasiness returns. Then and now, it was the people in church that made her most uncomfortable. It was the rawness of emotion—the *surety* of it all. When the people said prayers, did they really believe them? How could they know? There was no one to ask. She'd tried once and gotten hit for it. So she'd moved her lips during the prayers, closing one eye but keeping the other open.

Her parents, seated on the other side of Noelle, would be visible only in fragments. There was her mother's head, chin bent to chest, hands entwined in her rosary beads. Her father's long fingers rested on the pew back, loose, noncommittal. When it came to religion, Claire had always suspected her father was what she'd heard neighbors describe as a "tag-along husband." Claire had no idea what his beliefs were, or if he even had any. At Mass, Deirdre sagged reverently on her kneeler, head in hands, while Gene perched his kneecaps on the edge of it, almost but not quite letting his butt rest against the pew. He was an accessory to Deirdre, as they all were, and performed his designated role: digging in his wallet at the offertory and handing the bills to Noelle, because she was the youngest and cared the most, to drop in the straw basket, then giving Deirdre a chaste kiss on the lips during the peace-be-with-yous.

Now Claire is taken aback by how devout her father seems. He is leaned forward, collapsed over his hands. She is relieved when the priest's entrance summons the crowd to its feet.

"Please rise."

The rituals of the Mass feel familiar. Standing, sitting, listening to words she's heard a thousand times. There are slight variations, but they are essentially the same. *And also with you. Praise be to God.* Even if she doesn't believe them, there is comfort in the repetition.

"Lord, graciously hear us," the congregation repeats, as one by one people offer specific prayers, for the health of their sheep, their farms or families. At St. Cecilia's, these intentions were more formal, spoken from the pulpit and submitted in advance like the morning announcements at school. More than once, Deirdre's name had appeared in the lineup and Claire had felt the sorry eyes of the families around them. She wanted to crawl into herself and hide, because her mother was sick, but not sick enough that she couldn't place that call.

"Lord, graciously hear us," comes the chorus.

They stand. Kneel. Stand again. The priest waves the incense, releasing sweet curls of smoke. When he begins speaking in Irish, Claire listens more closely. This is the first time she's actually heard the language out loud. Though in writing it looks gnarled, jagged, the sound of it is surprisingly soothing. Smoke twines in and out of the stripes of light. *Incense*: another word that contradicts itself inherently—the noun designed to calm, the verb to anger.

The room is rising, row by row. When she was a child, the order of their entrance usually dictated that Claire sit on the aisle, so it was her job to initiate the merge into the communion line. Now it is Noelle who leads, sticking her tongue out when they reach the priest. "Body of Christ," he says. Claire opens her palms, places the host on her tongue, and feeling vaguely disingenuous, swallows it.

This is the part of the Mass she dreaded most: the most exposed and private, everyone on their knees, eyes closed. What are they thinking? Are they praying? Bits of dry host stick to the roof of her mouth. She fights the urge to pry them off with a finger. On either side of her, Gene and Noelle fold forward. When did their faith become so pure? Claire looks down at her hands, pads of her thumbs pressed together, making the tips fill with red. She pictures her mother's hands tangled in the rosary, the tiny blue Our Fathers and white Hail Marys like pills twined around acrylic nails painted in distinctly sacrilegious shades: Bahama Nights, Vegas Spice. But when she prayed, Claire thought, it was real: as if something were alive inside her, lips twitching, hands moving, rosary beads clicking like teeth. There was fervor in her hands, something bigger than the moment, and as much as Claire hated her mother's saying "I know more than you do," the truth was, she had believed her. Whatever knowingness Deirdre possessed, whatever divine insight, Claire had resented it and needed it at the same time, and now she is furious at her mother for leaving without first telling her what she knew.

Claire closes her eyes. Smoke from the incense catches in her throat. Maybe any mother is a kind of religion: the story of where you come from, the guidelines for what to believe. It is essential to have something bigger than you are there to guide and protect you and help you interpret the world. Claire hears bodies around her sliding back onto pews. On the outside, it must look like she's praying. Whatever prayer is, right now, she longs for it. For the capacity to believe in something, anything, absolutely. She thinks of the troupes of vacationers in Ocean City filling their plastic bottles with miraculous water. Of the Conneelys' kitchen, Aoife's magpie sighting and the family's automatic response. Claire has always associated that kind of faith with ignorance, but maybe faith is not a decision you can make with the mind. Some things you must believe without proof—the belief becomes the proof—and maybe this is the true bold thing, to have faith in something that you can't know for sure.

———

The sky looks rain-washed, soft grays streaked with indigo. They ride back across the bridge they came in on. On the other side of the river, the castle is illuminated with floodlights, its thick, bright reflection swimming in the water.

"Good-bye, Limerick," Noelle calls. The castle vanishes behind them, and the skinny road appears again, twining through the darkened green. Claire senses it is one of those permanent good-byes: They will not be back.

"I'm knackered," Noelle says, flicking on the headlights.

"What's that, honey?" Gene asks from the backseat.

"It means tired, in Irish," she says.

Claire leans the side of her face against the window. She is tired, too, the good kind of tired, the kind that befalls a car at nighttime as the buzz of where you've been is dying down, yielding to the comfort of heading home.

"Let's play a game," Noelle says. "We'll do limericks. There once was a man from Ballylickey. He woke up one day with a hickey."

Claire sighs. "God, Noelle."

"What? You rhyme it."

"Sticky," she says. "Picky."

"Doohickey," Gene says from the backseat.

"Good one, Dad," Noelle says. "Okay. There once was a man from Ballylickey. He woke up one day with a hickey. He said to his wife—"

"Gin rickey!" Gene shouts.

Noelle and Claire exchange a smile. "Um . . . okay. He said to his wife, I swear on my life, I'll cut back on the gin rickeys."

It doesn't make much sense, but has a good beat to it. Their laughter fills the empty road.

"There once was a woman named Claire," Noelle starts again. "With skin so Irish fair. She sat in the sun, she thought it was fun, now her skin is red as her hair."

"Hey, you're good at this, honey," Gene says.

"She's a shanachie," Claire says.

"Is that right?"

The sky is darkening. Houses appear here and there, glowing from within. Claire pictures the little house in New Hampshire, somewhere on the other side of the ocean. Already it feels like the product of a lonelier life. Still, she knows she has to go back, to talk with Bob, not just grab her things and run. Much as it scares her, she wants to end things right.

"Your turn," Noelle says, glancing in the rearview mirror. "You, Dad."

"Me?" Claire can hear Gene breathing, thinking. "There once was a girl named Noelle. People thought she was swell."

He pauses so long Claire thinks he forgot there was more. "She was having a wedding," she prompts.

"She's getting new bedding," Noelle adds. "Which I am, by the way."

Gene says, "And it's just as well?"

"Brilliant," Noelle says. "Maybe you should both help me with my vows."

Claire turns to look at her. "You haven't written them?"

264 { **ELISE JUSKA**

"Have I come begging you for help yet?"

"The wedding is in two days, Noelle."

"It is?" she says, feigning surprise. Then she reaches across Claire's lap, flips open the glove compartment. "That reminds me. Paul said he wants you to give a toast."

"Me?"

"It was his idea. Because you were such a hit at the pub last weekend."

"That's only because I was—" Almost thirty years old, she still doesn't want to say "drunk" in front of her father. "I was motherless."

Noelle shuts the door and smiles at her, a little sadly. "Here," she says, as a candy bar lands in Claire's lap. "Here, Dad," she says, pitching one over her shoulder.

"They're flaky," Claire warns him.

"They're gorgeous," Noelle corrects her, ripping hers open with her teeth. "So you'll do it, right?" She takes a bite and chocolate flurries in her lap. "The toast? You have to. You're the writer."

It was what they said about the eulogy, the night before the funeral, and the reality now is no different: Claire isn't a writer. She's barely a linguist, with a nonexistent thesis. Even cruciverbalist—much as she's criticized Noelle for exaggerating, all of these were liberal stretches of the truth.

"I'm not a good public speaker," Claire warns her.

"I'm not worried," Noelle says.

Claire opens her chocolate. Long shadows play on the curves in the road. She actually feels a faint excitement at the prospect of the toast, like she once did facing an important assignment for school. "What should it say?" she asks.

"I don't know. What do toasts say? Why you think I'm awesome, why Paul and me are meant to be together . . ."

"Does your heart go pitty-pat?"

"Of course," Noelle says.

Claire watches as smoke threads from chimneys. One road becomes the next and the next.

"Magpie," Noelle says.

"What?"

"Magpie."

"Where?"

"Over there," Noelle says, but gestures nowhere. "That's good luck for the wedding."

"I thought one meant—"

"Yeah, but one in flight is worth two in sight. It's only bad luck on the ground."

Claire searches the sky. Empty, except for the fading light.

"It flew away already," Noelle tells her.

"I saw," Claire says.

## CHAPTER THIRTEEN: Walking Stick

**T**here is the moment when simply stepping away from the cross-word puzzle yields insight. "No tricks," Gene used to tell her, sitting at the breakfast table. "Sometimes if you just walk away from it, it looks different." Whether doing a puzzle or constructing one, the same rule applies. Change your angle and a missing word can assume sudden shape, or shed new light on a clue once the grid is all filled.

Clueing, the last stage of puzzle-making, is Claire's favorite part. Once all the words are assembled, you can decide what they mean. Some words—the small but necessary, eso-

teric variety—are limited in their definitions. *Anil* (blue dye).
*Fala* (FDR's pooch). *Etui* (ornamental needle case). Most are
somewhere in the middle, allowing for more juicy but not terribly different variations. The hardest, and most interesting,
are the contradictions.

*Incense* (Sweet smoke or incite anger?)

*Temper* (Outburst or soothe?)

On a rainy morning in New Hampshire, a walking stick can
be a bug that melts into its surroundings. On a different day,
it can be a cane wound with green streamers, or a wooden
staff in the Irish countryside, or anything that helps a person
move safely from one place to the next.

Friday night, Claire sits at the desk in Graham's room, her
crossword notebook open in front of her. When she hears a
knock, she turns to see Noelle standing in the doorway. On
top and bottom, she is dressed like a housewife—pre-wedding
curlers in her hair, pink Isotoners on her feet. But in the middle, she is seventeen again: ratty T-shirt, sweatpants, chewed
fingernails. She clutches a piece of paper to her chest.

"I need help," she says. A blue pen smear has flown across
her top lip. "What's another word for *love*?"

"Affection," Claire says. "Lust. Ardor. Fondness."

"Not those kind of words," Noelle says, crossing the room
to toss the paper on the desk. "Help me."

"What's this?"

"My vows. They're shite. They're shite, right?"

"Hold on," Claire says. "Stop hovering."

*Paul, the first time I saw you across the bar at the Jersey shore I*
*knew I would marry you someday. Ask anybody that was there that*
*night—it's true! You are great craic. With you, "my heart is taken"*

*all three ways—loyalty, friendship, love.* From there the pen devolves into a frustrated dribble.

"They suck, right?" Noelle asks, from behind her shoulder.

"They don't suck."

"It's the same stuff everybody says."

"But you mean it, right?"

"Of course," Noelle says.

"Then—" Claire shrugs. "I think it's perfect."

"Really?" Noelle says. She picks up Claire's open notebook. "What's this?"

"Nothing."

"Is this my toast?"

"No," Claire says. "Not yet. I was just about to start working on it."

Noelle sits on the edge of the bed, thumbing through the pages. "What is this stuff?"

"Just some old puzzles," Claire says. "But I think I might be taking a break from puzzles for a while."

"Because you're writing your dissertation, right?"

"Actually, I think I'm done with that too."

Noelle looks up. "Then what are you going to do? Wait—are you moving here?"

Claire shakes her head. "I don't really know," she says. "I guess I'll go back and stay with Dad for a little while, until I find a place. After that, I have no idea." As she says the words, they become true. She has no plan, just a confident verb tense and a hesitant belief that things will work out okay. The feeling is equal parts giddy and terrifying. Her future is undecided, but it's the most decisive she's ever felt.

Suddenly a shout comes from upstairs. "Noelle!" It's Paul, sounding mildly stricken.

Noelle jumps up and cracks open the door. "Don't come down here! You can't see me or we'll be cursed!"

"I need to ask you something!"

"What?"

"Just come yell up the stairs," he says. "It'll be good practice for when we're married and rowing all the time."

"Shite." Noelle sighs. "I'll be right back. Work on my toast," she says, handing Claire the notebook, and slips out the door.

Claire turns back to her desk. She flips to a clean page, writes TOAST across the top, and stares at the blankness. She remembers her own wedding, Deirdre standing at the mike to deliver the blessing, cane in one hand and glass in the other. It was the most generic of blessings, the farewell blessing, the same one Deirdre shouted after the car every time Claire drove away. As she spoke, Claire had just wanted it to end. But now, as she pictures Deirdre, teary and broguing, she knows at least the blessing moved her mother. It wasn't the words she said, but the way she said them.

Claire tries it, tentatively. "May the road rise to meet you." Her voice sounds strange, alone in a room. "May the wind be always at your back, may the sun shine—"

She stops. It sounds as rushed and insubstantial as it did years ago, reading it out loud in a classroom.

"May the road rise to meet you," she tries again. She dwells in the pause, lets the image of a road rise to fill it. "May the wind be always at your back." She focuses on the wall, imagining the crowd that will be listening in the pub tomorrow, the ruddy old men propped on stools, musicians with instruments held quiet on laps, women sawing into sausages, babies jiggling on hips, children darting around the tables: the whole of life in one room. "May the sun shine warm upon your face, may the rain fall soft upon your fields—"

She hears a noise behind her and turns. Noelle is listening just inside the door. Claire feels embarrassed. Her mouth is open, mid-sentence, but the words are stuck in her throat. She knows Noelle is waiting to hear the rest, but can't bring herself to say it. It isn't that she doesn't want to. It's because of how exposed it feels, to be caught off guard by someone you love in a moment you truly meant.